QUEEN'S RETURN

BLOOD LEGACY SERIES BOOK 3

ELISE HENNESSY

Flutterbye Trail Press
797 Sam Bass Road #2541
Round Rock, TX 78681

First edition

Editing by Red Loop Editing
Cover Design by FrostAlexis Arts
E-book Chapter Art by Real Life Design
Published by Flutterbye Trail Press

ISBN: 978-1-7345137-6-9 (E-book)
ISBN: 978-1-7345137-7-6 (Print)
LCCN: 2020918783

Feedback: Encounter a problem with this book? Let us know at elisehennessyauthor@gmail.com

Books by Elise Hennessy

Books in the Altare World

GRYPHON RIDER ACADEMY
Second Chance
Chosen
Storm Front
Wild Flight

ROYAL SPY INSTITUTE
The Crown Heist
Five & Chance

Also by Elise Hennessy

BLOOD LEGACY SERIES
Dream Walker
The Winter Key
Queen's Return
Court of Illusions
Shadow Dance
Rule the Night
Dhampir's Wish

Blood Curse
Blood Legacy: The Complete Series

Queen's Return

Blood Legacy Series Book 3

Elise Hennessy

Chapter 1
Adrius

A WEEK PASSED, YET ADRIUS, KING OF VAMPIRES, WAS STILL dead. He preferred it that way. Wherever his soul landed in the between of life and death was a place of solitude and reflection, stirred by pleasant breezes and the occasional too-close brush of a fleecy cloud. He could stay there forever.

Except there was one problem.

Adrius picked himself off his back as his side soaked with water. "Sorry, didn't see you there!" called the only person to disrupt his paradise, an olive-skinned man who smiled with all his teeth in a sparkling, larger-than-life grin as he set aside an empty bucket. "Nice day for sky watching, but must you do it in my garden?"

Huffing a sigh, Adrius squeezed out the side of his shirt. Upon his death, he'd woken wearing modern clothes of a plain shirt and jeans that bagged around his legs. He began to trudge toward another peaceful spot. His new home was not lacking for places of repose, full of manicured greenery and the occasional tree grown to the perfect height for climbing.

"Not even going to say hello?" The other man was by his side in a few strides, whistling a jaunty tune. He stretched his arms behind his head, looking like he had not a care in the world.

Every time Adrius had died in the past, he came to a place much like this one, where his deceased friends waited to spend time with him. But that was a thousand years ago. Now, he only had this man and his garden. Maybe his friends had moved on, gone to where the dead go—Heaven, Hell, he had no idea.

He turned to the person who wouldn't let him rest in peace, clearing a throat gone dry with disuse. "Hello." Despite sharing the same space for a week, he had no interest in chatting up a stranger. Maybe if he gave the other man what he wanted, he would leave Adrius alone.

"Ah, you do talk! I was starting to worry about you." He slapped his belly with a hearty laugh, drawing a side glance from Adrius.

"Why worry? What's the point?" he murmured.

If his eyes didn't deceive him, the other man's smile dimmed. "When a soul that's supposed to be alive won't leave my island, I do get concerned. Why don't you tell me what's holding you back?"

Adrius gave him a hollow look. "How about we start with the basics?" the other man continued. "My name is Soren. I figure I've lived here longer than you've been alive. Who, exactly, are you?"

"I am not quite sure." But something in Soren's introduction gave him pause. Memories tickled at the corner of his awareness, flashes of insight he couldn't quite reach. He took a deep breath of crisp air laden with pollen and sweet flowers. The sun caressed his skin.

The sun. His gaze snapped upward, watching a cloud skim the edge of the burning disc. He looked at his body, which wasn't catching fire from exposure, and then to Soren, whose well-tanned skin suggested he'd spent too long bathing in the sun's rays. "What's wrong?" he asked.

"I'm a vampire?" It came out as a question.

"No, new friend. You're a soul right now, so enjoy the day like you used to." Soren spread his arms, the sleeves of his robe hanging loose at his elbows. "If you remember you're a vampire in life, what else do you remember? Your name, perhaps?"

"Adrius."

"What an interesting one," he said with a smile, drawing

Adrius down a brick path between garden plots. He seemed to meander now that he had company. "I wonder how your mother decided on such a name. If you were born in this day and age, I imagine you would be an Adrian. That's a good name, too. I have many friends named Adrian."

He started tuning Soren out as he started to speak of the Adriatic Sea, his voice dwindling to a buzz in his ear. Now that he remembered his name, memories pressed in, begging to be recollected too.

"Do you wonder where you are, Adrius?" Soren's next question cut into his attention before he could grasp anything concrete. He shot over an annoyed glance, only to realize something odd. The land was coming to an end, as an island meets the shore. Except instead of water lapping at the edge, there was an endless expanse of blue sky and a plunge into nothingness.

Adrius snapped his mouth shut before his awed expression could gather flies. "I know not of a place like this," he said quietly.

"But surely you can guess?" Soren coaxed.

If this was an afterlife, he had few options to pick from. Yet something told him he couldn't be here—that he was not good enough to make it to the place he first thought of. "Tell me," he demanded, not as lighthearted as the smiling man next to him. "Where are we?"

"The glorious kingdom of Heaven! Where else do you get views like this?" Soren shadowed his eyes to look into the depths of the sky, extending his other hand to wave to someone else too distant to make out.

Sweat trickled down Adrius's spine. "I can't be here," he said, but he didn't know *why*.

"Sure you can. You already are," Soren pointed out.

Adrius held in his distress as he leaned over the edge of Soren's island in the sky, wondering how far down the next section of land dwelt. He spotted nothing but endless blue. Maybe his enhanced sight was gone with his sensitivity to sunlight. Here, he was just a man, just a soul.

"Does that make you an angel?" he asked.

"That it does! Surprised?" Soren still smiled.

Maybe all angels are so jolly, Adrius thought. "Where are your wings, then?" He eyed the other man skeptically. Someone had once told him of Heaven and of the angels with burning light for wings who called it home. Great seraphs who served as soldiers in the infinite conflict between order and chaos and represented the very best in humanity.

"You don't believe me. Would seeing my wings convince you?" Soren chuckled to himself.

"I don't see why this is funny," he said, bristling.

He held up a hand. "I laugh because I see myself in you! One of the first lessons I learned upon my own death was that sometimes, you have to take a leap of faith and trust what you know is there." Without warning, he took a dignified step and went tumbling into the abyss of blue. Adrius jumped to save him but was too slow to grab anything but air.

Kneeling, he leaned over the edge. Soren floated a few yards away, buoyed by the sudden appearance of a pair of wings made from flame and light. Their radiance haloed behind his head and reflected in his eyes, rendering him as divine as someone he used to know. His mind supplied the name: *Gwendolyn.* A half-angel nephilim who could channel devastating light.

"My faith gives me wings," Soren said simply before flying back to the center of the island.

Left to his thoughts, Adrius turned toward the way he'd come. Remembering Gwendolyn reignited memories that he relived with every step. He was one of the first vampires, a guardian of mortal lives against a long-ago threat. Someone who had helped bring together an army to take on that threat before it could consume the world.

He was a warrior, a leader, and a king.

And then it all went wrong. Someone had killed him and stolen his throne. He discovered he could return to life thanks to the ring called the Shield Key permanently melded to his hand, but his body never fully recovered from the process without more magical intervention. He walked the world a shadow, waiting to die and be reborn again and again.

This time, his death was different, but his memories stopped short of explaining why. He marched up to the only house on this island, a quaint one-story with a plume of smoke rising from its brick chimney. Soren waited for him on the porch, leg crossed over knee in a rocking chair. Without his wings, he looked like a farmer relaxing after a long day in the sun, just missing a pipe and a wife to occupy the chair beside him. Adrius took it instead. "What do you know about me?" he demanded.

"More than you and less than I should." Soren's smile was back as he rocked casually. The sun was setting over his island, making way for an endless expanse of stars to glimmer in its place. "But if you are to be my charge, I accept the challenge without complaint."

He was talking too vaguely. Adrius was used to action and deed, not this trickle of information. "I don't understand," he admitted.

"Perhaps you will, in time," the angel said, a twinkle in his eye.

ADRIUS SPENT DAYS TENDING THE GARDEN WITH SOREN. Speaking with the angel reminded him of his life and the mess he'd left behind. How he'd died—cut through the heart to ensure others remained safe. He'd died numerous times this same way to keep the darkness within him from taking innocent lives. Death was a reset, a temporary and crude cure to exchange for his eternal existence.

"I want to go back," he said one day, his hands fully in the dirt as he packed tulips into neat rows. The easy labor helped him think, but now, he dwelled too much.

He'd nearly killed his brother, possessed by some terrible rage that drove him to try tearing Sirius apart. He needed to apologize. To confess that it hadn't been him in control.

"You're not ready." The same thing Soren had been saying for days. "You've had a brush with demon magic. It's time to take it easy and piece yourself back together."

"So, you're the one holding me back?" Adrius had never spent so much time in the afterlife. Two, three days at most, before his soul was yanked back into its cold mortal shell. Did his friends and family believe he was dead at last? Or did they wait for him even still?

"I have a say, yes." Soren flashed him a reassuring smile. "I am your guardian angel after all. It's my duty to ensure you are ready."

"I'm ready. My brother—"

"Will be overjoyed to see you. As long as you remain free of demonic corruption," Soren said, lifting a finger. "I can't imagine Sirius wants to see you if you try killing him again."

Adrius deflated. "So, you know about that."

"Your most recent death was the only memory the Council showed me before leaving your soul on my island." He lifted his shoulder. "Such things leave an impression."

Adrius mashed earth around the next flower's roots with his fists. Soren placed a hand on his shoulder. "Take heart, friend. I think you'll be ready soon." He left with his bucket to tend to another section of the garden.

They crossed paths again hours later, when Adrius went back to the house for a drink of water. There Soren was in his rocking chair, sipping from a glass dewed with chill. A pitcher rested next to him on a little table. He made to go inside and get his own refreshment.

"I've considered it. I could send you back now," Soren remarked, stopping him in his tracks.

He heard the catch to his tone. "But?"

Soren took a big, slurping gulp of water. It took all of Adrius's self-control not to stomp over and slap the glass out of his hand. Instead, Soren set it aside with a satisfied sigh.

"Why won't you send me back?" Adrius asked when he was sure he wasn't getting a timely answer.

"You may not feel it, but your memory is still damaged," the angel said, fixing him with the first serious look Adrius had seen him wear. "I fear it is not something that can be fixed except by time and experience."

"I need to apologize to my brother," Adrius said. It was urgent.

Sirius already hated him. It was past time for Adrius to try to mend the burning bridge between them.

"*Just* your brother?" Soren raised a brow.

There was someone else he had to apologize to?

Yes...he remembered the likeness of another person, a woman with eyes like molten gold and an energetic, bouncy way about her. His mind's eye flashed with her terrified face as she beheld him succumbing to the darkness.

"I will apologize to everyone if I have to," he said with gritted teeth. "Just set me free so I can get started."

"A difficult path unfolds before you," the angel warned.

He squared his shoulders. "I'm ready."

Soren shook his head subtly. "Go in peace, Adrius. Something tells me we'll be seeing each other again someday."

Adrius blinked his eyes closed, and all he knew was cold.

Waking from death was never pleasant. Waking after so long felt worse than dying the first time. He became aware before his body was ready to respond, trapped in the slow creep of warmth from the burning-hot Shield Key as its magic suffused him, restoring him nearly to where he was before his death.

When he finally opened his eyes and blinked away a film blurring his surroundings, it felt like his senses lagged behind. Distant voices slurred into an incomprehensible murmur. White burned into his corneas, surrounding him on all sides.

He flexed numb hands, realizing they were strung up over his head. He was a prisoner in a soft bed. It sheets chafed over skin tingling with revived sensation.

Some of the white was flung away, and the outline of a person stood in the gap, her feminine voice just out of reach. Whoever was tending to his body didn't know to leave him be in the first part of his return when he didn't know up from down or touch from smell. She rushed away, and he squeezed his eyes shut, focusing on grounding his senses. Something told him he may have to start apologizing before he could even move.

"Adrius?" A woman's sweet voice drifted over him, familiar in a way he couldn't place.

He opened his eyes to a blonde standing over his bed. Her features were out of focus, but he caught the hope in her tone and the crown that glinted on her brow. "Adrius, it's been so long," she continued, taking a step forward with a breathless gasp. "And I've missed you so dreadfully. The nights were long and cold, but now fate shines upon me to be at your side once more."

Adrius tried to inspect her more closely. He didn't recognize her, but what a rare beauty she was, her eyes sparkling at him with some wordless emotion he was too unfocused to recognize. Whatever he did, he couldn't take a stranger for granted. "Who are you?" he asked, forcing a dry throat to work without sticking to the words.

She recoiled as if he'd reached out and slapped her. Her hand flew to her lips. "I...I'm Nyah. Your lifemate? Your wife?" She sounded like she stifled a sob.

"I'm very sorry, miss. I would remember if I had a wife," he said as politely as he could muster. She was already gone, sealing him back in his white prison as she left the smell of saline behind.

Chapter 2
Nyah

NYAH WAS A WOMAN OF MANY TITLES BY THIS POINT IN HER life. She knew the songs that praised her bravery and strength in the face of innumerable odds. If only those composers could see her now, rushing from the bedside of a man who'd wounded her with only a few words.

I would remember if I had a wife.

Maybe she'd deluded herself in thinking she would one day make her way back to Earth and pick up her marriage right where it'd left off. She'd never forgotten what it was like to have her true match, her lifemate, on the other end of a mating bond. No one could fill the hole in her heart left by the trauma of parting with Adrius.

She ran headlong into someone solid, who checked her forward momentum with two strong hands. She looked up into the swirling clouds of Izell's eyes. "That was a faster reunion than I expected," the fae snarked. "What'd he do, fall asleep?" Despite her tone, she wiped the tears from under Nyah's eyes with gentle fingertips.

Nyah shook her head in denial. "He said he doesn't remember me," she murmured. "I just...I need some air."

"I'll shake some sense into him while you're gone." Izell flashed a wicked smile that betrayed her shifter nature. Eight canines made any display of her teeth a snarl.

Despite herself, she bared her teeth back. The instincts of her wolf rose up at inopportune moments, like this one, when she'd rather leave than have a fight for dominance with one of her oldest friends. "You will do no such thing. Once I catch my breath, we're seeking answers," Nyah said.

"Go on, then." In a flash, Izell schooled her expression and nodded to Nyah, satisfying her wolf and giving her an opening to disengage. Izell knew what it was like to balance an animal's nature and still be civilized, considering she had a dragon spirit's instincts to grapple with. While Nyah always had to win matters of dominance, Izell needed her solitude. They both got what they wanted as Nyah drifted from the room, her gait trudging as her worries heaped back on her shoulders.

Something was wrong with Adrius. Right? Some part of her wondered if he'd simply moved on without her. While she'd waited for him, maybe he hadn't done the same for her. Or maybe so much time had passed that he'd forgotten what they'd once had. Memory was fickle in such ways.

She navigated through the unfamiliar rooms of the mansion so politely offered as a residence away from home. The vampires who lived here were busy in the evening hours, leaving her to blessed silence as she stepped onto the back patio and breathed in the night air. Manmade scents wafted into her sensitive nose, still unusual when she'd lived so long in an isolated paradise of greenery. More people lived in this city than the population of her entire land.

This time, she noticed she had company before she could be startled again. "Evening, Sirius," she said to the man she'd scented. He carried a bit of wild in him as a shapeshifting vampire. She wasn't surprised to see him outside.

"You're crying," he said gruffly, standing from the patio furniture where he'd been sprawled. An undercurrent of anger ran through the air, tickling the hint of empathy she still carried after all these years.

"It will pass." She put on a smile.

His expression didn't change. "Was it Adrius? I warned you of him."

"You mustn't speak so negatively of your brother," she said, hesitant to answer him directly when there were obviously layers to their feud. Something she hadn't seen a moment of until it'd festered to its current hostility. The Sirius she'd known was Adrius's biggest supporter. However, this Sirius was feral. If he were a shifter, he'd be more animal than man.

"So, he's awake? I must have words with him."

She held up a hand, a command to pause that was second nature. He turned a leery gaze toward her palm. In the hierarchy of their family, she had been away too long to casually stop him. She dropped her arm when she realized she overstepped. "Before you go...can you tell me what happened to him?" *How could he forget me?* she wanted to ask.

"Dark magic." He shrugged like he didn't care, but bitter worry weaved around him as he took a pace toward the door. "Only one person knows for sure. You could always ask Lucia."

A soft growl rose in her throat. She'd heard about what Lucia had done, how she'd succumbed to madness. "If I must speak with Lucia, then so be it. I will have *my* Adrius back."

"Good luck," he said without conviction.

She followed him back into the mansion, bustling to keep up with his long strides. Sirius was a giant of a man because he'd consumed Fell blood from its source as one of the original vampires. Her stature had never caught up, so she remained a petite and high-voiced woman no matter the power she acquired over her long years.

Another Ancient vampire joined them inside, dressed for combat. *"Are we not sparring?"* Neala asked Sirius, though her gaze flashed between them. The woman was the only female Blood Prince still alive on Earth and of nearly equal stature to Sirius. She was also the closest thing Nyah had to a sister.

Neala had lost her voice as a very young child. Before she had a vampire's enhanced mental powers and mastered mental speech to communicate, she and Nyah had made up their own set of hand signals. As Neala's red gaze rested on her face, she flashed one of those old signs. The one to ask if she was okay.

"I must speak to Adrius first," Sirius was saying, apparently missing it as Nyah signaled back with a *no.*

Stepping aside, she swept out her hands. *"Go ahead, then. Try to cut him some slack."*

Sirius muttered uncharitably as he stomped off. *"I mean it!"* Neala called after him. *"He needs his brother, not his brother's anger!"* It didn't seem like he heard her, as there was no acknowledgement.

"He is not himself." Nyah heard herself speak as if from far away.

"Has no one told you what happened?" They went to find a bench to sit together. Neala put her arm around her shoulders for comfort as Nyah finally allowed the tears to flow freely.

The truth was that nearly everyone, even members of the band of vampires her old friends and family were living with, had tried to tell her about Adrius. But no one knew the full story or what would happen when he finally woke up. "I just thought it would be different," she admitted. "I waited for him for three thousand years, Neala."

"And he waited for you. He's been inconsolable since you were parted. One of the only good things to come of our long rest was that his pain stopped."

She'd been told of that event, too. How her own mother had sunk the island of Nyixa in a desperate bid to weaken vampire kind and the Fell Madness that manifested so quickly in the first generation of vampires. Gwendolyn had kept anyone from turning into a flesh-eating monster with the Madness for nearly a thousand years. But Nyah didn't know what to think of such a sacrifice of life to do it, especially since Gwendolyn was currently lying in a coma.

Neala's lips thinned. *"Adrius succumbed to the demon's whispers with your name on his lips. Minutes before the fae made contact with you in the Fell Lands, in fact."*

"How is it, then, that he just told me he doesn't know who I am?" she asked, wanting so desperately to believe her.

"The demon obviously did something to him. What it did is anyone's guess."

"Except for Lucia. She would know."

A scoff left Neala's lips. *"If she is sane enough to tell you. You are aware that she was behind locking you in the Fell Lands?"*

She nodded. She'd figured it out—not that it'd been hard when Lucia was the only Sorceress back when it'd happened. There was no love left in her for the old woman turned monster. "It's called Adrun now," she said, earning a raised brow from Neala. "The Fell Lands. It is Adrun, completely different from what you know. The last of the fae and I reclaimed the land once the Fell were no more. We became shifters, embracing a connection with animal spirits, as the combination is immune to corruption."

She stroked her chin thoughtfully. *"Is it true that you are a shifter as well?"*

"Yes. I paired up with a wolf spirit—a giant female timber wolf by the name of Night's Howl. She was an alpha in her time and still thinks she is. A queen is a different kind of alpha," she said with a smile for her old spirit.

"But...why?" Neala looked her over like she expected fur to erupt from Nyah's skin at any moment.

"After the Fell, it became something we all do. Vampires lose their blood hunger; fae grow more fulfilled due to their magic yearning for the bond of a familiar," Nyah explained. "I found my fangs taking the spirit trial and coming face-to-face with Night's Howl. She is my fierce side. Together, we're better..."

She snapped her fingers. "That's it. That's what can help Adrius. The trial makes you face your memories—your best and worst moments. Maybe it can help him remember me," she said, holding that hope close. "Maybe you and the other Blood Princes should take a trial too and clear the corruption from you once and for all. Would you like to try it?"

The other woman considered, though she struggled to hide a skeptical look. *"Perhaps later. After I see how it goes for others."*

Nyah drew herself to her feet, nodding to that. "I understand. It's a new concept after all." She offered Neala a hand up and headed back to the infirmary with new determination to her step.

They arrived to find an unfamiliar woman blocking Sirius's

way inside, her hands on her hips. She was brunette and bored-looking in an old-fashioned dress. "Don't come stomping in here like you own the place. And don't break him. He just woke up," she said. Her voice shaded from unfamiliar to Izell's tenor, startling him.

"This must be your glamor." He tried for a polite tone as he added, "Lady fae."

She waved him away impatiently. "I wouldn't look like a human right now if I knew it would be you three coming in." As she spoke, Izell's human illusion faded, replaced by pointed ears and skin festooned with the golden stars of an astral fae. Her dragon half had claimed her arms up to the elbow, laying down sandstone-colored scales, spines, and fingers tipped in wicked talons. A tail curled around her waist, whip-thin and twitching in annoyance.

Izell had not adapted well to Earth, Nyah reflected. The idea that fae didn't exist here—and if they did, they glamored their natures—didn't sit well with someone who never hid a moment of her true self. She stepped in before Sirius could take the fae's irritation as a personal insult. "We're going to visit Lucia," she told her.

Chapter 3
Nyah

"Delightful," Izell drawled. "We as in..." She gestured between the four people present.

Sirius jerked his chin toward the curtained-off bed where Adrius rested. "There's something else I'm more interested in."

"And you would not get much from Lucia with me present." Neala flashed Nyah a concerned look, and she tried to answer with a reassuring smile.

They were going into the Sorceress's prison for what would hopefully be a quick in-and-out. Taking Adrius for a spirit trial would do little if more demonic magic hung over him, something they needed to study.

Izell stood and started to make gestures to summon a disc of magic that opened like a rip in the fabric of reality. She paused before she made it large enough to pass through, tapping a claw to her chin. "Why are we going to see Lucia?"

"Answers, Izell." Nyah stood as close as she dared, her skin prickling so close to the half-finished portal.

"Unlike you, I have already attempted to talk to her. Note the *attempted*," she said as she finished making the portal a workable size.

Nyah walked through without another word. She schooled her expression as she took in the abandoned warehouse that was repurposed for the jailing of one of the most powerful beings in this world and the next.

Pressure popped behind her ears. Izell had made the portal right before a doorway that was freshly painted with two fae symbols. If she stepped past the threshold, she'd disconnect from all her magic. The wolf spirit within her, Night's Howl, stirred at their proximity to such powerful magic as a dead zone of this caliber.

"See you on the other side," she told her spirit before walking into the prison and shuddering at the unpleasant ripple of her magic being torn away. It was like being left without one of her senses.

The warehouse itself was full of pallets of boxed goods stacked over her head. It gave the prison a warren-like feeling. As far as Nyah knew, there were dozens of guards hidden and ready to act if there was any hint of trouble. "I don't like this," she grumbled, following Izell further into the warehouse and around several turns in the path as the pallets made an artificial maze.

"Imagine if they placed her in the infirmary. You'd have to look at her face every night," Izell said. "This way, all the little vampire covens can feel like they're doing their part in guarding her together."

"There is wisdom in joint responsibility." Though, she had to wonder on Lucia's ultimate fate, since the only true answer for her crimes was death. But because of the heavy burden of the curse she carried, Lucia could not be killed when it would pass on to the one holding the blade. She mused that the Sorceress could be left in this prison indefinitely.

Here and there were more symbols of fae magic. Her limbs felt heavier as they went further inside. The air thinned like they were climbing to the top of a high peak. By the time they reached Lucia, Nyah was filled with appreciation for the great oppression she felt, because that meant this prison would be impossible to breech.

Before one last pallet, Izell gave her an encouraging push and remained hidden. Nyah nodded, glad to know the woman was there but she would still have an opportunity to speak to Lucia alone.

Unlike a true jail, there was no cell. Lucia, in all her corrupted glory, was chained to a wall by all four limbs and her neck. She had enough slack to stand, and she did upon realizing she had company. The fae spells permeating the air took away her one advantage—her magic. To see her strung up with nephilim chains, irons that also stripped one of their extraordinary abilities, was another layer of safety.

Nyah drew on long years of diplomacy to keep her expression completely under control. While Lucia's expression lightened with hope, all she saw was a gentle smile on Nyah's face instead of her disgust at what the Sorceress had become.

Lucia wore her old robes of silver but was otherwise unrecognizable. She bore Fell Madness in every pore, her skin stained under the surface with black veins. Her eyes were deep pits of darkness above a smiling mouth lined with sharp, perfectly interlocking fangs. *This is the monster that locked me in the Fell Lands,* she thought. Now everyone could see it for themselves.

"I was worried you wouldn't visit." Despite her appearance, Lucia still had a voice like midnight silk, filling the space like she owned it. "None were as happy as I to learn that the beautiful Alchemyst Queen still draws breath."

If she still could feel her wolf, Nyah would've given herself away with an angry growl. There were some advantages to the dampening magic around them besides keeping the Sorceress before her docile. "It's been a long time...Auntie." It burned in her belly to refer to Lucia as family, but it had the desired result.

Lucia's face softened, her brow relaxing around her eyes. Her smile became more genuine. "Still the girl I remember," she murmured.

"You've made some poor choices since we last spoke, Auntie." And what an understatement that was.

Chuckling low, she asked, "Do you know when my trial will be?"

"A date hasn't been set." She watched Lucia bow her head

and took a guess as to why. "It must be hard not to see the future after you've grown so accustomed to it."

"Like putting out an eye with a lead weight," Lucia grumbled. "I don't suppose you're here to keep an old woman company?"

She was inspecting Nyah closely. Whatever she was looking for, Nyah made sure she only saw a placid expression and a stance that showed some tension. It wouldn't be believable if she presented herself as completely at ease with what Lucia had become.

"I had to see you for myself," she said quietly.

Lucia tilted her head, her tone thoughtful. "You must have questions."

Forcing herself not to blurt out about Adrius, she instead asked the other question burning at the tip of her tongue. "Why did you do it?"

"I have done...many things," Lucia said slowly.

"Three thousand years ago, you doomed the first expedition into the Fell Lands by causing the portal between our worlds to collapse." She straightened, looming over the other woman as she ducked her head in apparent shame. "I was at the head of that expedition. I, a woman who trusted you like family. You were my mother's best friend." How different Lucia and Gwendolyn were now as bitter enemies.

Whatever softness she'd cultivated with Lucia was gone when the Sorceress raised her head. A sneer showed sharp teeth. "You were in my way. Welcome back to Earth, Alchemyst Queen. Choose your new allegiances carefully."

"Says a woman in chains." Nyah bared her teeth back.

"There you are. The real Nyah." Lucia rested back against the wall, smirking now that she'd gotten a glimpse of the anger hidden under the façade of pleasantness. "I did regret leaving you behind, but you are still alive and clearly capable. My deeds have made you strong."

It's like she thinks she has bargaining power, Nyah thought, crossing her arms. Even bound and powerless, the Sorceress still held her dignity. She could see the queen in Lucia, the woman who took over the vampire throne in Nyah's absence.

"I attribute my success to myself and no other." And to suggest otherwise was an insult to what she'd achieved to survive in a hostile land. She had to change the subject before Lucia could raise her ire further. "Tell me what happened to Adrius."

Flashing a smile filled with fangs, Lucia met her gaze. "You disappoint me. Someone who survived the Fell Lands yet still cares for that waste of space."

Nyah kept a flat tone, knowing she'd miscalculated if she thought Lucia was done needling. "I will not repeat myself."

"If I'm honest, I haven't spoken to him since Nyixa rose from the sea." Her voice dripped with condescension. "What's wrong with him this time?"

"Mind your tongue before I have it ripped from your head," she said with clenched teeth.

At this point, she was sure Lucia wouldn't actually share anything of worth on the subject. She'd come and faced this monster for nothing but a bucketful of aggravation.

"Would you do it yourself, or would you bring in someone else to do your dirty work? What manner of queen are you now?" Lucia grinned, looking every inch a Fell in the moment.

She took a step back, away from that grotesque face, and turned on the ball of her foot, ready to walk away with her dignity intact. She didn't *need* Lucia to tell her anything.

"Wait."

She hadn't made it more than a few paces before Lucia called after her. Nyah closed her eyes, pretending the smooth voice behind her wasn't attached to a Fell Mad. If her ears didn't deceive her, she heard the rest at barely more than a whisper. "I don't mean to push you away..."

"Do you know what happened to him or not?" she asked with a sigh.

There was no answer until Nyah turned to see Lucia inspecting her talon-length claws. "Do you see me? Adrius is next. He won't fall the same way, but he will serve the same master." She wondered if she was witnessing a moment of clarity. Some part of Lucia was introspective and sober as she beheld herself.

"The demon," Nyah said, her stomach dropping with anxiety.

A cackle left Lucia's lips. It bubbled forth and rose like a geyser from the earth. "The great Jazrach, master of corruption. Able to crush the hardiest of wills. What chance does Adrius have? He's pathetic anyway!"

Nyah beat a hasty retreat as the laughter continued. She came to where Izell was hiding, listening to every word with an inscrutable expression. Lucia's bellowing voice followed them as they left. "Once he bows to Jazrach, you will be next!" The warehouse's acoustics bounced the words in an echo: *next, next, next.*

Chapter 4
Adrius

ADRIUS RESTED HIS EYES AND WAITED FOR HIS SENSES TO
balance. Not that he had any other choice, with his arms held
immobile over his head. He recognized it for what it was—a safety
precaution just in case he didn't return with his sanity intact.
Back in the day, he used to wait in a padlocked coffin until it was
determined he was back to himself.

He very much preferred the bed to that.

Behind his closed eyelids, he kept seeing the blurry face of the
woman he'd hurt. Maybe he had returned too soon, because it was
apparent he had more gaps in his memory than imported cheese.
He hadn't expected to forget a wife. And how could he explain a
stranger crying over him if there hadn't been some measure of
truth there?

He'd get to the bottom of this when he was coherent. Maybe
the memories would continue coming in even without Soren's
direct help. He'd obviously passed some sort of test to be allowed
back to life.

Sometime during his reverie, heavy footsteps approached his
bed. The lighting changed as metal hissed against metal. This
time, when Adrius opened his eyes, he realized that he wasn't
surrounded completely by white but instead a sheet torn aside by
a big man standing in the gap.

The newcomer was so tall he needed to duck under the

railing holding up the privacy screen. He paced forward like a predator, all deadly and focused intent. Despite his modern clothing, his dark beard was something of another age. It was groomed and braided, studded with wooden beads. It all had meaning—battles long won, courageous deeds sung of in a past too distant for anyone to remember. He had strong features under that beard, as if chiseled from stone and inlaid with white marble to match a complexion that hadn't seen the sun in centuries.

His brother Sirius's eyes were a dark maroon, practically burning with hostility. As a Blood Prince, one of the first vampires to walk the night, that feature was permanently marked with blood. Adrius looked just like him, with the exception of his own eyes, which were black with shadows.

"What did you do this time?" Sirius demanded.

Here was the man Adrius had returned for. He owed the biggest of apologies to him, but the words dried up as he realized his brother was speaking of something else. His confusion must've shown on his face, because Sirius amended, "With Nyah. What did you do to Nyah?"

"I...didn't do anything. I don't even know who she is!" he protested.

Sirius eyed him, his lip curling. "You don't know who she is," he repeated, his voice rising. "You don't *know* who she is!" He started slapping the metal bedframe to punctuate his words, shaking the foundation of Adrius's little haven.

"That's what I said." Adrius drew himself up as much as his manacled arms would let him, trying to take some dignity in the situation.

"I can't believe you. You are completely beyond help." His brother shook his head with openmouthed disbelief.

"I was warned I might have some memory loss—"

Sirius cut him off with a bark of laughter. "What a waste of time. You lost her and turned into the saddest shipwreck to grace the bottom of the ocean. Now she's back, and you've conveniently forgotten her."

"I'm sorry. Hear me out—"

He sighed with frustration as Sirius spoke over him. "You are a sorry sort, I agree. Do you remember who kept your sorry ass around the first time you lost her?" He hooked a thumb toward his chest. "*I did.* You died dozens of times, too consumed by your sorrow to notice a sword aimed at your chest. Who made sure you always had a warm bed and blood to return to?"

"You did," he said, because he remembered Sirius feeding him from his own vein to make sure Adrius didn't kill anyone with the barren bloodlust he felt upon waking.

"And now I'm done. Figure yourself out, Adrius, because I'm not doing it for you anymore." His expression shaded to a hateful snarl. "You almost killed me a week ago. I'm lucky Jaromir was able to mend me before I fell apart!"

"Please, accept my deepest apologies. I wasn't in control of myself." He was ready to beg. He couldn't remember his brother ever looking at him that way. It felt like hot daggers in his gut to be under such a stare.

Sirius took a step toward his bedside, his gaze never leaving Adrius's face. "I know. You allowed a demon to take control of you. Do you remember that at least? How you started menacing the new Alchemyst, who only tried to help you?"

"I didn't *allow* it. You're being unfair," Adrius sputtered. A hot kernel of anger stoked within the more Sirius hurled accusations at him.

"Unfair." Sirius chuffed like an animal. As the first shapeshifting vampire, that animal came to the surface every time he became impassioned. "The only unfair thing I see is that the strongest vampire in the world has the weakest will."

"How dare you," Adrius snapped.

"The facts don't lie. Only one of us has ended up a demon's puppet." The fight seemed to leave Sirius's face. He reached up and pulled Adrius's manacles off their hook, letting the golden chains fall into his lap. "Go ruin someone else's life for a change."

He stomped away, leaving Adrius with his mouth hanging open. He cursed under his breath, hauling himself to his feet with the intent to follow. Upon their first contact with the ground, his legs buckled, sending him into an undignified sprawl. For a moment, all he could do was rest his forehead on the cold ground.

How am I going to fix this mess? he asked himself as he struggled upright and walked in slow, shuffling steps. When he was around the curtain, he saw he wasn't alone in this place of healing. A bed across from his was curtained off, as was one at the back of the room. In the middle, someone familiar was strung up similarly to him.

"Jaromir?" he asked in disbelief. The man was awake, coherent...he must've heard everything. The only Blood Prince with the Gift, which manifested in the power to heal even the most grievous of wounds, he was the most skilled doctor Adrius knew. He was supposed to be on the other side of this, tending to patients rather than being one.

As he drew closer, he saw the black veins riddling one side of Jaromir's face. A sad smile split the gentle healer's face as realization set in. "You went Fell Mad?" Adrius asked, a dawning sense of horror gripping his innards. If it took Jaromir, it truly could take anyone.

"I was bitten. This particular strain is stubborn," he said. "But I'm about twenty treatments in, and it's working. Don't take my arms down. I chose to be restrained for everyone's safety."

Adrius shook his head in slow disbelief. He picked up a book resting on a chair by the other man's bedside, having a seat there. A muscular man's chest took up most of the cover, earning an eyebrow raise before he set it aside. "I couldn't help but overhear," Jaromir continued, clearing his throat. He sounded parched. It could easily be a side effect of his condition, as the Fell Madness induced levels of bloodlust that could hardly be quenched.

He warred with saying something of his friend's predicament rather than his own. "Are you comfortable?" he settled on.

"More so than you, I imagine." He offered a shrug. "I've spent the last week being fed fae sweets and read to by the most eccentric woman I've ever met. Meanwhile, you've been dead. That's not comparable." He shook his head, his expression sympathetic. "You really don't remember Nyah?"

"Should I?" When even Jaromir gave him a look of pointed disbelief, his shoulders drew in.

"It's not your fault. Perhaps it's a good thing, even. You both can rebuild from the beginning." It sounded like he was forcing a positive note on the situation. It chafed Adrius in a different way from his brother's yelling.

"I don't want to talk about her. Not when Sirius..." he stopped, feeling his voice start to shake. He would not get emotional. He'd figure this out.

He took a deep breath through his nose and again when Jaromir started talking. "He'll come around. You just have to earn back his trust." Adrius always considered the Gifted man the wisest of the Blood Princes. Hoping for some nugget of wisdom that would solve his problems in an elegant bow, he hung on to every word.

Jaromir's voice lowered as he grew introspective for a few minutes. "Well, how about I update you on what happened in your absence?" he asked.

Though disappointed, Adrius knew the task of winning Sirius's trust was his own burden. He nodded and listened as Jaromir recited a list of events more surreal the longer he spoke. In one of the curtained-off beds rested Taryn, Lucia's longtime victim, now freed of her control and hopelessly riddled with Fell Madness in his desire for revenge.

In the other one was Gwendolyn, in a coma as her body finished the transformation from vampire into human. "No one's ever recovered from vampirism," he interrupted in sheer disbelief.

"True, but Gwendolyn's different. The nephilim in her won when face-to-face with a demon." Jaromir's eyes sparkled with hope. "Many good things have happened while you were indisposed."

"Forgive me if I see only darkness." His memories were still patchy, Taryn was Mad, Gwendolyn may not wake... He dwelled on it as the pressure in the room changed.

A portal opened up at the front of the room. Out stormed the blonde woman from before, but now he could see her features clearly. Her chin was lifted and features pinched in a fit of pique. The sight of her took his breath away. Had he ever seen a prettier woman? She was lifted straight from his dreams.

Maybe she *was* his lifemate.

Chapter 5
Nyah

SHE FELT HIS ATTENTION IMMEDIATELY. SOMEONE HAD LET Adrius free from his bed, deeming him recovered enough to stand on his own two feet. Their eyes locked across the room, yet his expression betrayed no hint of recognition. It hurt worse than she expected, to see him that way a second time.

It was real. The damage to his memories was real, demon-caused, and potentially the first step for her to lose someone standing only yards, instead of a world, away from her. "It's time," she proclaimed.

"For?" Izell snipped.

She turned to her with a sigh. "Spirit trials." It hadn't been a long trip from Lucia's prison, but after leaving that dead zone, she'd become determined to see Adrius take one. He could not end up like Lucia.

"That's one way to push his memories back into place," the fae said thoughtfully, her tail swishing behind her as she went to check on Taryn. "I shall accompany this one. You will wish to take your mate, yes?"

She nodded, heart in her throat as she tried to swallow. She closed the gap between her and Adrius. Though his eyes were dark as pitch, she used to be able to read the emotions within as clearly as her own. Three thousand years later, with her empathy fading and their mating bond shattered, he was as inscrutable as a stranger.

She had to face the facts soon about her special ability. She had ignored or wished away her empathy so often when making difficult decisions as queen; it was responding to her whims by letting her go. In this situation, she wanted to beg its forgiveness if it would give her a helpful hint.

"*He hurts,*" said her wolf. Night's Howl was jostled awake after their visit to the prison. Most of the time, she slept, allowing Nyah full control. She had the ability to read quirks in body language Nyah couldn't see, determining true intentions within a blink.

"*So do I.*" She felt she could be selfish, at least with her wolf, who was as close as her own self.

"*We care for the weakest in the pack. That is what it means to be alpha,*" Night's Howl chided as Nyah stopped short of her husband. Could she really call him thus anymore? Former husband. She swallowed again.

"I would like to invite you to my home," she said. Her formal tone seemed wrong when addressing Adrius, but she held hope that soon this block between them could be removed.

His brow furrowed. "Do you speak of the Fell Lands?"

"It is called Adrun now. After..." After him, she wanted to say. "After three thousand years, we've long cleansed the land of Fell and reclaimed it for the side of life."

"Incredible," he murmured.

"Of course...you probably want to wash up first." Her sensitive nose picked up his odor, but she didn't fault him for it.

He glanced down toward his bound wrists. "Oh, let me take care of that for you," she said, taking hold of the glimmering chains. She hadn't seen a set like it since leaving Earth, but her mother had enchanted them, so she knew the release was somewhere in the middle links. With a press in the right place, they dropped from his hands with a *click.*

"I would be honored to see your home," he said, rubbing the circles in his skin and flexing his fingers for circulation.

"Maybe while you are there, you can experience some of our

magic." She walked with him out of the infirmary. "Has anyone told you what a shifter is?"

He spoke in a dull monotone. "If they have...add it to the list of things I've forgotten."

"My people had to take some extreme measures to survive in the early days," she said, glad she could at least share this with him personally. "There's a long history as to how I survived, but I won't bore you with that."

His brow furrowed as he glanced down at her. She stood nearly in his shadow, letting his bulk hide her from the lights burning overhead. Modern mortals really used too much of it now that they'd invented a way to capture it in glass bulbs. "I would like to hear it. Maybe later?"

"Maybe later," she agreed. "The early Fell Lands was a cesspool of corruption. A fae would transform into a Fell just by breathing in the wrong place. My purifying potions could change Fell to fae, but we had trouble keeping them that way. The solution fell from the sky one day. Literally."

They stopped in the foyer. His room, like the one that'd been lent to her for her stay, must've been on the second or third floor. "I'll tell you the rest when you've bathed," she said after an awkward pause. If he'd remembered her, she'd have gone up with him. "Dress in something durable. There's a lot of walking in your future."

Adrius nodded in acknowledgement. "I long to hear the rest," he said before bounding up the stairs.

She settled in one of the plush chairs lining the nearby sitting room to wait, sighing to herself. It was late evening by this point, and she was glad most of the mansion's denizens were off busy with their own tasks. She could be alone with her thoughts without worry that anyone would burst in to interrupt them.

Something Night's Howl was willing to do instead. *"You must let someone else guide his trial."*

"But I know him," she protested.

"You think you do, but he deserves a more neutral guide. You may lead him into a bad match," the wolf said. While others

would tiptoe around the point, she spoke her mind directly to Nyah.

Nyah and her wolf had never made a bad match between man and spirit. To imply that one was possible stung, especially from her permanent partner. *"We should guide Taryn, then. Izell and her dragon will need assistance with him."*

Night's Howl chuffed in agreement. *"Another damaged soul in need of a pack."* Judging by her estimation of Nyah's old friends, it would appear they were all damaged souls in need of a pack. Nyah yearned to show her wolf that her friends *were* a pack. That long ago, they'd been united enough to save the world. They didn't act like it anymore, but there'd been a time when they'd all die for one another.

She dwelled on that idea until Adrius returned, damp and dressed in something more rugged than a hospital gown. Her gaze skimmed him, not wanting to linger on the muscular shoulders and trim hips she thought she knew so well. It just further proved her wolf's point—if she could barely look him in the face, how was she supposed to guide him to finding a spirit animal to be his constant companion?

Distracted, she led him to where the fae had set up a semi-permanent portal in an unused closet to keep it hidden from casual visitors. Though this was a vampire abode, fae and magic were still a topic of whispers and superstition amongst a people experiencing a lack of exposure. Putting this means of travel behind a door was the ultimate "out of sight, out of mind" for most who came and went.

She closed the door after them before they took this portal to their next destination. The convenience wasn't lost on her as they traveled deep underground in a matter of moments. "So, what did you mean, that your salvation fell from the sky?" Adrius asked, taking a glance around.

He saw the room for the first time, the location of the first portal strong enough to pierce the magical veil between Earth and her land, Adrun. They were in a squat cellar cleared and deep scrubbed with the pungent tang of chemicals. Nyah's sensitive nose still picked up a hint of dried blood, enough to make her face wrinkle with distaste.

In the center of the cellar rippled a dark hole in reality. She stepped toward it, careful not to place her feet on any of the smears on the ground around it. Dark magic had created this portal, but an Alchemyst's blood had turned it from a doorway to Hell into a window to Adrun instead. Nyah gave quiet thanks to her junior Alchemyst, Olivia, for averting that disaster.

"Come, see for yourself," she said, extending a hand out to him as she backed into the portal, her feet moving from packed dirt to plush carpeting.

One side effect to Olivia casting a call into Adrun—she couldn't quite control where the other side of the portal landed. Thus, it was permanently in Izell's living room, an arrangement the dragon shifter was *not* happy about.

Nyah led Adrius from the house, breathing in the eternal night of Adrun with a smile on her face. It was wild, sweet, and free, her home made cozy in a land that the fae of Faerie had set aside as a place of eternal punishment. From behind her, Adrius breathed, "*This* is the Fell Lands?"

"Nobody calls it that anymore. Out with the old, in with the new." She stepped off Izell's porch. Izell lived on the outskirts of the city, Dragonhelm, where Nyah held court. Preferring solitude to politics, her friend had built a cottage out in the middle of the woods, where the twittering of birds and the rustle of wind through the trees were her only companions.

Adrius gawked, his head on a swivel. "Remember, three thousand years," she said gently.

When his attention turned back to her at last, he stared. "There's a..." he pointed to his own hair. "A butterfly."

"Just one?" she smiled, hoping this would stir some memory in him. Her first experiments with shaping life with her two Keys were the butterflies, bioluminescent creatures that were keen to perch on her as if they knew she'd made the first of them. She'd created them for fun, to be able to hold something pretty.

The old Adrius was endlessly amused that, given the power to create life, the first thing she'd done was make butterflies. Now, he smiled as if remembering before turning his gaze to the sky. Disappointment tickled her stomach as she did the same. "Look there." She inched closer and pointed toward a particular spot in the sky. She knew now that the glittering ceiling over her land was not stars and midnight ink, as it first appeared, but the shimmer of many multifaceted crystals only seen in a Faerie reef. There was one glimpse they had of the land above, in the shape of a torn hole the size of a finger pinch from their vantage, which leaked orange light.

"What am I looking at?" he asked.

"Adrun only exists due to the magic of Faerie itself. We are in a bubble of perfect exile. Nothing comes in, nothing goes back out." So as to not cause him further anxiety, she didn't mention that Adrun was the model for Nyixa in that it was an island capable of being submerged under the ocean. Unlike Nyixa, Adrun existed in a sizable dome of air and was stable at the bottom of Faerie's ocean.

"There was only one person who ever defied the odds and came from Faerie to Adrun. Izell, leading a host of willing spirits. She opened a hole in the enchantment for them, and to this day, it's translucent in that one spot. We call the day Spirit's Fall, and it changed everything." She felt herself slip back to old memories. Izell had shaken this little land with an earthquake and a gush of ocean water, falling for miles to join the land of exile.

"Why would anyone want to come here?" he asked. With a glance to her, he cleared his throat. "No offense."

She shook her head. "None taken. She came here because she knew what it was like. Izell has a storied past—you should ask for all the details, as it's not my place to share it all. When she was in Faerie, she discovered that the act of merging a person with an animal's spirit made it impossible for the combination to be Fell. It was an accident for her but purposeful for the rest of us."

"That sounds like quite the story," he remarked.

"Indeed. Izell didn't lead just any spirits here, though. Fae are more in tune with nature and the earth than we could ever be. They have a habit of forming bonds with animals and taming them into familiars. When the Fell swept through Faerie...one of many casualties were the familiars." Both of them took on grim expressions. He probably remembered it as clear as day, with his experiences fresher than hers. Fell would consume anything down to bones, man or animal alike. "So, Izell took the ghosts of the familiars to reunite with their masters. Thus was the death of the Fell and the birth of the shifters, formed from two souls already bonded in love and harmony in life *and* in death." Her eyes stung in remembrance of Spirit's Fall, a day of such joy for her people.

"There's something poetic about that," he murmured. "But you are a shifter as well? How did you find a spirit?"

She started down a path into the woods, beckoning for him to follow. "Many deceased Seelie familiars came with the first group. Izell promised a new start, and they took it. My wolf was one of them. We found that the animals I created from the Autumn and Spring Keys often take the magic that made them and become spirits in their afterlife. Not all choose to do this, and they rejoin the land like fae do when they die. But this is how we've been able to perpetuate shifters past the initial union. We have plenty of spirits for our children."

Adrius kept pace with her, a thoughtful expression crossing his face. "That is a lot to take in," he admitted. "So, you have a way to introduce new people to spirits? And you want me to do this too? Why?"

"Well, yes," she said slowly, knowing she had to pick her words carefully. "Part of the trial is reviewing old memories. Maybe you'll remember more once you've done it."

Maybe you'll remember me, she thought, hope thudding within to the beat of her heart.

Chapter 6
Adrius

He went quiet sometime during her explanation, finding it hard to believe that a world like this existed and was now connected to his own. A place where it was normal, and even expected, to become part animal in a coming of age ceremony that was once a necessity to survive. He needed to take the trial too. He'd decided the moment she suggested his memory would return.

But another part of him worried, and he finally voiced it as he saw their path join a white-bricked road sloping upward, toward a city marked by a palace of ivory rock, its towers stabbing high into the sky. It was so similar to the now-destroyed castle on Nyixa that he had to do a double take. "Will I lose my powers?" he asked in a hush.

He was known to possess some form of every vampiric ability due to his own folly in assuming he could hold the power of the strongest Fell within him. He was full to the brim with darkness, as signified by the shadows he could summon with hardly a thought.

"Probably," she admitted, turning to lead him down the road away from her city. They passed further into darkness, the forest thickening with trees and overgrowth on either side of them. "Most former vampires lose what makes them vampires. It's like wiping the slate clean. Starting anew as something else."

One thing stuck out to him: starting again. He wished he could wipe his worries away as easily as she made out this change to be. "No more Fell Madness?" he asked, certain of his choice when she confirmed it.

No more losing his sanity and, on top of that, a chance to remember what he'd lost. He would be crazy not to try it. "I will attempt your trial," he said.

"Outstanding. You will need a guide." She spoke briskly as her pace redoubled. He wondered if she worried that he'd change his mind. "Anyone bonded to a greater spirit can join you on your journey and explain what each animal spirit you meet represents. A guide is there to help you make the right choice the first time."

"The first time," he echoed.

"That's right. Sometimes there's a bad match. The person and their spirit don't get along, so they need to be separated by magic...something that is very painful." She shuddered at the thought. "Or you may run out of time. The potion that allows you to see and interact with spirits lasts anywhere from a week to ten days, but we have the occasional dud. Bad day in the alchemy lab." She offered a smile and a hesitant chuckle, like it was meant to be a joke.

"Are you bonded to a greater spirit?" he asked, earning a nod from her. "Why don't you be my guide?"

Her expression pinched like she tasted something sour. "Conflict of interest." With a face like that, he guessed she wanted to but really couldn't. Part of him ached with disappointment. She seemed to care for him despite his memory loss, a stark contrast to what he'd left behind on Earth. Surely that would make her a good guide for him.

"All trials start at a shrine. I'm taking you to one that serves the city," she continued. "If we're lucky, a guide will wait in the area. As a quirk to our animal sides, sometimes we can tell when a new person is in need."

Making a noncommittal grunt, he waited for what was in store. It was still shocking to see a land full of greenery when he knew the Fell came from a place of endless ashy desert. To think those monsters were completely gone. Now, they lived on as echoes in vampiric bloodlines as the evil lurking within that separated vampires from their mortal brethren.

They went off the white-brick path, following a rabbit trail her keen eyes spotted. As a vampire, he could pick out shades in the night to construct a grayscale understanding of his surroundings. The leaves and grass were tipped with dark green as they rustled from an errant breeze.

Nyah stopped short, her gaze turning toward a crunch in the underbrush. Out slinked a furry form, turning liquid-dark eyes their way. An odd tension filled the woman as the animal bounded ahead of them. "I see one such candidate already," she remarked.

"Is something wrong?" he asked, tempted to put a hand on her shoulder to rub some of that tightness away. But he didn't. It wasn't his place.

"Hmm? No, not at all. Here we are!" She put cheer to her voice and a bounce to her step as they emerged into a clearing full of broad, starlit sky. It didn't take him long to discover the shrine, which was a statue of a life-sized woman standing back-to-back with a wolf. He was surprised at how large the wolf was rendered, coming up to the woman's shoulder with a fang-lined maw drawn back in a fearsome snarl.

When they were closer, he recognized the features of the immortalized woman. "That's you," he said. She was dressed in a gown with a decorative, filigreed breastplate. Unlike the wolf behind her, this statue's rendition had a peaceful expression and held a bouquet of flowers and herbs. Someone had woven a fairy crown of real wildflowers to perch on the statue's head, and one of her butterflies perched on a blossom to complete the effect.

"I...yeah. This is my shrine." She sounded embarrassed as she knelt by the wolf's form and slid a wooden box out from under its paw. She retrieved a few items and replaced it after murmuring a few words of power. "There are four in total. They're full of magic, even if they look ordinary."

She stood, holding a vial and a glass ball the size of her palm. After giving it a shake, the ball ignited with warm light like a lamp. She offered it to him first, and he found it naturally bobbed a few inches over his skin. "Very helpful if you put it on your shoulder," she said while giving the vial a vigorous thrashing in her fist. He didn't question the strangeness of the lamp, instead perching it on his shoulder like a pet. It was obviously magic, and he didn't care to understand magic if it was useful.

In the light of it, he caught his first true glimpse of the animal who'd followed them into the clearing. A handsome red fox sat a respectful distance away, its plush tail curled around its paws. It didn't look like it was in any hurry, just observing him and Nyah with a tilt of its head. He wouldn't think it anything special if it weren't double the size of every fox he'd ever seen.

"And this will start your trial once you drink it." Nyah offered him the vial next. Now that it was properly mixed, it was as thin as water and left an oily residue on the glass.

"Is the fox going to guide me? And how will I find you afterward?" he asked.

She glanced to the fox, who slinked forward and placed a paw in the air. "I'll guide you back as well. We'll find her together." Her voice was higher-pitched, as he'd expect of a fox's squeal. "Shake on it?"

He knelt and shook her delicate paw. "Deal."

"I'm Swift, by the way, short for Swift Spirit. That's too much of a mouthful," she said. He heard the smile in her tone and reasoned that was why her muzzle crinkled as if she really was making a pleasant expression.

"And I'm Adrius."

Her gaze broke from his with a gasp, shooting a look askance to Nyah. As he stood, he caught the woman nodding to Swift in acknowledgement of something unsaid. He wondered if shifters retained their ability to speak mentally and what he'd missed if they did.

"Good luck, Adrius," Nyah said, taking a step away. "I can't wait to see what you make of this trial."

He nodded in agreement, eager to see what was next. Uncorking the vial, he drank its contents in an oily gulp. The only Alchemyst potion he was intimately familiar with was the blood purification potion, which was intense and painful as it scrubbed out corruption from the whole body. He expected something similar and ended up pleasantly surprised when all that happened was his belly making an uncomfortable roll and his eyes itching.

After giving them a good rub, he saw something new standing only a yard away. A tabby cat that would be unremarkable if it didn't have a ghostly white outline with trailing wisps at the corners of its body. It was obviously a spirit. He hesitated, wondering if he was meant to talk to it. Could spirits talk if they were just ghosts?

"Hi!" The cat ghost answered the question for him as it wound around his ankles, leaning against his boots like the living thing. He felt it purr, and when he knelt to scratch its ears, it was solid.

"Um. Hello." Now he just wasn't sure how to talk to a cat.

"I'm a shrine cat. Everyone's first spirit," it meowed. "The potion you drank briefly gives you the chance to interact with spirits as if we were still alive. See? I'm just like any other cat. But to anyone who isn't a medium or your guide, it looks like you're interacting with thin air."

Adrius glanced up to see if this was true for Nyah, but the woman was gone. He would have to figure out the trial on his own.

"You're the most intelligent cat I've ever met," he remarked.

"Yeah, well..." It sat back on its haunches. "Spirits are smarter than living animals, remember that. It's the magic. By the way, I like to be scratched on the back of my neck."

His lips curled in an amused smile as he took that unsubtle hint and started petting it too. "I'll take that under advisement."

After a few minutes, it padded away from him. "Well, what are you waiting for?" it asked, tilting its head. "Go find your match!"

Chapter 7
Adrius

THE FOX, SWIFT, LED HIM OUT OF THE FOREST AFTER THEY stopped to have a chat with a chimpanzee spirit. It barely gave him the time of day before it went back to its task of hunting for something to eat. "It's okay. Chimps usually look for brainy people. They represent intelligence," Swift told him.

Distracted from wondering if animal spirits ate other animal spirits, he furrowed his brow. "Are you trying to say I'm not intelligent?"

"No no!" She let off a squealing laugh. "Not at all! Just that your defining trait isn't your smarts, otherwise it would've been more interested in you."

He was pretty sure she'd just implied it. And he wasn't offended, because he knew he wasn't book smart. He'd made a career out of hitting monsters really hard after all.

"But I do need to find out what traits do define you, so I have a few questions." Swift frolicked as she spoke, bouncing on her delicate paws through the thick undergrowth. They were at the top of a hill, overlooking the land as trees grew sparser and gave way to endless waves of grass stretching as far as he could see. Just seeing how far they could go, combined with her energy, made him feel tired.

"Go ahead," he said.

"What animal do you think represents you best and why?"

He thought he was ready for a question and answer round, but this first one threw him. He'd considered heraldry before. As a king, he was expected to have a symbol to represent himself. However, he'd hardly sat on the throne long enough to design his own heraldry. He said the first thing that came to mind. "A badger. Something tough, nocturnal, and willing to take on things twice its size."

Swift giggled in response. "That's a good answer! Most people say lion or bear, like we all have to be big bloodthirsty predators." He opened his mouth and then closed it, realizing either of those animals would've been a better, more king-worthy answer. She was already a few yards ahead of him, her head popping out of a bush to see if he was still following. "So, you think your defining trait is toughness?"

"I would say so." Heaven knew he'd been through a lot in his long life.

"Good to know!" They spent the next hour or more with her asking more questions. Silly things. "Would you rather's" and "this or that's" that he wasn't sure actually helped her since he answered her immediately instead of giving any deep thought. It felt like she was asking more things than necessary and was keenly interested in every response.

He saw his next spirit in one of the last trees. It was a crow, watching them pass with beady eyes. "Aspirant!" it exclaimed, taking wing. The bird circled over him like a shadow in the night. "Aspirant!"

Swift went alert and stared into the underbrush. "Be right back!" She disappeared into the sway of tall grass, giving him a moment alone. He spotted horses in the distance, some with a ghostly glow mingling with other, living animals. A dog barked, leading a leisurely group of spirit sheep over the hill in front of him.

"Aspirant!" the crow cawed.

The furry figure of the sheepdog lifted its head, giving one last bark to its flock before loping his way. Adrius knelt down to meet it when it arrived, allowing it to lick his face. "Aren't you a sweet fellow?" he cooed. This spirit was a solidly built dog in the prime of its life, its fur black with a white stripe across the center of its muzzle.

"Hello, person." The dog's bark was gruff enough to be masculine. "I sense that you are very loyal."

He didn't know how to reply to that but didn't need to when Swift returned, leading a second spirit to him. He had to chuckle —she'd found a badger. "Oh! Well, I'm not too surprised." She giggled. "Do you want to test him?" she asked the sheepdog.

Placing a paw on his arm, the dog said, "Show me your loyalty."

He finally saw why Nyah mentioned memories when it came to the trial. Somehow, this spirit compelled a memory from him, as crisp as it happened moments ago. He was back-to-back with Sirius, blood pouring from a wound to his forehead.

"We're outnumbered!" his brother shouted. Most of their men were dead, savaged by Fell. On the horizon was a small village, and the two of them were the only thing stopping the razor-fanged Fell from consuming it down to bones and splinters.

"Press on..." The memory faded. It was enough. Adrius remembered how it ended. A narrowly-won victory and another knot in his beard.

His mind's eye shifted, and he saw her. Nyah dressed in a plain dress from another time, her hair a perfect fall of ringlets down her back as she applied cosmetics. Something like dread crawled up his back as he saw his expression in the mirror. Enamored by the simple motion of her primping. She was human in this memory, but...

No less beautiful, he thought. And like a kick to the heart, the memories continued to pour in. Nyah and him meeting at a formal dinner. She was the daughter of his commander, stealing shy glances across the table at him seated amongst the first vampires. A blush marked her pale cheeks after he caught her eye and winked.

He'd courted her like a gentleman, with kisses on her fingertips and stolen moments between fighting, strategizing, and training with his army.

How had he forgotten?

When he was crowned King of Vampires, there she was by his side in a wedding dress with a train of gold fabric as vibrant as a shooting star. He'd placed a crown of moonstone and silver upon her brow, marking her as his wife and queen. His equal, with her gentle ways and deep desire for peace.

They'd had months together. And then the unspeakable happened. He'd lost her and never looked at another woman the same way. That was the loyalty the dog spirit wanted to see, and Adrius blinked back into reality with wetness dripping down his cheeks. He shook his head in denial, his body flushing hot and then cold with chills to follow.

"*Why?*" he asked in a broken whisper. Why had he forgotten? Why didn't his time in Heaven restore his memory of her?

He'd completely blundered with her. His wife, miraculously returned from the dead. Something he'd yearned for with his whole heart for a thousand years! He saw her hurt expression anew. Sirius's disgust. Jaromir's worry.

Brushing his cheeks, he realized he was crying with a disgusted scoff. *Pathetic.* He was still the same person who'd allowed a demon to rearrange his head and take out the most important memories. Who'd let Lucia sit on the vampire throne for twenty years while he died over and over in pointless fighting and outbursts of Fell Madness from the futility of it all. The man who'd, time and again, let his little brother clean up after his every mistake.

Throwing his head back, he roared to the heavens. He'd shake the foundation of this little land—Adrun, named after *him*. He clawed at his face and hair, ripping a braid from his beard with a furious yank.

The sheepdog nuzzled his shoulder with a whine. "You are very loyal. You're destined for a spirit stronger than I," he said, pressing in to give Adrius comforting warmth.

His attention was on the braided hair in his palm. A relic of his past. "I'm...defeated," he said heavily.

Both Swift and the dog looked on in concern as he pulled the knife he'd secreted in his boot. He was never without something sharp, even when mingling in polite society. "What are you doing?" Swift asked in an uncertain whisper.

He drew the knife up, stopping at his throat with a tremor to his hand. *Am I really going to do this?* he asked himself. Swift exchanged a glance with the sheepdog, both of them pressing in for furry warmth. He realized at some point that the badger spirit had left, probably to find someone more worthy.

"Please don't do this," the dog said, pressing a wet nose to his wrist.

Adrius grabbed the ends of his beard and sheared through it a couple inches from his chin. He tossed the evidence of his past deeds away and sheathed the dagger. "It is time I started again," he murmured, grabbing the dog to hug to his chest and smiling wanly through a thorough face washing. He used the animal's coat to hide his tears as he wondered what was next.

How could he go on? What other, more unpleasant memories would he wake in himself by continuing this trial? "I want to go back. I need to see Nyah." He had to go apologize. He had to hold her and remind her what his love meant.

Swift was silent, watching with a somberness that reminded him that she wasn't really a fox but probably a fae thousands of years his senior. "She wanted you to finish your trial, no matter what."

"You don't understand," he murmured.

"The trial can be brutal for some. You have to look at yourself as a whole person instead of just the good sides." She stood and shook out her glossy fur. "As your guide, I saw what you just did. It may hurt now...but aren't you glad you remembered?"

"You saw?" He felt a twinge of embarrassment for her to see his more vulnerable moments in the swirl of his recollection. "I fear what else I may remember."

"The world never forgets our deeds. Come. You will be glad you did." She nudged the sheepdog aside, who cast a glance back to Adrius before running back to his flock. Swift padded away too.

Adrius knew she wouldn't leave him, but he still hadn't felt more alone than that moment. He beat himself up mentally for the colossal waste of space he was, deciding he wouldn't move because there was no point. If a spirit could call back his memories, they would all find something in him to revile.

It was just like the time after Nyixa had risen from the sea and he'd woken from his thousand year-long slumber. He'd dragged his sorry self to the throne room and sat, waiting for the world to go by. Because it would, it *had*, and he was a relic of the past too cursed by the Shield Key to die.

Wind pushed him forward instead as a massive form flew overhead. He went sprawling on his face. Spluttering, he pushed to his elbows in time to watch a scaled form swoop from the sky and grab two sheep spirits in its ghostly claws before flying off. The sheepdog barked after it furiously.

He finally stood, brushing himself off. "What was that thing?" he called to Swift. She'd stopped further in the grass to wait for him.

"You haven't seen a dragon before?" she asked.

He laughed in sheer disbelief. When Swift circled back to nudge him, though, he walked. Maybe he would see the dragon again if he kept going.

Chapter 8
Adrius

"WHAT DOES THE DRAGON REPRESENT?" HE ASKED.

He kept his eyes on the horizon, trying to make out where the creature had flown. In the dark, all he saw were seemingly endless fields of grass and the peaceful animals, alive and spirited, that called it home.

Swift padded by his side, keeping an eye on him as if expecting another fit. That's what he called them—fits—where he could barely string a coherent sentence with how little he cared sitting at the bottom of the pit he'd dug for himself. But it was out of his system. He had something other than his failings to occupy his mind.

"In a word, power," she answered. "Dragons are the most powerful beasts. Fae society reveres four dragon gods, one for each element. To have a living dragon as your familiar brings a fae great respect."

"And what does it mean to be a dragon shifter?"

There was a glimmer in her eyes. "It means you're Izell, the only fae old enough to have met King Oberon. There are no other dragon shifters."

"But there are dragon spirits," he said.

"One. There's one dragon spirit," she corrected. "And he's a bitter old man who doesn't want to pair with another."

She looked at him more closely as an idea budded in his head.

Something to prove his worth, if only to himself, and show Nyah he was dedicated to the trial she wanted him to finish. "It's not a good idea," the fox chided.

"I didn't say anything."

"I can tell what you're thinking with that grin of yours." She shook her head. "Zerenth will reject you. Besides, we'll never get to his mountain before your potion wears off."

"You underestimate me, fox." If there was one thing his shadows were good for, it was moving fast. "Even if he rejects me, I would like to look into the eyes of a dragon and tell Nyah of the experience." He had to do something impressive with this time apart. In the likely chance he was unworthy of the dragon spirit, he could at least tell her that he tried.

"Many have lost their lives wanting to do just that," she said. "The potion you drank makes it possible for you to interact with spirits in all ways. He can easily bat you off his mountain and send you plummeting to your death."

He barely gave that consideration. "Good thing I cannot die."

Swift sighed to herself. "It will take a fortnight on foot if we ran day and night."

"I can get us there in half the time. There's only one problem; I need blood." He felt the sharp tips of his fangs refusing to retract and the telltale dryness in his mouth like he'd gargled with sand. He hadn't had a drop since he'd last died. It was a wonder he'd made it so far without noticing, so caught up in his troubles.

"I'll give you some of mine," Swift offered. He could've kissed her furry snout. She was probably the only creature for miles that could give him blood rich enough for him to be able to call on his vampiric abilities.

"Thank y—"

"On one condition."

His mouth snapped closed. "First, you have to speak to three more spirits and seriously consider bonding with one of them," she said.

ADRIUS SPOKE TO A HORSE SPIRIT FIRST, REPRESENTATIVE OF endurance. Looking into the creature's liquid brown eyes, he recalled memories of his many deaths, starting from the first horrific time he'd ingested a poisoned potion that'd stopped his heart. "You have endured much," the horse said with sympathy, nosing Adrius's cheek. "You will make a good match to a spirit stronger than I."

As he stroked its velvet snout, an idea came to mind. "That's all right. Would you do me a favor?"

The horse spirit, Red, agreed to being his steed for the week. He rode bareback with Swift draped over his shoulders like a living scarf. All the easier for her to ask little curiosity questions to pass the time. They galloped through lush fields together until Adrius's lids grew heavy. Overhead, a voice cawed, "Aspirant!" to announce him. He strongly suspected it was the same crow who'd spotted him at the forest's edge.

He rested for the night with his tongue feeling like it was stuck to the roof of his mouth. Despite the way his mind threatened to replay the day's events the moment he closed his eyes, he dropped into dark unconsciousness as exhaustion overwhelmed him.

Then he woke to sharp teeth closing around his nose. He shot upright, startling Swift from her friendly nip. "Let's go!" she exclaimed. "I found another spirit for you."

He did a double take when he saw the ghostly creature waiting for his attention. "Where...did you find him?" he asked hesitantly. A lion with a full, dark mane sat on his haunches a stone's throw away. On the other side of Adrius, giving the newcomer a leery eye, was Red, standing at the alert.

"Does it matter?" Swift giggled and scampered behind him, giving him an encouraging push.

Lions, he learned, represented courage. Adrius woke up fully as he relived his most and least daring moments. The times he'd stood against impossible odds for mankind were soured by the moments he'd been seized by his fits, too apathetic to lift a finger even for his own benefit. He thought they'd balance out, but the lion kept drawing out more and more forgotten moments where he'd let down his friends and family by simply watching the world go by.

"I don't believe we're a match," the spirit said at last, cutting off the funnel of memories. After eyeing Red, he prowled away, leaving Adrius clutching his knees and gasping for air.

Swift pressed her soft fur to the backs of his hands. "You had to see it," she said.

"I had to see...that I'm a *coward?*" he spat.

"That's a strong word for it."

"That's the only word for it." He blew out a sigh, standing straight and cracking his neck. "One more to go." He needed that blood soon, but the thought of going through the memory process even one more time made him shudder.

He hoisted Swift to his shoulders and mounted Red, and off they went toward the spires of a distant mountain range. He rode in grim silence, sure they would come across another spirit willing to test him soon as the crow took up its distant caw of his aspirant status. It'd silenced itself while he was sleeping, just to resume the moment he was on the move again.

What creature would he end up taking with him? He saw himself somewhere between the hierarchy of a horse and a lion. Perhaps a lesser predator of some sort. First, he had to see the dragon. The starting point was so far from its den that he knew most aspirants never stood before it. But he had no illusion that the dragon would come with him despite representing power, the one thing Adrius had in abundance.

Doubts niggled at him as they thundered ever closer to the creature's mountain home. He knew he was holding on to a futile hope that, somehow, he'd succeed in winning over the dragon anyway.

He was tonguing the sharp edge of a fang when the next spirit swooped out of the sky. He only noticed it because the crow suddenly squawked in alarm and ceased its constant calling above him. "Missed!" it cawed instead.

Fluttering beside it on arrow-shaped wings was a spirit falcon. *Beautiful bird,* he thought. Not a feather out of place. He'd admired the sport of falconry from afar. Owning a falcon was one of many items on his old list of things to accomplish. It was a wealthy man's pastime, and at some point, he'd fancied himself so noble.

"If I wanted to catch you, I would!" the falcon called back, tucking its wings into a neat dive until it came in for a landing on Red's neck.

"Peregrine falcon, representing self-control," Swift said.

"What she said. Fastest diving bird, incredible eyesight, all of that," it said, waving a wing in apparent dismissal. "But that's not important. You're a human. We don't get many humans."

While he marveled at the bird a touch away, he got the impression it was doing the same to him. How surreal, to be the unique one here, when he came from a land that hosted a mind-boggling *billions* of humans. "You might be getting more soon," Adrius said. He couldn't imagine he'd be the only one slated for a spirit trial even amongst his friends, not to mention the countless other vampires who could also benefit.

"Well, you're here now." The falcon laid a wing on his hand to test him and bring forth memories of self-control. He hoped he would be worthy of it.

As the memories rolled in, his level of worthiness became apparent. He saw himself succumbing to Fell Madness, blacking out in a bar just to find himself surrounded by corpses drained of blood.

"I would not suffer a monster to live," he'd said, before plunging his blade into his chest.

His many lives balanced on the knife's edge of control. He was too much of a vampire, full to the brim with bloodlusting darkness that waited for a lapse in judgment.

The swirl of memories slowed as it showed him something more modern. Looking into the golden eyes of the second Alche-myst, Olivia, as she told him their resident fae were looking to scry the Fell Lands for Nyah. "Nyah's *dead,* you charlatan. How dare you make a mockery of her memory." He felt himself cringe in retrospect, seeing just how wrong he was. How fear crept over the girl's face as she watched him give himself to the whispering darkness.

Not his Fell Madness.

But the demon.

The same demon who'd constantly chipped him down. Called him worthless, pathetic. Told him that no one wanted him around. Laughed as it told him he ruined everything.

Adrius choked on a breath as he realized how much he'd internalized that voice. The demon was gone from him, but he continued to say those things for it. He was supposedly the toughest of his kind, yet he'd let a little voice within topple him like a house of cards.

It was as Sirius said. *The only unfair thing I see is that the strongest vampire in the world has the weakest will.*

He came back to himself feeling of two minds: torn and complete. His memories were whole again—on some level, he knew that—but he was suitably ruined by his own failings. "I'm sorry for wasting your time," he told the falcon, daring to brush its feathery chest with the back of his hand.

It regarded him with its head tilted. Despite how intelligent and expressive the animals he'd met on his trial were, its beak rendered its face as inflexible as its living counterpart. He expected its dismissal to be just as quick as the lion's. "I think we would be a good match," it said instead.

"You....what?" He scrubbed his ears.

"I think we would be a good match!" it repeated as if he were hard of hearing.

Red's hoof beats slowed, ears pinned back to listen for Adrius's response, which was caught in his throat. "You saw what I did?" he asked in a hush.

"Oh yes. It was quite awful." The bird gave a bob. "I sensed something else in you through all that."

Though tempted to quip back, Adrius waited out the falcon's pause for effect. "I sensed that you're determined to change that last part. And I can help! So, what do you say?"

He took in the waiting spirit of an animal he admired so highly. "Maybe," he answered.

Red, Swift, and the falcon all twitched in unison. "Maybe?" Swift repeated in disbelief.

"I have a dragon to meet."

"Zerenth the Fury? Do you *know* what he did to the last aspirant to go to his lair? He breathed fire all over that fae!" The falcon spread its wings with a dramatic screech.

Adrius lifted a shoulder. "I want to try, and I'm sure he will say no. That means you'll be my spirit. Will you humor the attempt?"

The falcon hesitated. "Well, all right. But only if I get to watch! You're the most interesting aspirant we've had in years."

Swift only offered her blood to him when it was obvious he needed it. He nearly fell off Red's back as weakness set in on the end of a hard day's ride. Red never tired as a horse spirit, so the constant gallop was simply a thrilling challenge for him.

Adrius's whole body throbbed even after he'd taken a careful meal of the fox's blood. But he went to sleep with a smile on his face. If he wasn't a dragon, then he was a falcon, and he was quite all right with either ending. With the falcon circling overhead, there was no longer a crow announcing his aspirant status, and thus, they crossed the plains without him having to face another spirit's test.

He traveled for days with only a horse, fox, and falcon as his companions on the way to see a dragon, a situation he would've thought impossibly bizarre only a week ago. Red carried him until they reached a rocky path that promised to lead to Zerenth the Fury's lair. "I think this is where we part ways," the horse said.

"Thank you, friend." Adrius patted down Red's flanks in appreciation. He wished he had an apple or sugar cube to offer, for in his trial, he'd noticed spirits still ate and predated just like they had in life. Swift had explained that prey species were reborn the next day so all spirits could still live like they used to.

"Thank you for bringing me some excitement." The horse nudged Adrius's chest. "Good luck to you." He shook himself out and galloped away, back to his herd, leaving Adrius to exchange a glance with Swift.

"Well, let's see what happens," she said, slinking ahead. He saw why soon enough, as the path ended and became a climb. She and the falcon helped him pick out the right ledges to reach for. Physical exertion like this was his element, though, and he excelled even after days of hard riding. He used his shadows to boost him, scrabbling up the rock face like some dark squirrel.

When they were close to the summit, there was a new path to follow. Swift stopped before him, blocking the way as her bushy tail flipped behind her. "If you really are doing this, know that I'm still with you. Just not too closely." Her nose twitched from the scent of wood smoke and burning meat drifting from what had to be the dragon's den.

He scooped her up for a hug, earning a yip of surprise before he set her back on her paws. "I know, thank you. I couldn't have asked for a better guide."

"Do I get one too?" The falcon watched them from a scrub tree. Adrius was very careful when he held it, considering the little bird's fragile bones. "I hope the dragon says no so you take me instead."

"We'll just have to see, won't we?" He placed it back on a branch and squared his shoulders. This was it, then. He had the chance to really impress Nyah and end his spirit trial on a high note.

He found the dragon sitting on its feet like a lounging cat. Zerenth the Fury's spade-tipped tail flicked while his red gaze narrowed in on Adrius. A warning growl rumbled in his throat. He was actually smaller than Adrius expected, being somewhere around double the size of a draft horse with his wings tucked like a grounded bird.

The light of Adrius's lamp glittered off onyx scales and a proud ridge of spines along the dragon's back and forelimbs. His head came to a point at the snout, permanently turned up in a superior expression as his nostrils flared.

When Zerenth spoke, his voice was deep and powerful, shaking the stone under Adrius's feet. "Another aspirant here to disturb my rest. I don't understand. Isn't it obvious I want to be left alone? I chose this mountain far from any of the four shrines."

"A challenge that I accepted. I am Adrius, King of Vampires." He bowed to the creature, sensing that some respect was due.

"A king? Here?" Zerenth leaned down on his long neck, blowing meaty breath over him. "Has no one told you that most aspirants who make it to this peak never return?"

"Yes." Up close, he could see every striation in the dragon's eye as it shaded to yellow around a slit pupil. A membrane swished over its glossy surface.

"And yet you persisted. Why?"

"I had to see you. I had to try," he said. "Will you test me?"

Zerenth's laugh made it feel like the earth quaked. "Do you think you are better than everyone else because you are a king?" He rose to his taloned feet, looming over Adrius. "Do you think I am the only spirit in this land worthy of you?"

"It's not that—"

"No?" The dragon tilted his head. "Let's see what your heart says." He touched the curved end of one talon to Adrius's shoulder, and the memories began.

Adrius didn't know what he'd expected Zerenth to pull. But instead of just the memories of Adrius's power, the dragon kept him pinned in place as he relived everything. *Everything.* From the first memory to the last, he was stuck in a swirling maelstrom of his own thoughts and feelings as Zerenth laid his life out like a surgeon.

He staggered back, his legs threatening to collapse. The surge of magic between them made it feel like his stomach had flipped over. "I see," Zerenth said. "You wish to use me as a trophy to impress your wife."

"No. I want her to see that I am worthy of a dragon such as you," he said quickly.

The dragon snorted. "You're no more worthy than any of the others. Did the crown cut off circulation to your head?"

"I wear no crown." He spoke through gritted teeth. This wasn't where he wanted the conversation to go.

"True. You only wore it for a few months anyway. The rest

of the time, you used the title like a crutch. You're not a king, Adrius Fabron. You're not even mated to Queen Nyah anymore. I won't sacrifice myself so you can win her back." The dragon turned a look his way, contempt clear on his lizard face.

Adrius balled his hands into fists. He took a breath and turned to leave, just for Zerenth to block his way. "You walked into my home, and I choose when you go," the dragon rumbled.

"Step aside," he said in a low voice.

"I have another question. A burning question." Zerenth held up a claw, a tongue of flame escaping his pointed maw. "What are you going to do when Nyah learns you married Lucia?"

"That was political. And unconsummated." He took a deep breath, squaring up with the massive creature. How dare he even mention that? He'd been at the peak of his desperation to try it some thousand years ago.

Zerenth leaned into his face with a laugh. "I think it'll break her heart. Again."

Adrius didn't think. Between one blink and the next, the dragon's head snapped back, and his knuckles ached from the impact with hard scales. "That's right, fight the truth!" His wings flared, and he lifted a foot from the ground.

His claws flashed past where Adrius was standing. With vampiric speed, he was on the other side of the creature, punching its other cheek. Zerenth flipped his tail around, its spade pointed straight at his heart. "Fight for all your worth," the dragon hissed, his eyes narrowing to pinpoints when Adrius caught his tail, the spike inches from his skin.

With a roar, Adrius called on his shadows and every ounce of his strength, dragging his opponent back to the ground. He climbed Zerenth's spines like a ladder, ducking between them when the dragon's snapping maw approached. As his wings opened and he took a running leap off the mountain, Adrius held onto the biggest spine while the change of air pressure nearly forced him off the dragon's back.

He jumped toward where wing met body and pulled, dislocating the wing with a loud pop and veering Zerenth from the open sky into a crash landing against the rock face. *You're wrong about me,* Adrius thought, thrown forward by the impact.

The dragon grabbed him as they went tumbling down the mountain. Adrius punched and kicked, struggling against the squeezing talons threatening to crush his ribcage. He couldn't avoid the next few bites that shredded his flesh. Blood flew from the wounds with each hard impact of their bodies on rock.

Heat mounted at the back of the dragon's throat. It glowed like a stoked furnace. Adrius shot out a thick tendril of shadow to wrap around Zerenth's throat to cut off his air before it became flame. Embers spat upon his face, smarting like wasp stings.

They cleared a rocky ledge, landing again on Zerenth's flank. It still smashed the breath from Adrius's lungs. Pointed stones lacerated him on the next impact, this time square on his back. He and the dragon grunted in pain, but they couldn't let up now. They were locked in a grapple, his hands holding the dragon's jaws and those teeth wavering toward his throat.

Weightlessness hit them both again. Adrius saw over his opponent's scaly shoulder that they were in free fall now, clearing the last ledge between them and the bottom of the mountain. He knew he was about to die. But he'd be damned if he wasn't taking this arrogant, overgrown lizard with him.

He and Zerenth jockeyed to land on top, spinning at a nose-bleed-inducing pace. He was sure he would win this duel, but the ground had other ideas. They landed abruptly in a tangle of limbs and scales with a bone-deep *crunch.*

"Hah...good fight..." Zerenth went limp, his ghostly form fading into wisps on the wind.

Adrius rested a hand over where it hurt worst, a laugh bubbling to his lips too. It *was* a good fight. He let the darkness take him from there.

Chapter 9
Nyah

She stripped behind a solid oak, placing her dress in a chest secured within its roots. Nyah called upon her wolf to take control and relished in the feeling of the change through her body. Her concerns and fears for Adrius faded to a dull ache under the fierce wildness of Night's Howl, who reared her head back and pierced the sky with her namesake.

"No need for dramatics. We're here," grumbled Izell as she stepped into the clearing Adrius had just left. By her side was Taryn, his black skin marked with deep corruption. "Decided you wanted to guide after all?" The fae turned to inspect her.

"I thought a wolf would be more agreeable than a dragon," Nyah said.

Izell shook her head and offered Taryn a potion to start his trial. The man didn't move to take it or even acknowledge her gesture. *"I do not think we will see much success here,"* she told Nyah privately with mental communication.

The old version of Fell Madness that gripped him was triggered by intense negative emotion. Nyah had seen it manifest from rage, fear, and hunger—the kind of hunger the Fell themselves carried, to consume anything living down to their marrow. She'd found that most cases of Fell Madness were curable in vampires, if not from her purification potions, then by resolving whatever had created the spike of emotion in the first place.

Taryn was a unique case. He didn't respond to potions, and the only resolution he'd accept was his fingers around Lucia's throat. Great depths of vengeance boiled in his blood until it ran in rivers of black through his veins. Even as he stood there with a seemingly blank expression, he was calculating whether what they offered would put him closer to his ultimate revenge. Nyah's empathy could feel the waves of rage simmering under his façade.

"If you take the potion, it'll help give you new powers to take on Lucia," Nyah offered. He nodded stiffly, holding out his hand for the vial.

Izell would've had to tell him something similar to convince him to walk all this way. As he drank the potion to take him into his own trial, Nyah wondered how much of this he understood. Was there a hint of the old Taryn hidden within, or had he withered away? He'd served Lucia only because of exposure to a stage three love potion, an outlawed brew that induced love so intense it was akin to servitude.

He was right to be angry. But Nyah feared his rage would ruin him, especially as the trial's magic slid into place between them with her as his guide. She saw into the spirit world with him, saw the shrine cat attempt to greet him. She was supposed to feel a cursory brush of his emotions and disposition, enough to form an opinion on what direction to travel in first.

Taryn was as expressive as a statue. He neither attempted to interact with the cat spirit nor gave a hint of himself to the trial's magic. It was like trying to guide a boulder to the river for a drink. Her senses jarred.

"*We need to take him to Chandra,*" she said to Izell, nudging his leg. He followed at a reluctant pace while Izell held up the rear with her keen gaze focused on him. Should he surrender to his Fell Madness in full and attempt an attack, Nyah knew that Izell would stop him in a heartbeat.

"*Straight to an extreme case, hmm?*"

"*Did you tell him what he was getting into?*" Nyah asked.

Izell wrinkled her nose. "*Of course.*"

"*And did he seem to care?*"

"*Not at all. But we have not attempted the trial with him past the potion,*" Izell pointed out.

Nyah shot her a glance, wondering if she was serious or not. Izell considered it her duty as an advisor to advocate for the other side of even the most obvious decisions. "*He doesn't need a spirit animal. He needs a new start.*"

"*If that is what you think is wise.*" The fae put her fist over her heart.

She led them through the forest, toward a dirt path lined on either side by white stone. They would head toward the heart of Adrun for the goal she had in mind. "Taryn, I'm afraid your healing won't be as simple as a week-long trial." She turned to see if there was any acknowledgement in his expression.

The Madness had rendered his eyes two flat pools of ink, making it difficult to read the minute changes that flickered over his face. "Whatever helps me kill her," he rumbled.

"It is what comes after that concerns me," she said. Confusion marked him as he was forced to consider an *after*.

And seeing as Lucia would pass on her curse to the person who killed her, Taryn needed to shake the Fell Madness before he tried going after her.

Though her mind was made up, over the course of the next few days of travel, they tried to convince Taryn to speak with various animal spirits. Their magic to induce memories was not strong enough to draw anything from him except disconcerting blankness. One by one, every spirit they attempted to match him with fled.

Nyah led him toward the refuge of Adrun, a place they called the Sanctum, lying within the heart of an untamed forest. They passed the outskirts of civilization, but she'd quickly led him away from view of any of her people. Adrun's citizens had deep scars from the devastation of the Fell. Even with everyone now immune to the Fell curse, to see someone afflicted with Fell Madness would be a dangerous situation for all involved.

They made the journey in near-silence, save for the occasional wistful sigh from Izell. *"Daydreaming of Jaromir?"* Nyah asked when the lack of interaction grew unbearable.

"Am I so obvious?"

"My friends talk. I've heard about your...courtship." It was hard to call it thus when Jaromir was restrained and a captive audience for whatever Izell wanted. Which was apparently to read saucy human fiction to him.

"That's not a courtship. That's entertainment."

She felt the urge to raise her brow, even as a wolf. *"He seems to think he's getting courted."*

"Don't be silly. If I were courting him, I'd do it in less clothing."

Nyah groaned, wishing she didn't have that mental imagery. *"Besides,"* Izell continued, *"he needs to be the one courting me. It is only proper."*

"I'm sure he'll get around to it." Now that she'd mentioned Jaromir, she couldn't help but wonder when they'd be doing his trial. If the Madness wouldn't fully clear his system, he'd need some help just like Adrius and Taryn.

She knew they'd arrived when there were two poles erected on either side of the path, connected to a stone fence marked with warnings in the fae language. Made of white stone, the poles were engraved with symbols of magic, their ends tipped with intricately carved pinecones. Green magic shot between them as the group approached, forming a sheet of light to pass through. It was one of four gates to gain proper entry to the Sanctum and the magic within. Nyah approached it first. Izell laid a hand on Taryn's shoulder, holding him back.

She stated their names and purpose—to clear Taryn of his Fell Madness. The magic would recognize her for who she was, but she was more concerned with formal acceptance to allow Taryn in. When the green light dimmed, she knew he'd gotten it and beckoned with her tail as she trotted inside.

The air changed, popping her ears once she'd passed the gate. "We are in the presence of magic that formed Faerie. This is our most sacred..." she drifted off as she realized Taryn wasn't listening.

He stood right outside the gate, watching her. "Will going here help me kill her?"

"Of course." She was glad to be human-born rather than fae, able to tell the occasional white lie.

He followed her with a soldier's marching intent, not stopping to admire as they followed the path down toward a building squatting in the middle of a bowl in the earth. The crater had once held an important tool that'd been transported to Nyixa—the dark Eye of Worlds—but it flourished still in the magic that made the Sanctum unlike any other place on Earth or Adrun. Multicolored flowers bloomed everywhere there was space. Even the building was covered in flowering vines and creeping ivy, surrendering to nature and the spirits that inhabited it.

A woman emerged from the building to meet them halfway up the path. She knelt and rubbed her hands through Nyah's mane. "Hello, friend. I've missed you," said Chandra. Formerly Prince Chandra, the Dreamer, the only Blood Prince caught in the Fell Lands alongside Nyah, she had flung off her vampirism and those titles in favor of another.

Chandra the Druid, leader of the small group that tended to the Sanctum and its magic. Druidism was one of the five virtues, alongside the empathy Nyah was familiar with. That Chandra manifested it was a little miracle, as the virtues tended to stay with Sorcerers and Alchemysts.

It was a life-changing gift for a woman who had not held strong vampire magic compared to the other Blood Princes. Her eyes now gleamed green instead of red, a striking color to match the leaves and purple flowers she'd woven into a sari to cover her elegant form. Nyah knew that her energy kept the living clothing alive and flourishing.

"I've missed you too. Have you gotten to see Earth?" she asked.

"I've been waiting for Swift to return," Chandra grumbled. Her gaze lifted, a small "oh" leaving her lips when she saw who stood there like a fresh statue amongst the meadow surrounding him. "It seems you've brought Earth to me instead."

She stood, nodding respectfully to Izell before turning to Taryn. "Remember me, old friend?"

He stared through her, lost in his own thoughts. "Taryn needs to commune with the spirits. Can you set that up for us?" Nyah asked.

"I see the Madness. Is it that serious?" Chandra murmured.

"I have a lot to tell you." Nyah did so mentally as they escorted Taryn inside, filling her friend in on what she'd found on the other side. Most importantly for the moment, what had happened to Taryn. She didn't mention Adrius, not wanting to re-open the wound of his amnesia.

The Sanctum was a circular temple, with quarters for the druids and visitors set around the font of magic within. Chandra and Nyah exchanged a glance as they passed into that place of power, which held a basin of water at its center. Nyah's fur ruffled with awareness.

Due to her connection to Taryn, who was still on his spirit trial, she could see the spirits amassed in this place. They winked into view once he spotted one, but they filled the Sanctum both inside and out. Fae spirits returned to the land and their mother element upon their death. What appeared to be a basin of water was instead full of souls swimming around like fish. The slight breeze stirring her fur was a playful spirit. If they'd looked more closely at the meadow, each flower could represent a formerly living being. And, rarest of all, flames burned and danced with a departed fae's fervor in the braziers that lit the room at four points.

What few Adrun citizens realized was this was another path for a spirit trial to take. Those with the worst trauma came here to lay bare their memories to the four elements rather than an animal spirit. To bond with a fae spirit was to gain elemental magic and a new start. The souls here did not cling to their memories in life, and they could help the living do the same. They nourished the land to all four points, as was sacred to their people.

Living fae emerged from their rooms to look on curiously. Amongst the green-eyed druids were others who'd chosen to stay upon receiving their fresh start rather than emerge and try to explain their lack of animal side to a land full of shifters.

Nyah stood with Taryn at the edge of the basin as the water began to froth with awareness at his presence. "Taryn, the spirits here can't do anything without your permission," she said. "You must allow them to look at your memories."

"Will it help me kill her?" he asked for hopefully the last time.

In the presence of so many Seelie fae spirits, she didn't dare lie. "No. But it will help you immensely."

He turned toward her, fury blazing across his expression. "You lied to bring me here. You wasted my time."

"Taryn, please. I only want what's best for you." She lifted a paw in the best approximation of a heartfelt oath. "The Sanctum is the one place in Adrun where you can cast your memories into the past. The land itself can help you heal."

She hoped he wasn't so far gone that the Madness would steal away all semblance of common sense. "You can be free of her. There will be no way she can take advantage of you again," she continued.

His lips went slack. There had to be a kernel of sense in him, some shining hope for the old Taryn. A hint of the man who wished to be free of Lucia instead of forced to serve her by the cage of his own emotions. She gazed into his flat eyes and wondered what horrors they'd seen because of Lucia. What she'd done to Nyah was heinous, but Nyah thought *this* was the truly unforgivable sin Lucia had committed.

"Take a look, then." His low voice was nearly inaudible, even to her wolf ears. His knees buckled from an unseen force, and he bowed his head over the water, forced to peer at his reflection.

Nyah yelped as the elements themselves cut her connection to him. She'd never witnessed a communion like this in person, so she didn't know what to expect as he sat there at length. "Yes, that's what I want," he said to the water.

He plunged his head into the basin. A firm hand on her

shoulder stopped Nyah from lunging for him. It was Chandra, shaking her head. "The elements have accepted him," she said. "This is what surrender looks like."

"How long must he do this?" Nyah worried that he would drown. Bubbles floated to the water's surface around him.

"The spirits of water are purging his blood." As she spoke, Nyah realized she was seeing black ink stain around his head. The water purified itself, leaving no trace of Fell Madness behind in the Sanctum once he reared back and took a gasping breath.

Water dripped from unmarked skin. His veins were clear, and his eyes gleamed Blood Prince maroon as they fixed on Nyah. "I asked them to spare my early life," he said quietly. "The spirits say I'm not done forgetting yet, but I wanted to remember you, Nyah."

She breathed out a heavy sigh of relief. She'd been reminding him of who she was throughout his trial. That he recognized her now, even as a wolf, was a great gift from the spirits.

"If you forget, I'll just have to remind you." She was grateful she couldn't cry, as the words scythed open her uncertainties surrounding Adrius.

He dipped his head in acknowledgement. "I am to do the rest alone."

The watching crowd left in a rustle of leafy clothes and excited murmurs. "Good luck," Nyah said, pressing her forehead to his wet arm before turning to pad away. Chandra sealed the entry to the room shut.

"Allow me to make you some clothing," she offered to Nyah.

SHE AND IZELL DINED WITH THE DRUIDS ON A FORAGER'S fare of fruit and root vegetables. The carnivore side of her balked at eating crunchy and sweet things, even though she was fully human again with Night's Howl passed out from such a long shift.

Chandra hosted them in their dining hall. They toasted with wine so rich Nyah could forgive the rabbit's dinner for another glass. She was dressed in a gown spun from flowers of all sorts, with a solid back of palm leaves so she wouldn't crush any pollen into her seat. Her retinue of butterflies was up to five the last time she'd checked instead of the usual one or two that liked to perch atop her hair.

They decided to spend the night and see if Taryn emerged victorious from his audience with the elemental spirits. If and when a spirit chose him, he'd need to stay behind and learn how to wield his new elemental magic. But at least they would know whether or not he'd be allowed to keep his more pleasant memories.

Chandra had worse news for them. "The spirits have been agitated of late," she said deep into her third cup of wine, relaxing into her chair with flushed cheeks. "It started when we connected back to Earth, but it's only gotten worse. There are new spirits in the mix that won't communicate with us until they're done letting go of their memories. But they certainly stir a frenzy into the rest before then."

"A lot of new spirits?" Alarm made her heart beat faster. In an immortal society, deaths were supposed to be rare. But Chandra spoke as if there were many dropping in and causing a disturbance.

"Yes. And we don't know why." She frowned into her cup. "I'm glad you came, actually. I was of a mind to send word to you soon."

"We will investigate," Nyah promised.

They were making plans to retire for the night when the stone door to the inner Sanctum slid open. Nyah was one of the first to lay eyes on the new Taryn. He appeared unchanged except for a singe mark on his shirt. "Nyah? Where are we?" he asked, looking around distrustfully.

Her heart soared to hear her name from his lips. She could burst with her joy for his second chance. "What is the last thing you remember?"

"Your wedding is tomorrow. I was getting my suit alterations finished..." He touched his forehead, brow crinkling. *The spirits must've erased his memory back to the moment Lucia gave him the stage three love potion,* she thought. "But this isn't the palace. And you smell of wine."

Despite herself, she giggled. Now that the giddy sound had escaped, it was hard to rein it in to reply, even under the disapproving look of someone who thought it was the night before her wedding. "I might've had a bit to drink," she admitted.

Chandra called an acolyte to soberly explain to Taryn what was going on. As they waited, she asked, "Which element did you commune with?"

Nyah held her breath as he considered, drawing on what had to seem like a fragmented and psychedelic dream to him. He held up a palm, cradling a bluish flame.

"The elements reignited his soul," Chandra breathed. Fire, the rarest element in Adrun, now burned in his heart. She turned to the nearest druid and raised her goblet. "A feast is in order! Pour the wine!"

Chapter 10
Adrius

Adrius expected to open his eyes and see Soren's garden in the sky. A groan escaped his mouth. Everything hurt, especially his side, where the dragon had dug its talons in deep. Yet the darkness persisted, which meant he wasn't dead.

Featherlight touches ghosted his skin, like the gentle press of a woman's fingertips. When he finally regained himself, the first thing he saw was the sky as a dark mantle full of sparkling stars. He'd never seen a night like it. Yet there was that little spot of orange light to remind him that they were under some sort of magic to keep Adrun separate from Faerie.

Someone sat next to him, waiting until he turned his head to look at her. Swift had her tail wrapped around her paws. "That was stupid," she stated matter-of-factly.

His muscles protested as he sat up. "What else was I supposed to do?" Judging by the ache in his body, the answer was anything else.

There was no sight of the dragon. As Adrius came into full awareness, their surroundings seemed empty. The scrub trees were bare, the sky clear. Realization hit as he turned back to Swift. "My trial is over, isn't it?"

"Yes. We need to find a way back to the capital now." She sighed as she stood, shaking out her thick fur.

He cursed inwardly as he pushed to his feet. They'd only

traveled this far because of Red, but without the potion to interact with spirits, there was no horse waiting to take him back. "I lost a lot of blood, but maybe I can carry us far with my shadows."

Swift looked studiously at the ground while he raised his fists, calling upon the darkness that marked his vampiric powers. He expected a surge of energy, a dance of tendrils to wrap around his form like covetous fingers. Instead...

Nothing.

"About that." Swift loosed a coughing bark. "Why don't you say hello to your new spirit?"

His new spirit? He thought he'd failed, run out of time as he laid on the ground unconscious. *"You are stupider than I thought,"* rumbled a voice in the back of his mind.

No. God, no.

"Zerenth," he said with loathing. The very last spirit he wanted to be bonded with after their fight. Yet he could feel the dragon as a presence within him, as much a part of him as a phantom limb.

"Congratulations. It seems I underestimated you." The dragon scoffed with derision. *"You will bring me out of my seclusion and impress your mate all in one go. You must be so proud."*

"What have I done?" He inspected himself with the words, looking for any scales or other sign that he was connected to a dragon. All he saw was skin and torn clothes. His wounds from the fall had already healed to hairline scars, as if he'd visited a Gifted healer.

Swift watched him with her head canted. "Can you shift?"

"How do I do that?" If he'd sacrificed his shadows, at least he should be able to assume a dragon's form.

"Would that make it all worth it?" Zerenth purred. *"Too bad. I refuse to merge."*

"You have to merge with your spirit. He'll show you the way," Swift said at the same time.

"And if he refuses?" He could feel the dragon's smugness. They may be bonded, but Zerenth controlled this aspect of their cohabitation.

Swift blinked in surprise. "Why would he do that?"

Before he could ask, the answer was already in his head. *"Because I didn't want this. I was content with my life as it was. The bar of who I would bond with was so high I didn't think anyone would ever reach it."*

Adrius repeated these words aloud, and the fox hummed. "Well, I guess we're walking," she said, striking off in a seemingly random direction away from the mountain.

"If we're stuck together, we might as well work together," Adrius said.

"Leave me alone!" Zerenth hissed.

With a grumble, he trudged along until they reached a brick-paved roadway. He wondered why they hadn't used this in the first place. "For what it's worth, I'm impressed you took him on and won." Swift broke the silence with a glance over her shoulder. "Powerful spirits like him don't go quietly. Maybe he'll come around."

"And if he doesn't?" Adrius muttered, kicking a loose stone like a petulant squire.

"There's a process to separate from a spirit, but it's a last resort. We require at least a month together before deciding if it's a bad match or not." He remembered Nyah using the term "bad match" and sighed in frustration.

Nyah wasn't going to be impressed. He was kidding himself to think the dragon spirit would somehow magically repair the damage he'd done to their marriage. *"Now you're thinking properly,"* Zerenth intruded.

"Leave me alone," Adrius echoed him, feeling uncomfortable with the dragon in his thoughts. What a huge breach of privacy.

"Get used to it."

Adrius pushed himself to a running pace not long after that, following the bend in the road as it veered farther away from the pasture where he'd found Red and the other horses. He savored the feeling of wind and hoped it wasn't his imagination when he thought he was still running with the agility of a vampire.

Swift ran with him for a time but started lagging behind before he tired. He stopped only to scoop her up and carry her over a shoulder, pushing his limits and courting the exhaustion he could feel coming. Wanting to know if he was still as skilled physically as he used to be, he only stopped when it felt like his legs were about to give out.

Gasping for air, he turned to see Zerenth's mountain a distant peak. He pumped his free fist. "Feel better?" Swift asked.

"I'll feel better when I hold Nyah again," he said honestly. That might be the only thing that could soothe the ache still lingering in his heart. "During the trial, it seemed like a distant prospect. Talking to her again."

He continued carrying Swift as he resumed down the path at a walk, cooling down before his leg muscles could seize up from overexertion. "I had time to plan what I was going to say and how I'd impress her best," he continued.

"But?" she prompted.

He shook his head. "All my plans seem stupid now. An unwilling dragon won't impress her. I don't think I *can* be impressive after what I've done."

"Have you ever considered just being your old charming self would be enough?" she asked.

Implying he was anything like he used to be. He scoffed at that idea. "I've changed."

"So has she." Swift turned so she was resting her paws on his chest, looking him in the eye. "You haven't damaged your relationship. You were nearly corrupted by a demon. I think I know her well enough to say she'll forgive you in a heartbeat."

"And how would you know?" he asked sullenly. It occurred to him that, for all Swift had seen of his memories, he barely knew her at all.

"Just trust me." She nuzzled his jawline.

He could do that. He *had* done that for his trial and continued to trust her as a caravan passed by them an hour later. The wagons were drawn by elk-like creatures as tall as him at the shoulder, with fur of a sumptuous midnight blue. Magical lanterns were strung between their antlers.

That was how he ended up sitting at the back of a wagon, dangling his feet and breathing in the smell of fresh oranges from a harvest. He preferred this seat to being up front with a gaggle of curious fae who stared at him as if he were the oddity when they were the ones with starry skin and butterfly wings.

Swift had him peel an orange. Her muzzle was stained with juice as she enjoyed its innards. "I should be leaving you soon," she said, staring off into the trees that began engulfing the road on either side of them.

"Surely you can come to the capital?" He wanted to keep the talking fox around, even though he knew she must be a fae under that fur. She felt like a close friend with how quickly he'd had to bare his soul to her in the trial. Not to mention her companionship during and after.

"I don't go into civilization." Rolling another orange to his side, she looked at him expectantly, and he peeled as she continued. "I'm a druid. Maintaining the life in this land is my duty. And now that your trial is done..."

It was time for her to return to her job. He sighed as he passed the peeled fruit back to her but not before stealing a slice for himself. The sweet juice rolled down his throat, helping to soothe a new, unfamiliar ache in his gut. *Hunger?*

How remarkable. He was hungry for solid foods.

"I appreciate your guidance. At least tell me if we will meet again," he said.

She sat close to him, allowing him to run his fingers through her soft pelt for comfort. "What kind of friend would I be if we didn't?" she asked.

But when the wagons finally rolled to the capital's gates days later, Swift slinked off into the wildlands without a glance over her shoulder. Adrius knew he was on his own once more.

Chapter 11
Nyah

After Nyah left Taryn in the druids' capable care to learn how to master his new flames, she returned to Earth. Izell remained behind to investigate why the elemental spirits were restless, leaving Nyah at loose enough ends to worry about Adrius and why his trial was taking so long.

Since time passed faster on Earth, she stayed there until a page found her. She was mid-lesson with Olivia when a fae boy burst into the infirmary, clutching his knees as he panted.

Olivia stared at him with her mouth agape. "Where are your wings?" she blurted.

The boy turned to get a good look at her, his starry fae eyes twinkling in surprise. Either shocked that he was in the presence of two humans, a rarity in Adrun, or recognizing that she was an Alchemyst too, he seemed spellbound by Olivia immediately. "Fae don't grow in their wings until they come of age," Nyah said.

"Oh well, you're still pretty." Olivia flashed a thumbs up. "Not like that. I mean, I have a mate. Just...all fae are so pretty..."

"Do you have a message for me?" Nyah spoke up before this could go on.

The page gave himself a shake and offered a scrap of folded paper. "From Advisor Firebrand," he said.

"I can tell," she said once she'd seen the message. Izell's message was short and to the point.

Adrius was back.

Her heart skipped a beat. *Adrius is back!* "Thank you. I will be there shortly." She nodded to the page, who ran off.

Olivia craned her neck to look at the note. "Get your furry wolf self back to Adrun before Adrius dies of angst?" she read.

"Izell," was all she said in explanation before she stood and brushed off her clothes. She'd changed from her druid-made flower gown into more practical leather embossed with fae symbols of protection and loyalty around the collar.

Nodding like that's all she needed to say, Olivia waved. "See you later maybe?"

"Until then," she agreed. Neither made any promises, but she hoped it was soon.

Nyah rushed through the portal and headed to the capital at a rapid clip. She projected her mental voice to Izell, connecting without difficulty, which meant that they weren't far from one another. *"Where is he?"* she demanded.

"Hello to you too. How was Earth?" Izell sounded remarkably cheerful.

Nyah's eyes narrowed. *"What's wrong?"*

"Nothing to do with Adrius. I have it under control." The fae sighed. *"Why don't you go see your mate first? He's in the square."*

"Does it have something to do with the unrest at the Sanctum?" she pressed. She simply couldn't let a problem dangle at the back of her mind. Focusing on it helped her avoid the what-if's piling up in her thoughts.

Though the worst one lingered. What if Adrius still didn't remember her?

"Yes. And I'll tell you everything once you've seen your mate," Izell answered.

She sighed, figuring that was for the best. *"Fine. Come find us."*

It wasn't long before she could see the city gates, currently wide open as most of her people considered it daytime. Fae lanterns were lit all along the white walls, casting a warm glow over her as she attempted a fast but more dignified walk. The last thing she needed was for rumor to spread of Adrun's queen running around like some green-eared page.

She avoided eye contact with the fae going about their daily tasks. Skirting a slow-moving wagon, she headed for the square that lay at the heart of the city. Two fae children stood at the base of the fountain, holding a coin between them and murmuring with their heads together. But there was no Adrius and nearly no citizens either. She had a feeling that wherever everyone had gone, that was where she'd find her husband.

The square was a crossroads of every major artery in the city, meaning he could've drifted anywhere. She worried her lip between her teeth before tapping into her wolf's senses. Closing her eyes, she relied on scent and hearing for anything amiss. *There!* A clamor of voices raising in a cheer.

A crowd of fae were circled around something close to a blacksmithing shop. Nyah drew herself up to her toes, trying to see around the press of bodies.

"Who's next?" Adrius's voice carried over the crowd. "You there! Try your strength."

Gasping, Nyah shouldered her way through, hearing some annoyance from those around her before the word "queen" started circling in her wake. The group let her step to the front, where Adrius was squaring off against a man she recognized as a bear shifter. Like Izell, he'd chosen to be half fae and half animal, retaining fur and massive bear paws. They were...arm wrestling? Someone had set out a table and two chairs, and there Adrius was, his hand locked with the bear shifter's paw, muscles bulging as he pushed.

"What's going on?" she whispered to the woman next to her, a tiger shifter whose skin was stained with orange stripes.

"This human is testing his strength. Isn't it delightful?" She tittered like a courtly fae and startled when she turned. "Your Majesty."

"Sure. Delightful." Nyah didn't know what to make of it. Judging by the crowd, he'd been doing this for a while. Maybe this was how he avoided his "angst," as Izell put it.

She had a few minutes to debate what to do next, because the bear shifter pushed Adrius to his limits. Their arms wavered, an inch favoring one side and then the other. She wondered what kind of spirit he'd bonded with since bears were known for their brute strength. If she'd been his guide, she'd have steered him toward a spirit of freedom or discipline, something usually seen in birds of prey, rather than something that could challenge a bear.

He didn't look like he'd allowed the spirit to take over part of his appearance. In fact, he didn't seem different at all, except he'd cut the beard he'd always been so proud of.

Adrius eventually won, left red-faced and panting as he sat back and the audience cheered harder. She didn't wait for him to call for the next person, sitting across from him with her arm extended across the table instead.

His eyes widened, and lips parted in recognition. The audience gasped for him on a long inhale to see the queen challenging the strength of this newcomer. "They didn't wear you out, did they?" Nyah asked, grinning from the thrill. She would win, of course. She was the alpha wolf here, and her instincts prompted her to prove dominance over a new shifter.

"Just a warm-up." His voice was husky and low as he grasped her hand. A spark of awareness prickled her palm, jumping between them like it used to. She'd forgotten that their touches were electric and *right* in a way she'd never experienced with another.

Instead of wrestling her, though, he ran his thumb over the inside of her palm. "I missed you so much, Nyah. You have no idea what I've been through without you..."

Her heart skipped a beat as he gave her a look of adoration, like the old Adrius she remembered. This was exactly what she wanted from the moment he opened his eyes. For him to still be devoted to her. That impossibly, despite the time between them, they were still the love-struck royal couple at the helm of a nascent nation.

She felt her smile falter. Her hopes were just dreams, and it had taken the lack of a miracle to realize it. "You have no clue of the hardships I've experienced." As soon as the words left her mouth, she wanted to grab them and throw them to the side. Her uncertainties held her heart in a vice grip. "I am not the Nyah you remember."

Adrius's expression shaded with his insecurity, so heavy she could feel it with her empathy. "What do you mean?" The question tiptoed out after he swallowed heavily.

"I'm saying..." She knew she had to phrase this right. "It's not that I don't love you. But you're right, I don't know what you've been through. We need to be reacquainted. Isn't that reasonable?"

He gripped her hand harder, like she was slipping away again. At the same time, his lips moved, repeating her words to himself. "This isn't what I was expecting." He smiled sadly. "But if that is your wish, then we can start over."

"Let's give the good people the show they came to see, hmm?" She put some pressure on his arm, and they started to wrestle. The crowd, momentarily confused by their interlude, began to cheer for her.

Nyah drew upon all the strength of her wolf and held him off with her teeth bared in a vicious smile. Adrius held back his full strength. She could feel it in the tension of his hold. "What spirit did you bond with?" she asked despite the strain. Very few could outmatch a predator's power.

He shook his head. A few moments later, his hand hit the table, and the watching fae clapped and cheered. "You let me win," she said under the sudden noise. It pleased her instincts of dominance, but she still wanted to feel how strong he was for other, more personal reasons.

Now that he was bested, the crowd dispersed quickly, leaving them standing in the street. "It's complicated," he said, scuffing his foot. "I bonded, but the creature refuses to cooperate." Which meant he'd beaten that bear spirit, and others, with what remained of his vampire abilities. *Incredible,* she thought.

"That sounds like a story. Come, let me show you around the city," she offered, taking up his arm to lead him. "It is unusual that a spirit doesn't cooperate."

He told her of his travels while she took him back toward the gates so he could see the grandeur of her city from the ground up. A chill brought goosebumps as she realized where his tale was going when he mentioned seeing a dragon spirit scooping up sheep for its dinner. "I knew in that moment I had to follow him," Adrius said.

"You went to challenge Zerenth the Fury?" she asked in disbelief.

Drawing his shoulders in, he snuck a nervous glance at her. "I, ah...I just wanted to be tested by him."

"He's a dragon, Adrius. The most dangerous spirit." She clutched at her collar. "*And* secluded for a reason."

"I didn't know."

"Swift should've told you." Her brow drew together. Why hadn't Swift mentioned it? Everyone in Adrun knew of their resident dragon spirit who slept at the peak of the highest mountain, far out of reach of the average aspirant.

Adrius was obviously not an average aspirant, though. "I think she tried, but I wasn't listening. I wanted to impress you." He continued his story as she reeled from that emotional gut punch.

Spirits above! Just being here is enough, she thought. She guided him under an awning next to a fruit vendor as he spoke, because she was sure he wouldn't remember anything about the city until he'd gotten everything off his chest.

"He drew out every memory I had and taunted me with one of my worst moments," he said of the dragon. "I lashed out, and we fought. I'm sorry, I killed him. Again."

"You what?" she breathed.

"I won the fight. He died, and I didn't. Which apparently means—"

"You didn't kill him! You proved yourself worthy!" she exclaimed, slinking free of his hold to grab his shoulders. "Do you realize what you've done?"

By the shock she felt through his skin, she knew he didn't. "No one's been worthy of Zerenth in three thousand years," she whispered, glancing to see if they'd garnered any attention other than the usual to see a human-born outside of the palace.

"Well, I'm still not there. He refuses to merge with me," he muttered. "If I try to talk to him, all he says is to leave him alone."

The reminder brought her elation back to the ground. "There's something you need to see. Let's continue our walk."

"Your city reminds me so much of Nyixa back in its glory days," he said, stepping out from the awning. She could see the resemblance as well, especially with the white-stone palace looming in the distance with its pointed minarets.

"The city itself could be rolled into a giant ball and stuffed into Nyixa's palace, to give you an idea of size," she said, earning a low whistle from him. "Everything in Adrun is smaller. The fae reproduce slowly, and most of my original honor guard passed away fighting Fell. We're small but stable. Few births, few deaths."

Except recently, with what Chandra had told her. Concerned thoughts rose up to plague her as she showed Adrius the open-air market where various vendors hawked their wares. "Is that why everyone, including the spirits, find my humanity an oddity?"

"Yes." She smiled up at him. "The fae are so extravagant that it's nice to see someone as mundane as I am."

"Mundane," he echoed with a laugh of his own.

"In appearance only. Did you know the fae call humans 'flat-skinned'? Just because we're not made of elemental magic..." She slowed as they reached the square and its iconic fountain. Now there were several fae going about their day, and the children had cast their wish and left.

"Is that him?" he asked, heading straight for the sculpture that flowed endlessly with water from a simple fae spell. It depicted a dragon, detailed down to the scale in onyx stone, curled around a tiny version of the city. His arrow-shaped muzzle was permanently pointed downward toward the pool below. Next to him was his bonded fae from when he was alive, whom the dragon mourned, some say to this day. He was one of many who'd died in the Fell's onslaught of Earth. As a fae who'd kept Zerenth as his familiar, he must've been powerful indeed.

"You tell me. You saw him for yourself." She sighed. The dragon, so known for his fiery temper, always seemed miserable in this memorial.

He paced a semi-circle around it before nodding. "That's him. But why is he here?"

"My city's name is Dragonhelm. The fae insisted," she said, her gaze on the rubies standing in for Zerenth's sculpted eyes. "To them, dragons are spawn of the divine. The fact that a dragon came during Spirit's Fall and took up residence was a sign that the fae gods hadn't abandoned them."

"Swift mentioned something about that," he murmured. "What do I do, Nyah?"

She knew what he was asking and didn't speak her thoughts aloud. If her people learned he'd successfully merged with Zerenth, he'd be lauded as the king he was meant to be. But if he continued to mishandle the spirit that was such a symbol of faith and hope...

"You must speak to the only other dragon around. You need Izell." And for that matter, so did she.

Chapter 12
Nyah

Izell was not hard to find once Nyah took him to the palace. While Adrius admired the tapestries covering the foyer walls, Nyah's gaze zeroed in on the dragon shifter eating grapes while lounging across a perfumed divan a stone's throw from the entranceway. There usually wasn't furniture there, but Izell had moved some along with an enchanted palm frond to fan her.

"In days of old, monarchs had servants to feed themselves grapes," she said as she approached the fae.

Izell offered her the bowl, eyes twinkling with merry stars. "That's what you're for, yes?"

Sitting in one of the two chairs set across from her divan, Nyah took the bowl and began eating the fruit instead. "Mmm. These are fresh." She offered a handful to Adrius as he sat too. "This is Izell, my advisor."

"You have a dragon problem, do you?" Izell asked before he could open his mouth for a more polite greeting.

He cast her a distrustful look. "Has word spread that fast?"

She tapped the space between her brows. "Future sight."

"From Sorsha's history lessons, I thought your virtue was true sight," he said.

A smile stretched Izell's lips enough to bare her eight sharp canines. "It is."

"But you have..." he paused, brow creased in puzzlement.

"A fae can have more than one. Who knows, maybe I have more tricks up my sleeve yet—"

"She has all five," Nyah interrupted, earning a scowl. "Sorry to ruin your fun, but the man is confused enough."

"All five," Adrius echoed. "That's just incredible. How...? No, tell me later. I do have a dragon problem."

"And we have a problem here at home too?" Nyah pressed.

"There are three problems, actually, but who's counting?" Izell inspected her talon-like fingernails. Sitting forward with a growl of impatience, Nyah motioned for her to continue. "I've taken care of one for now. One of the fringe villages is empty. It's like they all abandoned their homes and walked into the wilderness. But since the spirits are so restless..."

"You think something killed them," she supplied.

"I do. And I've dispatched a company of the guard to go investigate. In the meantime, we have Adrius. And this note just arrived a few minutes ago." Izell gestured lazily, floating a piece of paper with ink staining through the back.

Adrius leaned over as she gasped, hand covering her mouth. Someone had dashed this off in a hurry—saying that Gwendolyn was regressing. "I...I have to go to her. If she's rejecting my magic, maybe I can do something..." She shot to her feet. With Adrius tying up all her thoughts, she'd barely spared a thought to her ailing mother.

"I'll help Adrius," Izell volunteered.

"Can you?" she asked, glancing to him. He just seemed confused, which made sense. He had been unconscious when Gwendolyn went into her coma. "And explain what's going on?"

Izell smiled with all her teeth. "Oh yes. I think Adrius and I will get along great." Nyah shot him an apologetic glance and rushed out of the palace.

NYAH ARRIVED TO AN ARGUMENT. SHE SUPPOSED ARGUING was just the way of things on Earth. She chafed at the feeling of discord in the infirmary as her empathy picked up heightened emotions in the room and rubbed them against her skin like shards of glass. "What's going on?" she bellowed, forcing a few vampires to startle apart.

They'd congregated at the end of Gwendolyn's bed. Jaromir was standing, still shackled, his brow drawn as he pulled his chains away from Olivia. The resident Gifted, surgeon Melanie Rainey, had her hands on her hips.

By the bedside was Sorsha, sweat dripping down her brow as she held a pose with both hands twisted at uncomfortable angles. A glowing fae symbol hovered over the bed, pulsing in time with Sorsha's breathing. Her companions and guards, Keegan and Ash, were watching Nyah's approach. She'd only met the trio of fae briefly, but even the glimmer of relief from the two guards told her she'd arrived at just the right time.

"Thank God you're here!" Olivia exclaimed.

Sorsha spoke from between gritted teeth. "Heal first. Talk after."

Seeing the wisdom in that, she shouldered past the group and took up her mother's hand. Gwendolyn's skin was cool to the touch. Her mouth was parted in the midst of her deep coma, breath coming shallowly. As she'd feared on her way there, Nyah could tell her life magic hadn't taken or simply wasn't enough. The woman was wasting away.

Gwendolyn had done the impossible in becoming mortal again after centuries of vampiric existence. But as Nyah tapped the Spring and Autumn Keys on her fingers and began forcing raw life magic into her mother, she wondered if the miracle could end in any way other than Gwendolyn's body rejecting its new conditions and perishing from old age.

She felt the attention of everyone in the room as Sorsha eased off her spell. It must've been suspended animation, because it was like she poured energy into an empty pit rather than stabilizing her patient. "Feels like something is eating up my magic," she muttered.

Sorsha watched them for a moment. "Ash?" She turned to the only Unseelie in the room.

Approaching on cat-silent feet, the other fae took Gwendolyn's free hand. Nyah was accustomed to token Unseelie amongst her people, listening in for Ash to say the opposite of what she meant, as all Unseelie were cursed to find the truth painful or impossible to speak aloud.

"Angels verses demons is my forte," Ash commented, lifting a shoulder with a frown breaking her stern features. "There is magic here I... I can't..." She swiped at her nose, catching a drop of blood and glancing down at it with a grunt. "I mean, there is much magic at work inside this woman, and I can cancel every single piece of it."

"Huh?" Olivia muttered, scratching her head.

"She's saying there's something at work here that she cannot use her Spellbreaker abilities on," Sorsha explained for her as Ash pulled out a kerchief and pressed it to her nose. "Which is our barometer for demon magic."

"What? No!" Olivia's eyes were round as saucers as she listened in.

"This is why we trust the fae on these matters," Jaromir commented from where he stood a pace away from her. "Gifted magic heals wounds, not matters of supernatural importance."

She scrunched her face. "Implying vampires aren't supernatural."

Nyah turned to her with a sigh. "You were there when my mother was attacked by the demon. Was there any opportunity for him to leave something in her?"

Olivia paled, turning instinctively to the doorway, where her mate Julian walked in and surveyed the crowd around Gwendolyn's bed. A pang of jealousy hit Nyah, which she quickly tried to beat off like a smoldering ember on her clothing. As a newly mated pair, they were sensitive of each other to the point she wouldn't be surprised if he'd come running from feeling his mate's distress.

A comforting cloud of cool air followed in his wake as he crossed the room to put his arm around Olivia. He was learning some control of his Winter Key abilities. Like Gwendolyn, he held the immense power of his Key within him rather than in a ring that could be taken on and off at a whim.

"Yeah, I think there's a chance he did something," Olivia said, taking a deep breath of the cold. "He reached into her to pull out her Portal Key magic. Like, shadows under her skin."

The two fae women exchanged a glance. "We should have expected this," Sorsha said.

At the same time, Ash said, "We shouldn't have expected this." The words were laden with the heaviest sarcasm she could muster.

"What should you have expected?" Nyah felt how sharp her question was as she clutched her mother's hand. If they'd missed some latent threat within Gwendolyn, she didn't know how she'd forgive herself for leaving her bedside.

"It's how demons work," Sorsha murmured, her hands flashing through a few gestures in a complicated fae spell. An after-image of purple light followed her movements. "Especially corruption demons like Jazrach. If they can't kill something, they leave behind a parting gift they might use later."

"And you didn't think to check." She growled low in her throat.

"I did check. But Gwendolyn's magical readings have been all over the place." Sorsha spread her palms, her eyes flashing over a jumble of fae writing glowing between her hands. "Jazrach is a creature we cannot underestimate. He must've hidden a kernel of his magic within her Portal Key capabilities when he stole from her."

Ash pointed toward a cluster of symbols wordlessly.

"I see it," she answered, a grim twist to her lips.

"What do you see?" Nyah felt her patience wane as the two pressed closer together and exchanged a glance.

"The spell I just cast gives me a list of the magic within someone. We use it on fae youth to see which spell schools they have within them," Sorsha explained rapidly. "It doesn't work as well on humans and vampires, but this reading identifies that approximately one percent of Gwendolyn's current magic is demonic in nature."

It was like she'd doused Nyah in ice water. The hair on the back of her neck stood on end as goosebumps flushed her skin.

"Fifty percent of her capabilities are nephilim-based, and forty-nine are the Portal Key, so it's obvious the seed is growing from—"

"Can you stop it?" she demanded. The hand in her hold twitched. She turned to see her own magic finally working, drawing away the age from Gwendolyn's features. Keeping her alive just a little bit longer. She was sure that even a tiny seed of demon magic was enough to keep someone as pure as a nephilim on the cusp of death's door. With a thrill of horror, she wondered if her own life-based gift was helping it flourish, with how she'd first felt like she was healing an empty pit.

"I can isolate it for now. That will keep her stable," Sorsha said. She began to cast another intricate spell over Gwendolyn.

"What about removing it?" She'd heard the "but" in Sorsha's tone. Her empathy picked up a whisper of discomfort and fear as the Archfae shifted her weight.

She met Nyah's eyes. *"Can we speak privately?"* They had a rapt audience by this point. Except for Keegan, who'd disappeared. If she weren't sick with worry, Nyah would be surprised to see him leaving his post. As it stood, she couldn't bring herself to care about anything else except the matter at hand.

"Of course," she answered.

"I don't have the answers you seek, but I know where to find them. Izell speaks of her library quite fondly." Of course. The Fell had left Dragonhelm's library intact, considering there wasn't anything to eat amongst the dusty pages.

"I shall accompany you." Though, it troubled Nyah that, for all Sorsha's power, the only thing she could offer was a flimsy promise of stability. Nyah feared that meant there was some truth the fae didn't want to give voice to.

Chapter 13
Adrius

Izell ushered him back to Earth like she was smuggling something shameful. They spoke to no one upon coming to Coven Rehnquist's mansion. In fact, he'd barely gotten his boots on the ground and his eyes stung by the influx of light before the ancient fae was shoving him through a second portal.

He dusted himself off with a muttered curse. Izell hadn't followed him through to this place or given any word of warning, but he recognized where he was instantly. The grassy clearing was as wide as a battlefield and secluded far from mortal eyes. It bore patches of burnt grass and blackened earth from magical training.

He was alone, so he let his feet take him to the far end, where he could eye the shattered remnants of the Eye of Worlds. A demon's prison, he now knew. Haphazard shards of glass, some larger than him, lay strewn and glinting in the moonlight.

"You thought it was unbreakable." Zerenth's voice drifted through his head.

"I did," he agreed out loud. The dragon had surely read that thought off his memories. In his time, he'd considered the Eye of Worlds to be an unknowable monolith and a permanent fixture on Nyixa—what a joke, in retrospect.

"I was there, you know."

"Where?" he asked. He wondered how long his dragon would

remain pleasant, expecting a verbal sucker punch now that he'd let down his guard.

"For the forging. The glass is dragon-forged. It should not have broken the way it did." Zerenth sounded lost in his own thoughts. *"I wonder how Jazrach weakened his prison beforehand."*

"I wouldn't know," he admitted. He hadn't understood much about it when it was intact. In retrospect, he'd always felt unsettled in close proximity to it. The shadows right under the glass had seemed to form a coalition of laughing ghosts, pointing and mocking him.

"Why educate yourself in matters of magic when Lucia did it for you, right?" the dragon said waspishly.

"We don't say that name here," he answered in kind.

"What name?" Izell came up to his side silently. He twitched her way, wondering how he hadn't noticed her or Keegan behind her.

The male fae had his lips drawn tightly. Surprisingly, he wasn't with Ash or Sorsha. They were always within an arm's reach of one another. "Well, call her. We don't have all day," Izell said to him. "You want to get back to your Blade duties, right?"

"I need to be doing those right now, Grandmother," he said through gritted teeth.

"Nonsense! She has your little Unseelie friend. What was her name again?" Izell tapped her chin.

"Ash," he sighed.

"That's right, she has Ash." Izell waved dismissively.

Keegan shook his head, resignation drawing over his face. He brought his fingers to his lips and whistled into the woods, where it echoed through the empty space. As they waited, Adrius tried to perk his hearing like he used to as a vampire. The two fae were staring in a specific direction, as if they could hear something coming, but all Adrius could pick up on was the wind and a sudden stillness of any other natural sound.

A form broke through the tree line. He scrubbed his eyes, but no, they told the truth of what trotted toward them across the field. *"Dragon Blade,"* grunted Zerenth in apparent approval.

Pacing their way was a dragon, its scales gleaming scarlet. It was about the size he recalled Zerenth being, towering over them at the shoulder. Unlike the other dragon, though, this one had a back free of spines. Its arrow-shaped face was complimented by two pointed ears that trailed in the wind.

"*She's gorgeous,*" Zerenth purred.

"Adrius, meet my dragon, Vidia," Keegan said, rubbing her snout when she dipped it toward him.

Face-to-face with a living, breathing dragon had robbed him of words. He found himself agreeing with the dragon spirit within him—she *was* beautiful. A sleek, giant predator of a creature with intelligent yellow eyes narrowed to slits as she inspected him. Smoke puffed from her nostrils while she leaned in to sniff more closely.

He dared to reach out and touch her scales, which were dry and warm like snakeskin. She recoiled, her jaw snapping in warning. "You smell of dragon." Her voice was a bass rumble, just like Zerenth's. There were a few subtle differences between the two, but she didn't sound feminine.

Adrius turned to Keegan, his awe apparent. "Dragon spirit. Not living dragon. You own...?"

"Ownership is a fickle word," Vidia answered. "I am his familiar, his equal. He was worthy of my fire. As you were worthy of a dragon...spirit?"

"Not quite." He was loathe to admit it to this magnificent beast.

She sat, lowering herself to eye level. "Interesting," she commented.

"I thought you two might talk while my great...how many greats is it?" Izell asked.

Keegan answered automatically. "Five."

"Great-great-great-great-great grandson and I start salvaging this dragon-forged glass," she said.

Adrius glanced at his long-suffering expression and her smile, wondering how he could be tired of someone who'd just returned from a long exile. He supposed there was more history there. "In a minute," Keegan said.

"I need you now," she insisted. Their gazes met, a clear challenge arcing from one dragon tamer to another.

Eventually, Izell nodded in approval and went to go stack glass. Keegan turned to him, clasping his hand. "Congratulations," he said. "I can sense that you're holding a powerful spirit."

"Should I be saying the same for you?" Adrius gestured to the living, breathing dragon. "Zerenth called you a Dragon Blade."

If he didn't miss his guess, Keegan looked practically embarrassed as he stuffed his hands into his pockets. He was different without Sorsha to speak for him. Since protecting her was his duty, this moment was the most relaxed he'd ever seen the male fae. "There's a lot I don't talk about. Were you aware that I and my companions are fae nobility? The fact that we're on Earth, trying to help you fix your problems, is...odd."

"I understand better than you may think," Adrius said. In his brief time as king, he'd chafed at the idea of letting others handle the more dangerous sides of running a nation. "And you know what? I'm not surprised that Neala's kids are the ones here to help us."

Keegan started to smile. "True. We've been odd all our lives. But having an affinity for dragons has been in my family line all the way back to King Oberon." His expression faded back to his usual neutral as he glanced toward Izell.

He dropped his voice, as if wanting to keep the words from her ears. "If you hear anyone questioning why I'm still just a Blade, that's because I should be taking Vidia and sitting up in a castle, waiting for my servants to pay their taxes. Blades are somewhat common—anyone with magic that augments physical performance can be a Blade."

"But by staying a Blade, you've gotten to avoid the castle," Adrius said with a nod. "What does adding 'Dragon' to your title mean?"

A mischievous look crossed his face. "Means I can do this." His blade shot from its scabbard. Within a blink, he was holding it upright while flames licked up and around the metal until it glowed molten white. Adrius took a step back and gaped, impressed anew when Keegan ran his hands up the flat side and gathered up a handful of fire, manipulating it between his fingers like putty.

"Quit showing off!" Izell called crossly. "I still need your help."

Keegan still looked like a child who'd gotten to share his favorite toys. Upon sheathing his sword, the flames all faded into smoke. "Being a Dragon Blade means no one in their right mind would fight me," he said proudly. "Now, if you'd excuse me…"

"Of course," Adrius murmured, still dazzled by that performance. Now it was just him and Vidia.

He also felt his tongue go dry at the thought of talking to the dragon. Izell was supposed to be helping him, and it seemed like she'd stopped one direction short of what he needed to do. *"It won't work, no matter how many instructions she gives you,"* Zerenth hissed.

"I have a problem," he told Vidia. She tilted her pointed head.

"Why don't you sit and tell me everything?" she suggested.

He dropped into the grass with a sigh, wondering if *everything* included how he'd apparently taken Zerenth from seclusion against his will, worthy or no. Before he could get a barbed reply from the dragon, he acknowledged that it was important information if the other dragon was to help him. The moment he was sitting down, all his worries came in. The things he couldn't fix—Gwendolyn's coma, Nyah's reluctance, Zerenth's hatred, his brother's hostility.

Vidia rested her chin in his lap, holding still when he rubbed her snout. Her eye was as large as a dinner plate as it rested on him, waiting. "You seem troubled. Take your time." He could feel her rumbling voice down to his bones like this.

They watched Keegan and Izell for a few minutes. He was holding up plates of glass, and she was fusing them together with fire directly from her mouth. Though he wasn't half-dragon like his ancestor, he handled the glass without a flinch or singe. He didn't touch the molten parts, just guided them together once Izell melted the edges and barked orders at him.

Adrius found himself telling Vidia everything once he relaxed. If two fae could become glassblowers without any of the proper tools or precautions, he could have a reluctant dragon spirit living in him. Anything was possible to an unsettling degree with fae magic.

"You said his name was Zerenth the Fury?" she confirmed once he'd confessed it all.

"Yes."

"We still tell his story." She released a wordless rumble. "We remember you, Zerenth."

Left as the middle man as the dragon within him responded, Adrius said, "He is honored."

"We are honored. The great dragon of the Sorcerer Calinhes, who died defending the Astral Fae Academy," she said with awe. "It still stands because of him. Its walls sheltered countless astral fae during the war!"

He'd stopped listening at a certain point. "What did you say?" he murmured.

"He died—"

He felt himself struggle to breathe. "He belonged to whom?"

"The Sorcerer Calinhes," she answered, lifting her head as she beheld his reaction.

Calinhes. He knew that name all too well.

"You killed him. You butchered him for his blood," Zerenth accused.

So, that was the fae immortalized next to Zerenth in Dragonhelm? Adrius reeled at the truth that'd been so close to his face.

"Tell me that's a lie. Tell me it was anyone but Calinhes," he said, ready to rip the dragon from himself with his bare hands if he had to.

"Why?" Her brow pulled in confusion. "He's a hero. He also saved countless lives during the war."

He shook his head in denial. Suddenly, the loathing he felt from Zerenth made sense. It wasn't just that he'd taken the dragon from his home. He'd won their fight; he was worthy. But Zerenth had read every memory from his head—including the ones about his former master. "Maybe he was a hero to you. But to my people, he was known as the Fell Emperor and led the slaughter of man, woman, and child."

And Adrius had *gladly* killed him.

"I don't know anything about that," she murmured.

"Tell me one thing. What do you feel for Keegan?" he asked.

"He is the most important person in my life. I would gladly die for him," she answered without hesitation.

This was the information Izell had brought him here to learn, because undoubtedly, she already knew both sides to this conflict. "*I don't understand,*" he said to Zerenth privately.

"*Of course you don't,*" he growled. "*Worthless idiot that you are.*"

He clenched his jaw from a biting remark, forging on with the other half of his sentence. "*If you saw the Fell Emperor like I did, you know what a monster he was.*"

Zerenth didn't reply for a few long moments. He thought, perhaps, the dragon was reliving those memories. He could forgive the dragon if he could look at the memory of the Fell Emperor's throne of clean-picked bones and acknowledge that Calinhes was the worst kind of creature. Spawned from the pits of Hell to dine on human flesh.

When he did reply, his voice was low. "*I know one thing for certain, Adrius Fabron. I participated in Spirit's Fall to see him made whole and untainted, but he'd died on Earth without me. For three thousand years, I've mourned, just to find his murderer was the one person who could best me in a fight.*" He breathed an angry roar, giving Adrius an instant headache. "*I don't care what he did as a Fell! That wasn't him! I could've saved him! And you took away that chance.*"

He clutched at his head as the last words rung in his ears. "*I hate you,*" Zerenth snarled.

"*The feeling is mutual. You can rot atop that mountain for all I care.*" He would tolerate Zerenth only for the time it would take to throw him back into Adrun, where he belonged.

Chapter 14
Nyah

Sorsha walked Dragonhelm's streets as a fae, her arms behind her back and tucked under her starry wings. Her iridescent eyes gleamed with wonder. "No one in Faerie believes you all could've survived this place," she said to Nyah.

Despite the urgency gripping Nyah's chest, she allowed Sorsha a curious stroll once they'd reached the city. The Archfae had explained that she'd isolated the seed of magic trying to germinate in Gwendolyn, giving them the time they needed to research another solution. And since time ran so much slower here than on Earth, they technically had triple the hours.

Nyah still worried. She wanted to hold her mother again, whole and hale. How cruel fate would be if she were to perish before a proper reunion. Or worse, to wake after demonic magic had eaten up the good in her. She struggled to focus on Sorsha, realizing the inquiry in her words. "Surely your father told you of Spirit's Fall," she said.

"Yes, but the life here...creating your own animals, spreading biodiversity..." She shook her head in awe. "You and your druids pulled off something even our most distinguished scholars couldn't predict."

"In my youth, I would be proud to hear that. But down here, we have already gone in circles about our accomplishments. How it was like threading pure chance through a needle," Nyah admitted. She no longer had that pride in her heart. Old accomplishments were like ash in the face of new, serious threats.

Sorsha nodded. "I understand better than you might think. You made thread of chance, and I was a child of prophecy."

Nyah had caught but a glimpse of newborn Sorsha when she was thrust into the arms of her best friend to take back to Earth. As she and Caladorn Nightweaver, Sorsha's father, bonded as fellow survivors, she'd learned all about the fateful prophecy that'd led to that moment.

"Your father was very brave," she said, feeling it was an understatement of the sacrifice he'd made. He and his late wife had called for a seer before the Fell crisis to tell them of their future child's life. It was the way of fae nobility, to peel back the curtain and give their heirs a leg-up before they were even born.

What a shock it must've been to learn that Sorsha was destined to be raised by a vampire and hunted due to her true sight virtue. Caladorn had told her the story one long, cold night as they commiserated with their small band of survivors. The seer had fled their estate in terror and not long after, the Fell curse came for them.

As if their words summoned him, the man himself was waiting outside the city's public library. She assumed Sorsha had invited him, as she seemed completely unsurprised. Nyah let them have a moment alone as she paused on the sidewalk, watching him place a hand on his daughter's shoulder in greeting.

Caladorn's stoic face broke into a brief smile. He was dressed in his customary uniform of a navy tunic and dark pants belted low at the waist. His rank insignia was hidden under the folds of his cloak, but no one would mistake him for anyone but the general of their small land. Though he'd traded in his rank of Blade when his Sorceress wife passed away, he still kept his Faerie-forged rapier on his hip. Sorsha and he shared little resemblance, leading Nyah to believe she took after her mother in more than just magic.

Nyah let her gaze stray to the library behind them. It was a pristine time capsule from Faerie, or so she'd been told. The monolithic structure and all its information had survived in the heart of the Fell invasion. She'd heard of Faerie's grand library, a place for all the knowledge of the long-lived race. Her own archives were just a smaller version, sure to have *something* to help her remove the demonic magic attempting to worm its way into Gwendolyn.

She eventually made her way to join them, inclining her head as Caladorn saluted with his fist over his heart. He rarely forewent the formality. "I understand we are researching demons today," he said.

"Namely removing demonic magic from a nephilim." She headed for the stone doors of the library.

"Nephilim. Where did you find one of those?" he asked. He fell into step as a defensive shadow. Nyah would never question that he'd once been an effective and deadly Blade. Even after he'd taken his promotion, he still had a protective streak.

"I'll tell you the story, Father." Sorsha spoke in a hush as Nyah panned the stacks on the first floor. The library twinkled with fae lights, a few floating down from the ceiling to halo her. It was one of the best-lit areas in Dragonhelm, though it still did not approach the eye-offense level of Earth buildings. Sorsha continued to whisper as they followed Nyah up a staircase and toward the back of this level.

She wasn't playing around. She opened a door with a white-stone key from her belt and took them into the restricted section secluded from the public's eye. The hair on the back of her neck stood on end at the proximity of some of the texts filling the rectangular space. Sorsha paused in her explanation and glanced around with her mouth gaping.

"You have the thirteenth tome of Archimedes the Mad's collection!" Her starry fingernail pointed unerringly toward a black spine in the middle of the archive. She started naming more rare works on sight before her countenance fell. "The great library had to hide or burn most of this knowledge. It's from astral fae scholars."

"A good thing it's still here, then," Caladorn said, frowning in concern. "Do we need to send copies to the Library of Faerie?"

Nyah let them discuss the possibility as she started reading spines for a hint of what she wanted. She didn't dare touch them —some books were back here for the protection of the patrons rather than the knowledge they contained. Most had spells of understanding over them, meaning that the cryptic fae letters rearranged themselves into a language she could read the longer she stared at their spines.

"—There may not be a Library of Faerie left if we don't succeed," she caught Sorsha saying as she ducked to study the spines of the bottom rows to this stack.

"Very well. We will hoard our knowledge for now. Perhaps Adrun will be the only safe haven if the Everlasting War returns to Earth," he said. "Wouldn't that be something?"

Sorsha made a noncommittal sound. "Let's not take that chance."

Shaking her head, Nyah continued her search until she'd combed through a full stack. She called Caladorn over to remove promising titles that suggested they were about angels, demons, or their conflict accurately labeled the Everlasting War.

"It's going to be a long night," Sorsha commented, placing half a dozen more books next to those Nyah had found.

"There's a study in the back room." Nyah pointed it out, determined to go through each book until they had some definitive answers. The library had supplied pillows and blankets in the back as well, as it was the kind of location a scholar could get lost in for days. It was a cramped space for three of them, but she took the desk while the two fae sat on a pile of blankets, and they all began reading.

Fatigue only reared up the moment Nyah relaxed into the task with a fresh sheet of parchment, quill, and inkwell set before her. Between Adrius's reappearance and the news of her mother, she'd pushed herself nonstop and felt the consequences as words danced on the page before her.

Focus, she hissed to herself. She'd only stuck to the basics when it came to the Everlasting War in her own studies. With a nephilim for a mother, she'd had the religious education to under-stand the spiritual connotations to her heritage. Angels killed demons, and demons killed angels. Foolishly, she'd thought that was enough on the subject.

Her quill scratched sluggishly across the paper as minutes dribbled into hours. When Sorsha sat up with a cry, Nyah's sentence ended with an irregular ink blot from her startle. "I knew I could count on the old man," she said, holding aloft the black-spined thirteenth tome of Archimedes the Mad.

"Are you sure someone with that name is an accurate information source?" She stifled a yawn behind her wrist.

"He's just a little dramatic." Sorsha waved dismissively. "Listen to this: 'Angels and demons are restricted by a draconian set of rules. The most important of which is an understanding of balance. If an angel breaks through the veil to set foot on Earth, so too must a demon.'"

"And vice versa, I would assume," Nyah commented.

"Exactly. So, an angel has to be coming." She continued reading out the rules to them as Nyah shrugged to herself and took notes. Demons act, angels defend. Only demonic taint can permanently kill an angel, and thus, only an angel's light can remove a demon forever. Angels make oaths, demons strike pacts. As she looked at the list, she wondered what would truly help them in that moment.

"So, we cannot kill the demon." It was the opposite to what she wanted to hear. "We need an angel to come down from on high and do it. An angel we do not have."

"Because angels defend and are careful they don't send too many angels to fight off a threat," Sorsha said, stroking her chin. "At least, that's what I'm reading."

Caladorn interrupted with a faraway look in his starry eyes. "It makes sense. Demons are incredibly destructive."

So Nyah knew from her mother as well. She'd never seen one for herself, and of that, she was glad. "Is there anything in that book of yours about the specifics of demon magic?" she asked.

"I'll look." They all returned to their reading as Sorsha delved deeper into the book. Nyah glanced up occasionally to mark her progress, watching her eat up half its contents from rapid skimming. It was the best lead they had so far. Caladorn had set aside an occult tome for summoning demons, while Nyah was halfway through an account of the early days of war as told from a fae's point of view.

As fascinating as it was to see how far divorced fae were from Everlasting War, which was ultimately a conflict for humans by former humans, it wasn't what Nyah needed. That was, until she skimmed the name "Jazrach" and paused, touching the word with her finger.

Picking up her quill, she wrote part of the passage down. "King Oberon sealed a willing Archangel into the Light Eye, did you know that?" she asked her companions. "Jazrach was forced to power the Dark Eye."

"It's why I think he's still around," Sorsha murmured, not taking her eyes from her studies. "Oberon destroyed his body and harnessed his magic, but some teeny tiny part of Jazrach survived and rallied over time within the Dark Eye, biding its time until it found the perfect puppets to dance to its whims."

"Lucia," Nyah growled.

Sorsha marked her page with a thumb and met her gaze. "Earlier. The Unseelie Queen who bent a knee to him first. The general populace doesn't know, even to this day. But...I think she is the real reason why Jazrach survived Oberon's spell. Demons are like Fell. They need something to suck on until they're reduced to nothing."

Nyah rubbed a chill from her arm. She continued reading of the demon and took notes of its attributes, hoping to find some weakness secreted within the pages. What she documented suggested that Jazrach was a forgotten evil. The kind everyone wanted to move on from. She eventually read a passage that encompassed what it truly was aloud to the fae.

"'Jazrach was selected for the grim honor of powering the Dark Eye from a lineup of the worst criminals of demon kind. King Oberon decided that his crimes were the worst, having witnessed Jazrach's ascension from common underling to greater demon by his own clever manipulations. He led an army of angels he'd personally coaxed into falling and laughed as they slew their fellows with demon-forged weaponry. Most scholars agree that

Oberon's selection was of a more personal nature, as Jazrach's corruptive powers were likely behind the Seelie-Unseelie split of fae kind.'"

Caladorn and Sorsha exchanged a glance. "We wouldn't have this problem had he picked any other demon," she muttered.

"Perhaps he felt the worlds would be safest with Jazrach contained," Caladorn said. "We know Unseelie happened because of demon influence. Why else lock the Everlasting War from Earth *and* Faerie?"

"The only good corruption demon is a dead corruption demon," Sorsha sighed.

"How many kinds are there anyway?" Nyah asked, continuing to thumb through the history book for any other mention of the demon's exploits.

Sorsha flipped back through her book and scanned a page. "Most represent the seven sins, but there can be demons for every negative aspect of human kind. If they're not sins, they're rare."

She was glad corruption was rare at least. "Fun fact, but angels are the converse. Anything good about a person can be the grace of an angel, who is expected to uphold it to the highest," Sorsha continued. "Demons of corruption and doubt are the highest cause of angels falling since too much of either causes an angel to fail at their grace."

"It was a fun fact until the end," Nyah said. She wished she'd invested more of her time into learning this. Her head was already hurting from all this knowledge at once. After Sorsha was through with that book, she would need to study it and share its contents. One downside of the two Eyes of Worlds was that few knew what to do when encountering either a demon or an angel.

Her eyes started to droop as silence fell over them again. It was only a matter of time before Sorsha found what they needed to know, so she finally set aside her book and waited. Hopefully Adrius would find somewhere comfortable for the night. Their schedules wouldn't sync up well if he stayed on Earth for long.

She needed to call him to Adrun. If she had any hope of reconnecting with him, they had to see each other more.

She thought of his smile, the electric warmth of his palm in hers. How his face had softened with intimate recognition. Her mate was back. There was no need to punish either of them any further by being on opposite sides of the portal—again.

A gust of wind startled her. Her cheek was lying on the hard line of a book's edge, and she sat up quickly, like she hadn't drifted off for an extended moment grasping her most recent memories of Adrius.

Sorsha lowered her hand, a nervous smile tugging the corner of her lips. "I think I found something," she admitted.

"Mmm?" For a moment, she was more annoyed that Adrius's scent had left the moment her dream did.

Raising her book and finding a section with her finger, Sorsha launched into a litany about demonic magic that shocked all the warmth of sleep from Nyah's self. The surface-level magic, she already knew. Demons could inch their way into their victim's thoughts. They fed off of souls and savored the taste of ones they'd corrupted the most. "...But there's something even I didn't know in here," Sorsha continued. "That even the lowliest demon has a kernel of their soul remaining from life. It's called their spark. Sparks can attach to someone's soul and slowly bleed into it until the victim's soul resembles that of the demon's."

Even Nyah breathed a low curse at that. "You don't think he put his spark in my mother, do you?" she asked, her fingernails making crescent moon patterns in the meat of her palm.

Sorsha dropped her gaze. "It...is a possibility."

Chapter 15
Nyah

After resting on a lumpy pile of books, Nyah rose the next day feeling like her burdens had been tied to her back. The two fae had left at some point, but a pile of notes rested on the corner of her desk, written in flowy script. She rolled the parchment and held it in a loose fist as she marched from the library.

She must've looked a state, since she could still feel the imprint of her book pillow on her cheek. Her hair had come down from its coif to bob on her neck with each step. Passing the palace and the chance to not become gossip for bored city fae, she instead made her way to Izell's house and the portal within. She had to see Gwendolyn, if only to hold her hand and pray that Sorsha's magic could keep isolating the spark of demon magic within her.

This time, Earth was under the natural lighting of the sun when she emerged from the portal. Coven Rehnquist's mansion was still and shuttered from the day. She crept to the infirmary, stopping short when she saw two new beds were occupied. Had something happened in her absence?

On second look, neither of them looked ready to stay there for long. The curtains weren't even drawn around their beds. Fully dressed and sleeping on his back was the coven master, Alexander Rehnquist. She'd met him briefly to thank him for hosting her and Izell, but a whirlwind of matters had kept them busy separately since then. The bed next to his was occupied by Neala. Her brow was drawn and lips were smacking as if in the midst of a nightmare.

Nyah hesitated toward her, wanting to at least make sure she was more comfortable. A hiss sounded from further in the infirmary, where Jaromir met her eye and shook his head. The manacles were off of him at last. But he was still dressed in a shapeless white robe, covers pulled to his lap as if he were in his bedroom. He beckoned to her.

"They're dream walking," he told her in a private mental whisper.

She nodded and headed for his bedside instead, standing at the foot of it. *"I've done my fair share of it with Chandra."* Despite Chandra's change into a druid and bond with an elemental spirit, they'd been able to preserve her strongest vampiric ability, to walk in dreams with lucid clarity for walker and dreamer alike. *"What do they seek?"*

"Ah. That is a long story. But he's helping her remember someone she was forced to forget."

She glanced to her mother, who was as still and pale as she last remembered. *"Perhaps we can share information,"* she said, heading over to take Gwendolyn's cool hand. She set aside Sorsha's notes and concentrated on funneling more life magic to help keep the elderly woman breathing just a little while longer.

She had Jaromir tell her of Neala while she stood there. Another tale of Lucia destroying some else's life, but Neala wasn't just any victim. A growl rose in Nyah's throat to hear of Lucia stealing her lifemate and destroying her memories with the Mind Key. The dream walking was to reclaim them in full, to make Neala whole again. And apparently, it wasn't going well; thus, she needed to sleep close to their only dream walker to bend her reluctant mind into remembering.

"She has the strongest mind out of all of us. It's possible this also won't work." He finished his explanation with a shrug.

She raised a brow. It was unlike him to be morose, but she could see it in every line of his exhausted face. *"I noticed you are free,"* she said, rotating her wrist.

"I am clear of the Madness, yes." He looked down at his lap. *"But it has taken my Gift."*

Jaw hanging open, she was at a loss for what to say first. Jaromir's Gift defined him as the only doctor amongst the Blood Princes. Even in her absence, she could tell that he hadn't changed from the steady hand and voice of reason amongst those vampires who'd survived the Fell. *"Oh, Jaromir,"* she murmured.

"I know you have...a lot going on." He gestured to Gwendolyn. *"If it would not be a bother, I have need of your Alchemyst services to return my Gift."*

"Of course." She didn't offer a potion on the spot because, well...there were no potions to grant the Gift. In the early days of vampire kind, she'd brewed many an elixir that changed and sharpened the abilities they'd inherited from the Fell. Without her, there would be no vampire blood lines, just a muddled collective where everyone had a bit of everything.

"The Gift is the only benevolent power we took from Fell, you know," she remarked. Others, like dream walking, could be used for good—but could also plague someone with nightmares or spy on the memories in their head.

"And I was the one who found it. But...let us not dwell upon it." Even though she imagined that was exactly what he wanted to do. *"Do you know more of Gwendolyn's condition?"*

She parted from her mother on a murmured prayer, drawing the curtain around her again. *"Read the notes if you like,"* she offered. As he did, she explained what they'd found in Dragonhelm's library.

"Have you read this?" he asked, raising a page along with an eyebrow. *"It is instructions on how to summon heavenly light."*

"Oh?" She forced herself to sound interested. *"Find my grace, uphold it, and I, too, can harness nephilim power?"*

Jaromir paused mid-read to glance at her. *"That is the essence of it, yes."*

Muffling a groan of frustration, she began to pace. *"Dare I admit that I have tried even to this day? Mother was so disappointed when she realized I didn't have enough angel in me. I'm not a nephilim, Jaromir. Certainly not now."* She drew her arms apart and shifted her hands into wolf paws.

Wordlessly, he held out one of the sheets to her.

It was the end of the notes, a few lines printed on the page. "Most nephilim do not reach their full potential until face-to-face with a demon. Keep trying!" She read those words over and over again, fatigue suddenly layering atop her shoulders.

Keep trying.

Nephilim no longer existed because of the Eyes of Worlds. But now she had to wonder—was that because there were no angels to have relations with, or was it more the fact that there were no demons to face?

Two sentences had re-opened her uncertainties anew. She'd long accepted that she was many things: Alchemyst, shifter, queen. But *not* nephilim. She hadn't had the light in her when it mattered, when the Fell were trying to ravage Earth.

"I'm sorry. This is too much," she said, pushing the sheet back into his hold. The last thing Nyah needed was to have her thoughts filled with graces and light. She had enough to carry already.

Immediately, she felt selfish. If she could summon light, she could burn out the demon seed trying to take root in her mother. She would need to resolve the issue another way. *"Do you know if Adrius is here?"*

"I heard his voice from the portal. Izell came by for a bit too," he said with a nod.

She couldn't help but grin. *"Oh, did she now?"*

"You know about her and me too?" He breathed a sigh aloud. *"It's not like...that. She is just helping me through this difficult time."*

She reached out to pat his arm. *"Izell doesn't 'just help' anyone. I think she likes you."*

He struggled to keep a neutral expression. *"If you say so."*

She flashed a knowing smile and drifted to the front of the infirmary, where there was metal equipment she couldn't make heads or tails of. Sitting in a rolling stool, she gave the beds her back and picked out a glass vial from the rack she had balancing atop some expensive box-like implement.

Growing herbs and other greenery for her potions was as easy as holding out her palm. Enough lavender and chamomile for a sleeping tonic popped into her hand at her whim, courtesy of the Keys glimmering on her fingers. She crushed them into the vial along with water and a drop of her blood. She went and offered the mixed concoction to Jaromir. *"Take it. Sleep. You need it,"* she said.

"Okay, mother hen." Though he teased, he also drank, and she took the empty glass as it sent him off to sleep nearly immediately. Hopefully his Gift returned with the dawning of another night, because all she had to offer otherwise were small consolations like the sleeping tonic.

She padded from the infirmary and shifted her nose to a wolf's sensitivity. The smell of many people co-mingled and stung her nostrils. Picking Adrius's scent out was easier than she'd expected, however, with a hint of dragon's breath and char planting a clear sign for her. She followed the trail up the stairs and to a doorway, which she tried with a ginger knock.

At this hour, she could wake every vampire in the mansion with a more aggressive motion. So, when he didn't answer, she tried knocking with a pattern they'd developed together. It was their secret signal to let the other know who was at the door or entering the bedroom.

The door flew open with her knuckles still resting on the wood. Adrius's bulk filled the space, and he blinked down at her. Shock passed over his expression, like he was reminded she was back. He stepped aside for her to enter.

"What's wrong?" he asked in a hush.

As soon as he latched the door behind him, she felt foolish. She was rested, yet here she was disturbing Adrius for her own comfort. "Nothing's wrong," she lied. "I just wanted to see you."

His brow drew in confusion. "In the middle of the day?"

"I've just woken. It's night in Adrun." She realized he was staring and felt the need to babble her intentions when he took a step forward. His thumb skimmed her cheek. Reaching up, she realized she still sported a little valley on her skin from her book-shaped pillow.

"Was your night as eventful as mine?" he asked.

"Are we back to small talk and even smaller touches?" Like they were still strangers, she thought.

He tilted his head, watching her as if she were a puzzle he couldn't quite figure out. "My night was quite something," he offered. Stepping past her, he went to the small kitchen provided in most of the guest rooms, hers included, and drew out a brightly-colored package that had her mouth watering the moment he opened it.

"Mortals call this wrapping plastic. They put it around everything," he told her as they snacked on beef jerky. It was highly pleasing to her wolf side, even rousing Night's Howl from her slumber to enjoy the taste.

"It doesn't smell natural," she said. Honestly, neither did the jerky, but she still liked it. "Does this mean you've gotten in tune with your dragon side?" He had to be craving meat as well, as dragons were apex predators.

His expression darkened. "Let's not speak of him right now."

So, no, he hadn't. A frown creased her lips. "Very well."

As they tore through the jerky package together, she let industrious chewing save her from speaking. Either she had nothing to say or she wanted to tell him everything, and soon, she would need to pick from those contradictory thoughts.

He seemed to be doing the same, his dark gaze dancing over her face and form as he thought. Eventually, there was nothing more to eat, and he broke the silence first. "What is troubling you? Don't say nothing. You always rub your lips together when you're upset about something."

She paused, realizing he'd caught her doing exactly that. "I do have a few worries." An understatement. She let him guide her to a couch, where they sat without touching as she aired them all to him.

<h1 style="text-align:center">Chapter 16
Adrius</h1>

HE BARELY MOVED AS NYAH TALKED AND TALKED, unconsciously drifting closer to him until she was resting her weight against his shoulder. If he touched her, he feared she'd spook like a frightened rabbit. It nearly felt like a dream to have her here in the middle of the day, going on about Jaromir and Neala and Gwendolyn, with some demons verses angels for added flavor.

The things she spoke about were too real to be part of a dream, though. The grogginess of rest faded fast to sober reality. He worried for the people she mentioned, friends and family alike hurting as much if not more than he was.

"You think you're hurting? How rich," Zerenth rumbled in the back of his mind, having taken an interest in the conversation.

"I thought we agreed we weren't talking to each other," he snapped.

He had the impression of the dragon hissing then silence. Until they could be separated properly, it was the best compromise they had. They would coexist until Zerenth could be released to go mourn a murderer for the rest of eternity for all Adrius cared.

"I think I speak for everyone when I say we don't expect you to solve all our problems," he said once Nyah was finished. Her head lay against his bicep, her eyelids lowering. Despite saying she'd slept in Adrun, it was apparent it wasn't restful.

"It's what I do. What an Alchemyst does," she sighed.

"What a queen does," he mused. It's what set her apart from Lucia, this deep care for others. "How many worries have you shouldered so your people wouldn't have to?"

"I've lost count."

He nodded, daring a touch at last. A stroke of her silky hair, which he relieved of a leather tie keeping it knotted low on her neck. "You've cut this shorter," he remarked, smoothing the fall along her side. If she were standing, it would be to her mid-back.

"And you've done the same here." She tugged at the remnants of his beard.

"New start, new me." His neck felt practically drafty without it.

Her touch lingered, stroking his jaw and sending goosebumps in her wake. "When have you been defeated?" Nyah laughed like it was impossible, and his heart sped to double-time.

That this woman still had so much faith in him meant she'd never seen him at his lowest. "The moment you left me, until now. It's been one long defeat," he murmured.

Her sigh was wistful as she leaned up. Realizing her intentions a split second before it happened, he sank into her kiss like time and space didn't matter. Like they were still the young king and queen of a new nation, bursting with promise. Hungry for every moment alone.

He nipped her bottom lip as they parted for air. "I thought you wanted to—" He stopped himself abruptly. *No, I won't put my foot in my mouth.* If his woman wanted him, he wasn't about to remind her that she asked for time to be reacquainted.

Reality stole across her features all the same, taking away the edge to her expression, as if she were about to release her ravenous wolf self upon him. *Please do,* he thought, sad to see it go.

"It's too easy, isn't it?" She touched her lips, her gaze seeming far away. "Especially since you've slept nearly all this time. Does it seem like just yesterday to you?"

"No. I'd rather have died than be parted from you." At least he could admit this. "I feel like I withered while you thrived. Yet you still waited for me...for three thousand years?" he asked in a hush.

"Suffering isn't a competition. This won't work if we keep measuring our trials like one has had it worse than the other," she said, rubbing the back of her knuckles across his cheek.

He leaned into the graze of her soft skin and her husky voice so close to his ear. "But yes, I've waited that long. There was never another for me."

"I, too, never turned to another," he whispered.

Pulling her closer, he kissed her with singular intent. She'd come here to forget, he thought, to lay her worries aside for something good. He had every intention of supplying it and drawing them back together in the process.

That is, until Zerenth decided to speak up again. *"Aren't you forgetting something?"*

Ignoring the thought, his hands kneaded Nyah's curves. He pressed a kiss to her collarbone, savoring the breathy moan drifting from her lips.

As he moved to lift her tunic, suddenly his mind was a thousand years away, hands lifting a different piece of fabric. The memory intruded on him so fast it was like he was in a dream and some dream walker had plunged him into another scene of his life.

Before him was Lucia in a wedding gown, the most frivolous and expensive thing he'd ever seen. Miles of silver and white silk, her train lifted behind her by three serving girls. Her bodice was decorated with seed pearls sewn into the crest of Nyixa, and the veil he lifted from her face was decorated with diamond shards.

It was the worst day of his life.

Lucia's affliction had been recently treated, revealing a face as lovely as the full moon. Ruby-red lips pursed as she formed the words, "I do."

He was supposed to kiss those lips, sealing their vow before the whole vampire court. If he didn't, by the end of a fortnight, they'd have a civil war. Either Lucia was queen or Adrius was king, but this way, they could share and avoid the bloodshed.

Blessedly, Zerenth released his mind before Adrius relived the awkward moment their lips met. He came to his senses with his lips hovering over Nyah's and his hands stilled on her hips. A cold sweat gripped him before he erupted into a rage he contained to an expletive-filled mental rant.

"How dare you! You know that was unconsummated. You know it was political. And Gwendolyn sank Nyixa right afterward, so it didn't even matter!"

Panting, Nyah watched his face with a bewildered expression. "Adrius? What's wrong?" she whispered, walking her fingers over his muscled bicep.

"It matters. Tell her. Don't take advantage of her," Zerenth rumbled.

"Damn you. Damn you to Hell," he practically snarled, still caught up in that past moment. The humiliation of being forced into a union with someone as vile as Lucia.

"If you don't tell her, someone else will…"

"Adrius?" Nyah wiggled out of his embrace, her brows furrowing.

"I…I need to end my union with this dragon. Can you help me with that?" he asked, focusing on her face. He was here with Nyah, not Lucia. And the only problem was that the dragon had to go.

Her eyes widened. "Why are you bringing this up now?"

"I need him gone," he said. It was the stark truth. First the attack over the Fell Emperor's fate, now this. Zerenth could cripple him at any moment with a painful memory from his past, and he just couldn't have that.

Fixing her clothes back into place, Nyah took her time with answering. "Did Swift tell you what happens to the spirit when there's a bad match?" she murmured.

"No?" Not like he cared what Zerenth would do without him.

She met his eye, as grave as he'd ever seen. "The spirit dies. We don't just remove spirits on a whim." She stood from the couch and gave herself a shake. "Especially when that spirit is the mythical protector of Dragonhelm, who hasn't found a worthy match in three thousand years. Can you imagine telling my people that their dragon died on first exposure to Earth?"

"Nyah..." He swallowed his words, seeing her playing out the worst scenarios behind her eyes as they flickered.

She turned a despondent look his way. "Just...try to figure it out, okay? Don't make me choose between you and my people. I will go find rest elsewhere. See you later."

"I would never—" The door banged behind her as she left with haste. "—make you choose," he said to himself.

But he would if Zerenth died by his own fault, wouldn't he? He didn't know much of the fae she'd lived with for so long, but their reverence of Zerenth was obvious.

He was of half a mind to chase her but decided against it. He had to make some decisions first.

My people, she'd said. Not their people. Hers. He was no longer part of her life in that way.

Well, it would be *their* people soon. If he had to suffer this monster-loving, spiteful creature to have Nyah back, then he would.

Chapter 17
Nyah

Nyah waited out the daylight hours, unable to rest any further with the trembling in her hands. She didn't need any more worries, not with the threat to her mother's life and soul looming over her. Were it any other day, she would've stayed, talked through the problem with Adrius. Like any relationship, the shifter-animal bond needed compassionate communication on both sides, and she'd become skilled at making sure a bad match couldn't fester.

As night fell at last and the shutters closing the mansion off from sunlight creaked open, she knew she was being foolish. Adrius needed her help, not for her to flee at the first sign of trouble.

She left her appointed room in search of him and found Izell instead. At least, she thought it was Izell by scent, though what she saw was a stranger lounging across a loveseat, petting a plump cat as it nuzzled her hands for more affection. "Can't you stick to one form?" she sighed by way of greeting.

"If I must pretend to be human, at least I can have fun with it," Izell retorted. She was currently a Black woman with a stately halo of graying corkscrew curls, wearing a surprisingly modern getup. At least, Nyah thought it was modern, but she had no finger on Earth fashions except that the textiles were soft and fragile compared to what she was used to.

Nyah made a noncommittal grunt. "You look terrible. Want a glamor?" Izell offered cheerfully.

Pushing the fae's feet from the cushions, she sat next to her instead. "No. I just want you to tell me everything will be all right."

"When have I ever coddled you thus?" Izell scoffed.

Nyah put her head in her hands and re-told her woes to the fae, starting with her research and findings at the library. "You think Gwendolyn has Jazrach's spark?" Izell interrupted the litany of words.

"Well, yes. There's some seed of magic within her," Nyah said.

"That's true. But..." She let the word hang as she stood and placed the cat back on its paws.

"But...?" Nyah drew out the word.

"But never do magical research without contacting me first. I could've saved you some trouble," Izell scolded, walking away and talking over her shoulder, assuming Nyah would follow. Which she did after rolling her eyes. "It's true that demons have a spark of magic that behaves in a corruptive fashion. But the victim has to give consent for it to attach to their soul. Do you really think your mother did that?"

"Of course not."

"Therefore, she has some weaker form of corruption within her. But your spark theory has given me an idea." Izell raised a finger as they descended to the ground floor of the mansion.

"Do you think you can take it out?" Nyah asked hopefully.

"Do I look like an angel to you?" Izell countered. "No, a different idea. I need a blood purification potion from you."

She couldn't help her disappointed expression, though the fae didn't turn to see it. "No problem," she said.

"But first, I need to deliver this." Izell lifted her hand again, this time holding a sweet wrapped in bright paper.

Nyah didn't follow as the fae veered into the infirmary, knowing who that was for. She leaned into the banister instead and rested her eyes as she waited. However, she cocked her ear toward the unlatched door and listened in for how she actually spoke to Jaromir.

"Is that for me?" His voice drifted to her only with the help of her wolf's enhanced hearing.

"Yes. I have business to attend to today, but I couldn't go without visiting my favorite vampire." Considering Izell was speaking without snipping, Nyah thought, *yes, there's something there.*

Jaromir chuckled, his tone turning sly. "Are you trying to get me fat, lady fae? Is your preference—"

"Queen Nyah?"

She startled. The speaker had approached silently. Awake now, Alexander Rehnquist stood at a polite distance away, wearing a fine suit and fiddling with the cuffs. "Sorry to bother you," he said, flashing a lopsided smile.

"Hello, Alex. Were you able to dream walk with Neala last night?" she asked.

"I was under the impression Neala wanted it to be a private matter." He focused on smoothing invisible wrinkles in his crisp coat.

"She's practically my sister." Nyah frowned at the deflection before seeing the strain in his expression. "Did she ask for discretion?" She hadn't known a thing about it until Jaromir had told her after all.

"Yes, but I make for a terrible doctor," he admitted with a chuckle. "I've been meaning to seek you out. She is not taking this transition well. Perhaps she needs a confidant more her..." He gestured vaguely. "Equal?"

Nyah bit back a sigh. Of course Neala needed a confidant and didn't want to burden her with the task. "I will speak with her," she promised, turning to do that, just to see Izell returning, sans sweet and smiling broadly.

The line of Alex's body drew taut with hostility. "Who are you?" he demanded.

Izell raised a brow. "Who do you think?" She turned to Nyah. "Night's a-burning. Let's go."

"You're going to give me a right heart attack with your glamors," Alex commented.

She flashed him a grin with her fangs un-glamored. "It's not my fault you vampires are paranoid. Can we borrow a...?" Now she was waving vaguely. "What do you call those metal boxes?"

"A phone?" He took one from an inner pocket.

"I know what those are," she scoffed. Alex glanced to Nyah for help before Izell clarified, "The boxes you use for transportation."

He raised a brow. "Oh, a car. I'll call an escort for you." He started tapping his fingertips on his phone screen.

"You can't help her right now," Izell said as Nyah made to head to the infirmary. "And she'll just tell you about Sirius, which will get you even more worried."

Nyah paused mid-step, her brows drawing together. "What's wrong with Sirius?"

"Just that he's been missing for days."

Great, now Nyah was wondering about her brother-in-law too. "Oops," Izell said, licking her lips. "I didn't mean to tell you that right now."

"Uh-huh. So, where is he?" she sighed.

"Having some private time. Sulking. You know how men can get."

Nyah was sure of one thing in the moment. Izell's dragon was awake. Like Nyah's spirit, Izell's slept most of the time. But when he was awake, she lost her sense of social decorum and even blurted out things she'd seen from her future sight out of turn.

It wasn't her fault. Nyah still rubbed at her forehead and suppressed a groan. This quirk had its charms but not when there was so much at stake. "And why is Sirius sulking?" she asked her palm.

"Ask him," she said, indicating the staircase. Adrius was descending it, wearing a faraway look and a set of modern clothing that looked out of place on his muscular frame.

Alex turned to her. "If you head outside, I have a chauffeur waiting to take you where you need to go," he said. "I must excuse myself. I have a trial to arrange."

"Lucia's?" she asked. She so sorely wanted to attend it.

"No. We're stalling that one," he admitted. "Can't bloody kill her because of her curse. And execution is the only thing that'd come of it. We're putting one of her conspirators on trial, a nasty man by the name of Bryant Collins."

Her interest waned to a polite nod. "Let me know when Lucia's trial is."

"Of course." He inclined his head as he escorted them to the front door. She could feel Adrius behind her, following them out.

"Where are we heading?" his deep voice rumbled behind her.

"I don't remember inviting you," Izell said sharply.

Nyah offered him a tentative smile. "Apologies for leaving you like that. It was not a mature reaction. I would love to help you make a connection with your dragon."

His stoic expression broke with the beginnings of hope. "I would appreciate—"

"Could you two quit flirting?" Izell asked.

"Try not to strangle her. It's the dragon in her," Nyah told him privately as they piled into the backseat of the car.

"I understand completely," he sighed.

She ended up squeezing in between Izell and Adrius with her smaller size, wondering why they needed an escort of two people, who introduced themselves as Armando and Charlotte, two of Coven Rehnquist's enforcers. "Where are we heading?" Armando asked, his arm slung over the wheel.

"Lucia's prison," Izell answered, earning pointed looks from Nyah and Adrius alike. "What? I have an idea!"

Adrius muttered uncharitably as the car lurched into motion.

"Here, make me that potion." Izell produced a glass vial from her sleeve. Nyah chafed at the thought of brewing in this confined space when she realized she recognized the woman riding in the seat up front.

"You're Olivia's friend," she said.

"Yes, ma'am. I mean, should I be calling you Your Highness or something?" Charlotte asked.

Almost everyone from Coven Rehnquist asked some variation of that question, but Nyah tamped down her impatience for a quick answer. "Nyah will do. Do you have a blood purification potion?"

Charlotte repeated the question facetiously and opened a compartment up front with a dramatic flourish. It was full to the brim with the shimmering potions. "Trade you?" she offered with a grin, taking the empty vial in Nyah's hand and offering her a larger one that was full and corked.

"We believe in being prepared around here, *amicos*," Armando said.

"If you're going to rough up Lucia, can we watch?" Charlotte asked.

"Oh yes, please. Let's bring popcorn!" He turned to her. "Do we have popcorn too?"

"We're not *that* prepared."

"Would you two...?" Izell took a deep breath. "Why am I surrounded by couples? Why is everyone coupling up all of a sudden?"

Adrius glanced to Nyah, and they shared a look and apparently a thought, as they reached for each other's hand at the same time. His broad palm gave hers a squeeze, and he kept her in his gaze for the rest of the car ride. Their escort quieted up front after sharing a look of their own. Nyah assumed if there was flirting, it was now being conducted more privately. She knew when they arrived at the prison when her skin rippled with unease. She could feel the magic wards even from a distance.

"We won't be long," Izell told their escort. Her nose wrinkled as they walked up to the seemingly abandoned building. "I hate dampening wards. Makes my dragon all...quiet." She put a hand to her forehead before drawing herself up with prim posture.

"Welcome back," Nyah said. "So, what was this idea of yours?"

"Nothing you're going to like. In fact, perhaps I should have gone on this venture alone..." The fae frowned over at Nyah and then up at Adrius as her glamor faded upon closer contact with the prison wards. The stars that danced across her skin and scales dimmed.

"You may as well tell us." Nyah hushed her voice as they

entered the warren of cargo crates and felt the oppression of her magic smashing to uselessness as they passed the first fae rune. Night's Howl woke with a yip of displeasure before their mental connection was severed.

She rubbed her arm to ward off the goosebumps, leaning into Adrius's strength as he drew her closer. "More that you'll see for yourself," Izell remarked, pushing to the front of their group. "Stay out of her sight, and let me do the talking."

Sharing a shrug with Adrius, they both seemed all right with it. She was cautiously curious to this idea, though anything involving Lucia was bound to be a wreck at best. She and Adrius stood close enough to the central prison to listen but not see the chained Sorceress.

Adrius was taut as a drawn bowstring as Izell continued walking and greeted Lucia with an acerbic, "Do they not wash you?"

Chains clanked as Lucia shifted. "Did your mother make love to a beast?" she asked, her voice too dry to be forceful.

"Oh yes, very original. I've never heard that one before," Izell said, her tone implying a roll of her eyes.

Adrius cast a glance to Nyah that practically said, *what is she doing?*

She held up a finger to wait, tilting her head toward the conversation as Izell said, "You are cursed, hmm?"

"Just look at me," Lucia sighed.

"I am. But I've recently seen many vampires just like you. The only thing that makes you different is your silver blood. Well, formerly silver."

"That is because I shared my curse with them."

"How kind of you, sharing. We must all hope to gain such magnanimity."

There was a pause. "Go ahead and mock. Get your punches in while you can," Lucia muttered.

"On the contrary, I'm here to help you."

Nyah bit her lip to muffle a gasp. While she trusted Izell, the moment she helped Lucia was the moment Nyah had to reevaluate their friendship. "You have a *spark* of something in you," the fae continued. It felt like a pointed message directly to her for her falter of faith.

"Of course," Nyah breathed. "It makes so much sense." She was tempted to draw Adrius farther from the discussion, but she didn't want to miss a moment of what Izell did next. Instead, she made her lifemate bend down and whispered to him what a spark was.

"If you're offering to remove my curse," Lucia said in the meantime, "don't bother. I've long grown accustomed to it. It's had a thousand years to fester under my skin."

"You think the curse is...?" Adrius whispered.

Nyah nodded. It made sense to her and answered the *whys* still surrounding Lucia's fall from grace. Her shift in personality. The obsession with the throne to the point she'd kill to have it. And her actions in modern day, which had achieved at least one thing—freeing Jazrach from a nearly unbreakable prison. Lucia's curse went soul-deep.

"So, you don't want to be pretty again? I've heard the stories," Izell cooed. "You could be beautiful and wear your own face. Free of the whispers."

Free of Jazrach, Nyah thought, wondering how Izell would do this. Maybe she could send the spark back to where it came from.

"That...would be nice," Lucia said. Nyah imagined a leery look on her face to go with the hesitance.

"How much would you give to go back to your old self?" Izell asked.

"Anything." There was no reluctance there. "To turn back the hands of time and be myself again. I would give anything."

"Then I offer you a new pact. I will relieve you of your curse if you agree to fulfill one wish of mine at a time of my choosing."

"Considering my days are numbered, you have yourself a deal."

"Then I accept the burden of your curse," Izell said.

Nyah leaned around to watch them shake on it. The first of her misgivings bubbled to the surface as she realized what Izell was truly offering. She wasn't returning the spark; she was taking it into herself!

"Become yourself again," Izell said, giving Lucia the blood purification potion, uncorked. She went to breeze past Nyah, who caught her sleeve with a hiss.

"What have you done?" she demanded.

"Strategy," Izell said with a wink. "You trust me, do you not?"

"That spark corrupted her so fast." Nyah dropped her voice to a horrified whisper.

Izell pulled away. "You can trust a Seelie. I have more defenses against magic than she would ever dream of," she said quietly. "If you want to see a future without Jazrach, first we must take the teeth out of his servants. I'll be back. I need to leave the wards to make sure the deal went through."

She breezed away, leaving Nyah to watch, numb. Mentally scribbling Izell's name to the bottom of the list of those she worried for, she reversed her hand to hold her face instead.

"Was that Nyah's voice I heard?" called Lucia. She tapped sharp fingernails against the glass she held.

Nyah came out from hiding, pointing at it. "Drink that. I will not replace it."

The chained Sorceress was starting to wither. Maybe it was the Fell Madness, but she looked smaller. Frail. Deep half-moons marked the hollows of her eyes as her skin dried to a corpse-like pallor. She understood Izell's crack about bathing as she caught a whiff of body odor mixed with decay. Yet Lucia was smiling over-wide, glancing over Nyah's shoulder as Adrius stepped out behind her.

"Cheers, husband," Lucia purred, toasting him with the potion.

Adrius put a hand on Nyah's shoulder. "We should go. No good comes of talking to her," he said. His fingers were trembling ever-so-subtly.

"Oh, did he not tell you?" Lucia said, taking a breath of the fumes from the open potion and making an expression of bliss. "We wed before the thrones. The whole vampire nation was in attendance."

"Nyah, let's—"

"No." She held up a hand, a sinking feeling in the pit of her stomach. "You two...married?" Glancing up at Adrius in the hopes of stone-faced denial, she saw he was instead ghost-white and looking far too guilty for this to be a coincidence.

The Sorceress cackled. "We sure did. What delicious irony."

"It was unconsummated," Adrius blurted. "Gwendolyn sank Nyixa that night."

Nyah shrugged off his touch, seized by wide-eyed shock. She'd been told the story of Nyixa sinking and her friends, the Ancients of this time, sent into a thousand-year sleep. They'd been attending a wedding, but no one had done her the courtesy of mentioning it was *Adrius's* wedding.

"It was purely political." Adrius was following her, his excuses turning to white noise in her head. She fled, putting as much distance between her and the laughing Sorceress as possible. They re-emerged into the night air, and their escort started the car, seeing all three of them out of the prison.

Adrius tried to take her shoulder. She spun, hissing, *"Don't!"*

Chest heaving, her shoulders hunched in defensively. "Of all people. *Lucia.* You married Lucia."

"Let me explain." He put his hands up.

"The person who locked me away from Earth! Who all but murdered me to sit on the vampire throne." She shook her head in sheer disbelief. She thought she knew him, but this just proved how wrong she was.

Izell was suddenly at her elbow. "What did he do this time?" she asked, glancing between the two of them.

Nyah had no more words, but her emotions were bubbling over in the sting at her eyes. She turned away so he wouldn't see them. When Adrius went to explain for her, Izell put her palm up. "I didn't ask you. Why don't you give her some time to process...whatever happened?"

"But I haven't explained—"

"I waited for you," she said, hating how broken the whisper sounded. "I could have wed hundreds of times for politics. But I refused every single one."

"It was different this time. I *had* to." Heaven help them both, he sounded nearly as wretched as she felt.

She didn't turn around. She couldn't see his face right now and acknowledge what he was saying. "Could you just...leave for a while?"

She was doing it again, pushing him away instead of facing the gulf between them. If she didn't have plans to grill Izell, she'd be the one running. But she needed some distance from Adrius and the problems he brought with him.

Maybe she wasn't ready for a relationship after all.

"Nyah..." he murmured.

"Go, please," she said more quietly. "I can't right now."

She turned to Izell, who was waving him toward the car. His footsteps signaled his retreat, but she didn't watch him leave.

Chapter 18
Adrius

"I couldn't help but notice…" Armando broke the silence with all the delicacy of a creeping spider.

Adrius sat in the back, curled in the spot where leather met metal. His body jostled with every bump in the road.

Stupid. So stupid.

"What happened?" Charlotte asked more directly.

She hadn't listened to him, that's what happened. Because she'd heard the truth from the wrong person and formed her own conclusions because of it.

"I can't escape it," he whispered, finally lifting his gaze to meet hers. "My past."

Instead of judgement, those chocolate-brown eyes were filled with understanding. "I know a thing or two about that," she said.

That moment of warmth in a stranger's eyes was what he needed. "I need a better future," he said, though he still didn't know how to grasp it. But he had to do something for Nyah, to prove that his devotion was to her and never to another. Before he lost her permanently.

He couldn't think of any worse fate than to see Nyah give up on him too. A blow like that would turn him into the most desperate wretch.

Charlotte flashed a smile. "The first step to change is knowing it has to happen."

The pair escorted him into the mansion and made small talk on either side of him. As he trudged inside, he realized Zerenth had been strangely silent. He could feel that the dragon was awake, active, and thinking hard, but there was no interaction between them. Didn't the overgrown lizard want to rub his prediction in?

Whatever. He meant to tell the two enforcers that he appreciated their presence but would be okay on his own. That was, until he noticed the door hiding the portal to Adrun had come ajar and a young fae face was peering around the corner, his sparkling eyes widening with awe.

"Excuse me, do you know where I can find Queen Nyah?" The fae addressed him, coming out fully to reveal his page's uniform. He held a sealed scroll between two fingers.

"She is away, but I can take that for you," he offered.

The page gripped the scroll in a loose fist. "I really should deliver this directly to her..."

"Hey, *amico*, let me show you what you'd have to do to deliver that to her." Armando slung an arm around the fae and took him to a window, pointing out the roadway and how far he'd have to travel in this strange new land to meet up with Nyah at the moment. He ended the explanation with the scroll in his hand and a grateful page bowing away, heading back to Adrun. "Too easy." He flashed a bright smile Adrius's way as he passed it over.

He hesitated in breaking the seal and reading its contents. It was addressed to Nyah after all, the person whose trust he wanted back. But he knew there was something troublesome happening in her kingdom too. What if he could solve it for her? Wouldn't that prove his devotion?

The letter was signed *Caladorn Nightweaver* with a wax crest and contained an official request for her presence. Adrius couldn't help the beginnings of hope stirring in him as he realized Nyah had a problem that a company of her guard had failed to fix.

"There are fae going missing in Adrun, and a company of Nyah's guard has done the same," he told his two new friends. "Do you know what this means?"

"Demons?" Charlotte ventured.

He paused for a moment. "Possibly." That hadn't been his immediate thought, though. "You know, probably. Can you imagine if I singlehandedly brought him in?"

Armando and Charlotte exchanged a glance. "What?" he asked.

"That sounds incredibly dangerous," Armando said. "Like, I think it's brave and all, but you're still one guy."

"The King of Vampires," he reminded him. Even though he didn't feel like it and he'd lost his fangs, he still had that title to his name.

Armando considered him, rubbing his chin. "Can we at least give you some tools for the job?" He went to inspect the size of the portal and nodded to himself. They parted ways for the moment, the two enforcers promising "goodies" to help.

Adrius went to his room and fitted himself in his old, kingly armor. The metal was a dark gray, embossed with an old heraldry symbol he traced with a fingertip. A horse rampant, the mark of someone who'd served old Gabriel Legion, Gwendolyn's deceased husband. "If only you could see me now," he said to his reflection. The armor didn't quite fit, because he wasn't in tip-top shape anymore to fill the metal with muscle. Long ago, he'd also lost the tabard that marked him as a knight.

A joke anyway. Adrius had never been so honorable, even when he'd served humanity as its bulwark against Fell invasion. He'd tried, though. Back then, he'd truly believed he could be better than a scavenger who liked the taste of monster blood and the power found within.

He knew that same desire now, to be *better*. "I will be," he murmured, turning from his reflection and going downstairs to see Armando and Charlotte working together to wheel the love-child of a bicycle and car through the front door. He'd seen a few on the road, zooming in and out of traffic with a single person maneuvering boldly.

"I'm lending this baby to you, but you gotta promise to take care of it," Armando said once they had it resting on a stand on the underside.

"What is it?" he asked.

"Let's get it through the portal, and I'll show you."

He and Armando went through the portal together, but not before Charlotte loaded him up with several guns and more ammunition than he'd need. "Put one through its brain for me," she said, waving goodbye as the portal enclosed them, bringing them to the basement and the other portal taking them to Adrun.

"Damn, this place is dark," Armando muttered. Once they wrestled the vehicle onto the forest path that Adrius remembered led the way to Dragonhelm, Armando taught him how to use it.

Adrius was pretty sure he was about to destroy this motorcycle by crashing it into a tree. However, he focused on learning what he needed to do as he weighed down the poor thing visibly with his bulk. "This is a clever vehicle," he said once he had a handle on the basics and zipped back and forth on the same stretch of ground. He appreciated the headlight, illuminating what was directly in front of him.

The beam caught a glimpse of red fur. He stopped the machine and twisted. A familiar figure approached cautiously, sniffing and wrinkling her muzzle as if the motorcycle was the most dreadful object she'd ever smelled. "Swift!" he exclaimed.

"What is this thing?" she asked.

Armando gave him a strange look when he zipped by a few minutes later with a fox riding in the seat behind him, her muzzle lifted to the breeze the machine created. "I think I got it," he said, giving the vampire a grateful glance. "I'll try to take care of it."

"Good luck, *amico*," he said, slapping Adrius's shoulder and waving as he took off, taking the path cautiously until it widened into a proper road. He told Swift his intentions as they approached Dragonhelm and startled the guards into drawing their weapons at their fast approach.

"And why are you doing this on your own?" Swift asked the part he'd omitted, that Nyah needed him to prove himself. Addressing the guards was the distraction he needed.

He dismounted the vehicle and approached with his palms up. The fae seemed familiar and thankfully seemed to recognize him. "I need to speak to..." He took out the scroll and consulted it. "...Caladorn Nightweaver."

Exchanging a glance between them, the fae sent a runner into the city, a magicked lantern bobbing behind him. Adrius stayed with the motorcycle, just in case the denizens would try to damage it. But that meant Swift was still waiting, her tail tip starting to twitch. "This isn't just to impress Queen Nyah, is it?" she asked. "Please tell me that's not why you're doing this."

He made a noncommittal grunt. "What did I tell you before? Putting yourself in danger isn't the way to her heart," Swift chided.

"It may be the only thing I have left," he admitted reluctantly, telling her of the misunderstanding as they waited.

Swift rested a paw on her muzzle and shook her head. "She just needs some time. Why don't you wait instead of do this?"

Adrius was glad when a new trio arrived a moment later, saving him from responding. He didn't do well with *wait and see.* He did a double take to see Sorsha and Ash accompanying a tall and graceful fae man who wore a displeased expression already. "Stand down. The Earth...thing won't harm you," the man he assumed was Caladorn snapped to his men.

"Motorcycle," Sorsha supplied, along with introductions. The man was her father, he learned. "Adrius, what are you doing here?"

Adrius took a long breath to steady his surprise and nerves. "I, ah, received this," he said, showing the message to them.

"That wasn't meant for you." Caladorn's face hadn't changed from its stoic mask.

"Nyah is my lifemate."

The mention of Nyah made him scowl and eye Adrius anew. "Then you would know that it is bad manners to read her correspondence," he countered, crossing his arms. "Well, you are here. What did you want?"

He certainly wasn't expecting a warm welcome, but the fae leader was practically frigid. Was there already some bad blood here? *A spurned suitor of Nyah's, perhaps,* he thought, bristling. "I came to help. I just need an escort to the village having trouble."

"You're going on your own otherwise?" Caladorn raised a brow.

"Maybe my fox friend will also accompany me." He gestured to Swift.

"Can I speak to you privately?" the fae asked abruptly, turning on his heel and walking toward the forest without hearing a response. They turned back toward the road, though Adrius imagined the fae was watching his daughter, while he was more focused on the motorcycle.

"Adrius, I've been around a while," Caladorn began. "Queen Nyah was just researching demons. Why would she be so interested in that subject if there wasn't one around? I cannot in good faith help you start your mission, because you are not an angel nor blessed with an angelic weapon."

It was at that moment Adrius felt Zerenth stir and speak. *"Tell him that demons can be disabled."*

"Demons can be disabled," Adrius parroted.

His lips twisted. "You mean to capture it."

"I mean to see it for myself," hissed the dragon.

"Yes," Adrius said, tamping down a note of uncertainty as he wondered what Zerenth meant.

"That is a legitimate option." Caladorn glanced to the sky. "I can lend you one man to the task before I march my whole army down there personally. Honestly, do you think you are strong enough to take down a demon?"

He fixed piercing, starry eyes on Adrius. Any hesitation, and this tough old fae would rescind what little he meant to offer. "I can," he answered. Though on the inside, he thought of how easily Jazrach had bent his will on their first encounter. A cold sweat beaded his back.

"Hmm." For his part, Caladorn didn't seem convinced. But his words gave Adrius a measure of hope. "I have an artifact you can borrow, but it will only work for one person. You will have one man, the artifact, and your wits. If you can but scout out what is going on in that area...I would be in your debt. But don't say the demon-word around my people." He turned away, shaking his head. "We are all afraid of what they can do."

Chapter 19
Nyah

away, taking Adrius with it. She felt hollow in the moment, unsure of how to feel.

It took Nyah a few moments to realize what she was talking about. The pact, right. The spark she had just willingly lifted from Lucia's soul. "Why?" she croaked, feeling her tears spill over. "Why would you help her?"

Izell scoffed. "Sooner or later, that demon will return for his spark. He'll never return to full strength without it."

Nyah swiped at her nose, realizing the fae's eyes glimmered with her usual cunning. "*And,*" she continued, "unlike those who held the spark before me, I know exactly what I'm dealing with. Come along. Let's see if Lucia can give us any information now that she's of her own mind."

Though she felt washed out, she welcomed the idea of information on the shadowy demon that lurked somewhere, waiting to cause havoc. They re-entered the prison to find Lucia slumped in her restraints, unconscious. Her Madness was receding, veins clearing and fingers twitching as they reduced from talons into less threatening fingernails.

"This would be easier if I could use my magic," Izell remarked, walking up and slapping the Sorceress hard enough to send her body lurching. They'd given most victims of Fell

Madness a day to sleep off the effects of the purification potion, which could be as painful as placing fire in the veins to clear out the darkness.

A vigorous shake had her waking with a cry of agony. The last remnants of black blood were pooled in her eyes, and even that was fading as she beheld the two women looming over her. Her face still looked practically skeletal, though, so the potion didn't work quite as fast on the details.

"What? What do you want now?" she rasped.

"You're going to tell us about Jazrach," Nyah said, folding her arms.

A spasm seized Lucia. "Jaz...rach..." she gritted out, the silver in her eyes flashing through. Her wrists pulled their chains taut as she writhed through a wave of cleansing pain. Once it passed, she could speak again. "Jazrach, of course. What do you want to know about that conniving scum?"

Nyah's brows raised at the wording. "Does that shock your delicate butterfly sensibilities?" Lucia sneered. "I'll tell you *exactly* what he did to me, and we'll see if you think he deserves a worse title."

"By all means," she said, gesturing for her to go on.

"Mind that I'm only talking so you do the honors of ending him," she muttered. "I can tell you hate me."

Nyah bared her teeth. "For good reason."

Bobbing her head in acceptance, she echoed it, "For good reason. I apologize, for what it's worth." She looked almost human as she met Nyah's gaze. "I did care for you. I simply...cared for your throne more."

Izell nudged her when she went for a waspish reply. Sucking in a breath, she recognized the faraway look in Lucia's manner. She swallowed her words, thinking it more prudent to let the woman talk.

"Whatever you did to me has pulled the wool from my eyes. I recognize so many things now as his doing," she began. "That voice, so close to my own, whispering my virtues. He was in the Grand Occultarus...I mean, the Eye of Worlds. Whatever we are calling it now. When Nyixa sank, he continued talking to me.

Guiding where my third eye looked. We constructed a plan together, even though I thought it was of my own doing."

She bowed her head again. "He promised I would rule the world, but all he wanted was to escape his prison and build a way to make contact with Hell. Every one of *my* wishes slipped out of my fingers. The throne, my...Neala's...lifemate, my beauty, even his approval, he didn't allow me to keep any of it."

"Control," Izell said, nodding.

"And now that you have me here, I am no use to him. He has abandoned me," she said, cringing through another wave of pain. "Since you have my curse, fae, I presume my head will be leaving my neck shortly?"

"Not while you owe me a favor. And trust me, I won't need it for a while," Izell answered. Nyah bit her tongue harder, because the Sorceress had a point. If they wanted to kill her for good, now they could.

Lucia leaned back in her restraints. "Pretty words. You need to find him before he whips up a problem you cannot fix. He's a demon of corruption, and in our short time together before he took his vessel and left, he bragged about how he can corrupt *anything.*" Her gaze turned to Izell pointedly.

Dread coated Nyah's throat. "What does he want?" she asked.

"I already said it, a portal to Hell. Wants to elevate his status. Rule below instead of serve above, if you know what I mean."

She chewed on that thought. "He gets something if he helps destroy the world?"

"He gets to rule the Earth that remains after his fellows pillage and rape and destroy everything in the apocalypse."

Nyah pulled a face of disgust. Of course that was a demon's end goal. "One more thing," Lucia sighed. "We both know you're going to try reuniting the Fell Keys and construct a new Eye of Worlds. He will do everything in his power to distract you or get his hands on a Key or two to make it impossible. He only has to wait you out until midwinter."

Releasing an unladylike curse, Nyah paced the small space before the confined Sorceress. They *had* to find Jazrach. This was the problem she needed to give her full attention and resources to. "I can help you," Lucia said after Nyah did a few laps. "Release me, and I will gladly hunt him and the Keys."

She held out her arms and the shining metal confining them. Despite herself, Nyah considered the offer. If she spoke true, Lucia had solid reason to want Jazrach permanently confined to a new prison.

But.

"I cannot forgive your actions because of one good deed," Nyah said. "Nor can I make that decision for others who would kill you on sight. Here you shall remain."

Disappointment glimmered in Lucia's eyes. "Very well."

"We should be going," she continued, glancing to Izell. She wasn't sure if she could take any more revelations today. The fae nodded and turned to go.

"Nyah, how is Gwendolyn?" Lucia asked.

Frowning suspiciously, she said, "Unwell."

"Won't you tell her for me...that I miss the people we used to be?" The fight seemed to leave her until she was just a miserable husk.

The last thing she needed to know, if she didn't already, was that Gwendolyn still battled for her life. She could give Lucia this bit of closure. "I'll tell her."

Nyah took the car ride back in silence. She watched the world scroll by, faster than riding on any horse or fae-bred elk, and embraced the numbness within. The two enforcers accompanying her and Izell were quiet, and she could feel them glancing at her occasionally. They'd returned from escorting Adrius, and she couldn't meet their eyes for fear of judgement that she'd sent him away like a coward rather than hear him out.

In truth, she didn't know what to say to him until she was before his door and knocking, to no answer. "Adrius?" she called, trying their secret knock next.

Nothing.

"I'm sorry I overreacted. Again." She spoke to the cold wood, resting her forehead against it. Maybe he was listening, and if so, she would at least express herself from the heart. "I'm ready to hear what you were going to say. That it was a political arrangement? I can see that now. She took my throne, and you must've abdicated for a while when I...when you thought I was dead..."

She took a deep hiccup of breath, feeling a tear finally leak down her cheek. "I never thought we'd see each other again, and you must've done the same," she continued. "It's just, I waited for you, and at the time, I thought you cracked within, what, twenty years? That's nothing..."

As she drifted off, she realized there was someone else on this floor, attempting to ignore Nyah as she dusted the corners of the corridor. A maid. She'd completely overlooked the maid. Color flushed her cheeks as she imagined what exactly she must look like, desperately spilling her heart out to a closed door.

Well, if Adrius was there, maybe he'd take her words to heart. She flashed a nod to the other woman and headed up to her own room to rest so she could tackle the next day with the verve it would require.

Chapter 20
Adrius

Adrius sped through the gloom on a trade road with a fae guard in the seat behind him and Swift sitting in the space between his lap and two outstretched arms. The fox had her head up, enjoying the moment. The guard, a stuttering astral fae with his grasp around Adrius like an iron vice, was named Vistral. He sported the spots of his beast, a jaguar, over his exposed skin.

Adrius had met someone on Earth who'd worn a shirt with purple animal print, and that's what Vistral's skin reminded him of. One spot haloed his left eye; another blotched along his cheek. It had a certain charm to it, he decided on the few times he glanced back to see if the other man was still okay.

"What does a jaguar signify?" Adrius asked to break up the monotony of his trip. The motorcycle's headlight illuminated a jagged oval of tree limbs braided and manicured until it seemed like they were following the path of one very long tunnel.

"Patience," Vistral responded. "My boss thinks it's laziness, though."

He wondered if that meant the fae man was chosen for this trip as punishment. "Are you a fighter?" he asked.

"I'm a guard."

"But are you a *fighter*? Have you been in many fights?" Adrius pressed.

"Well, no. Just shoplifters so far. I enlisted about a year

ago." His response made Adrius stifle a sigh, realizing he really was on his own if it came down to a fight. Swift and Vistral were along for companionship and to guide him down the right route.

His tongue worried at a space between his gums and back teeth. The artifact Caladorn had let him borrow was a bead the size of his pinky nail. It was made of cloudy glass, with a curl of light dancing within like a candle flame. The fae general had not-so-gently wedged it into the back of his mouth, where it seemed to disappear except for a tacky feeling against his gums.

Even with the gift, his opinion of the fae general was quite low, to match the derision that filled everything the man had said and done in their short acquaintance.

"It's the only angelic artifact I have," Caladorn had said. "Don't take it out until you return, and you'll be immune to demonic corruption."

He certainly liked the sound of that and wished he'd had the little bead sooner. Maybe things wouldn't have gone this far. Maybe he'd be falling asleep with Nyah by his side right now.

They traveled for the bulk of the night, not that the sky lightened as a reminder of rest. He'd spent most of the time either making small talk with young Vistral, getting lost in his own thoughts, or trying to get Swift to stop giving him a judgmental side-eye. *Maybe that's just her face,* he thought. They encountered a few traveling groups, who watched him maneuver by them with gaping stares.

"Swift," he said as they broke from the forest tunnel at last. There was civilization ahead, but they passed right through it with Vistral loosening his death grip to manage a wave to those who came out to see what the motor noise was.

Adrius waited until the road took them further into the gloom of Adrun. The fox had turned to look at him, her ears cocked at different angles.

"I've been wondering," he continued, grasping for a way to phrase this and not cause insult. "Earth is so different now. Technology, cars, phones..." He realized she didn't know what those things were and gestured to the machine under them. "Motorcycles. Yet, here in your land, it's like no time has passed at all. Where is your advancement?"

She tilted her muzzle back and forth thoughtfully. "Magic. We have all our needs met by magic," she answered. "And...if this thing is anything to judge by, Earth has more metal than Adrun. Metal is scarce here."

"What do you do for coin?" he asked. "And armor? And weapons?"

"We use paper bills, and other things are magically fashioned from wood," she said.

He glanced down at her in disbelief. "Are you wearing wood?" he asked Vistral. The fae revealed he was actually wearing padded cloth. Nearly worthless as armor, he thought.

"Our weather comes from magic. Drinking water, too," Swift continued. "Adrun wasn't designed for life, but Queen Nyah and the druids make it work."

"Remarkable." His admiration was for Nyah alone, though. As they crested a high hill, giving him a glimpse of rolling frontier far into the darkness, he was proud for what she'd accomplished. They couldn't let it be undone now.

Vistral spoke up as Adrius revved the motor, speeding them along since he saw no one sharing the road with them. "The druids keep the plants alive too. Even though there's no sun." He could feel the fae's curious gaze. "Are you from a place with the sun? What is it like?"

He thought back with a wistful twist of his lips. He hadn't experienced the sun in so long that his only answer could be, "I don't remember. The sun is deadly for vampires."

As he explained what a vampire was to the clueless fae behind him, he felt Zerenth wake and listen in with a rumbling at the back of his mind. The dragon said nothing, fading to a sense of deep thought.

"What is it?" he asked with a mental sigh.

"None of your business," Zerenth snapped. *"Don't talk to me."*

Adrius was just happy the exchange happened in his head, because he imagined walking away from the dragon missing a few fingers. He kept his own company as they finally saw another settlement coming up. "This is it," Vistral said. "Emberglen. And there's the barrier." His spotted arm shot out to indicate a direction, but all Adrius saw was darkness studded with sparks like stars in the sky. He wondered what was out there.

He decided to park the motorcycle behind a farmhouse abutting the outskirts of Emberglen Village, just in case. The three of them walked the rest of the way, no sound around except that of Adrius's armor clinking. His legs were sore from the extended trip atop the vibrating vehicle, but the discomfort was fading, as if he still had regeneration despite losing his vampiric powers.

"Look for any signs of struggle, but stay close," he whispered to them. He inspected the ground and tried doors, finding most of the buildings empty and the ground undisturbed.

Vistral rubbed his arms as they passed each other on their search. "Something feels wrong," he murmured.

"I don't smell anything off," Swift reported as she rooted around with her nose to the ground like a hunting dog.

"Keep looking," Adrius said, rubbing at his eyes. He worried his fatigue would make him sloppy, but he pressed on, thinking they could re-check the area later.

Swift lifted her tail, pointing out trampled land. "Elk. They passed through here," she said. "The company didn't stop for long."

Great, Adrius thought with a sigh. "We can follow the trail tomorrow." He turned toward the cozy, two-story inn situated in the village square. "Let's get some rest and start this up again when we're fresher."

Swift stepped into his path. "Not there," she said. His brow furrowed in puzzlement. "We know this place isn't safe. Unless you want to disappear too?"

Reluctantly, he found himself bedding down for the night by shredding a fresh bale of hay into a bed. They'd found a barn to match the farmhouse on the village outskirts, and while it wasn't the most comfortable of arrangements, Adrius was reasonably assured it would be safe for a night.

Vistral made himself a similar bed in the stall next to his.

There were no livestock, which struck them both as odd. "I don't like this," the fae kept muttering under his breath. "Not one bit."

"You'll be okay, friend. Anything that comes in will find me first," Adrius pointed out. He left his sword unsheathed by his makeshift place of rest and piled up his armor neatly to the other side. They'd drawn straws for watch, and his was last. Swift's furry form was somewhere in the shadows to keep an eye out while they fell asleep.

Despite himself, he fell hard to a dream of Nyah in the dark. She was...*aroused*. Shadowy hands grasped her hips, and a pair of lips materialized to kiss the soft column of her throat. Her phantom lover turned toward Adrius, flashing a pristine smile of too many teeth.

His eyes shimmering with cunning, it was Caladorn who kissed Nyah like he owned her. *I knew it!* The fae disapproved of him for a reason. In his rest, he completely believed there was something between them. Something Nyah had had and kept from him.

Adrius watched, hapless, until the sound of rustling hay brought him from the sight that would burn in his retinas. Disorientation gripped him.

No, that was a dream, he corrected.

He blinked up to see the star-flecked and spotted skin of Vistral looming over him. "My watch?" he croaked, clearing his throat and beginning to sit up.

Vistral tilted his head to an unnaturally cocked angle, his whole form trembling. He caught the handle of Adrius's blade with his foot and flipped it up with the grace of a master, not some guard so young his ears were still green. Adrius was still shocked when the steel pierced his throat, killing him instantly.

Chapter 21
Nyah

Nyah's first trip was to the infirmary the next day, just in time to watch Neala manhandle Jaromir from bed and dump him on his rear. Shocked, she stopped at the doorway. *"Sulking time is done. Go get dressed,"* the female Blood Prince said gruffly, arms crossed.

"You don't have to be so rude," he grumbled.

"Consider it tough love."

Neala turned, and their eyes met across the room. Nyah could tell what Alex meant immediately, as shadows smudged the hollows of Neala's face and haunted her eyes. Reaching for her empathy to see just how bad it was, to her surprise, she came up empty on that front. It was like she was still in the prison, still hollowed out by the revelation of Adrius's wedding. Her virtue was snuffed like a candle at the end of a long night.

"Where have you been?" she murmured, crossing the tile to hug Neala and then coax Jaromir into the same before he left the infirmary, perhaps for the first time in weeks.

"You know, around," Neala said with a vague wave. *"Just like everyone else. You and Adrius have been running back and forth between that portal. Sirius and Korin are off doing God knows what. And every time I catch someone, they're sulking. Why are you sulking?"*

"I'm not..." She stopped herself with a chuckle. Her face

must've said otherwise. "I was just in a fight with Adrius yesterday and haven't seen him since."

"Trouble in paradise?" Neala raised a brow.

"What paradise?" Nyah sighed. "It's like he's a completely different person."

They found a more comfortable place to sit, with Neala watching the stairs, apparently for any sign of Jaromir. *"If Jaromir is to be disabled like me, then at least I can help him,"* she said.

"There's a big difference between a voice and a Gift, though."

"Not on the inside." Neala shook her head. *"Have you considered that you, too, are a very different person?"*

"Of course I am," she said.

Neala made a mock bow, as if that proved her point. *"I'll trade you tasks. If I find Adrius, you can be the judge at the trial today."*

Nyah wrinkled her nose in distaste. "That's today?"

"It is. And guess who was the only non-sulking Blood Prince Alex could find?"

"Maybe it'll be fast," she suggested.

"Oh, doubtful."

As they lapsed to companionable silence, she wondered how to broach the subject that seemed to weigh so heavily on Neala. The other woman's red eyes drifted to hers, and she frowned. *"There's nothing to pity here. I am just feeling sorry for myself."*

"I heard a bit about it..." She scrubbed at her face, making sure no sign of concern remained in her expression.

"Alex accidentally reminded me of deeper memories than of my deceased husband," Neala offered, even her mental voice hushing. *"I can now recall events from when I was a toddler."*

Nyah cursed under her breath. "When you lost your voice?"

"Yes. No pity. I am still here to remember after all."

"It is not pity to be concerned for your wellbeing. Do you want to talk about it?" The other woman had squinted her eyes closed, as if to shut out those thoughts.

"Not yet," she murmured.

"When you are ready, Chandra makes for an excellent counselor if you don't wish to speak to me," she offered.

Neala shook her head. *"I don't know which thought is worse, you thinking I won't talk to you or that I need another dream walker."* Going rigid for a moment, Neala's lips pressed into a tight line. *"I must go. The trial awaits. See you later?"*

"Definitely," Nyah said, seeing her off with another hug and a wave. She sat back in her chair and relaxed until she noticed a fae page peering around, shading his eyes as he crept from the room concealing the portal.

Upon seeing her, he nearly tripped over himself to deliver a note and hovered anxiously as she unfolded it. "Would you like to send a response?" This must be a more experienced page, for he forwent the formalities she hated so much.

"No need," she said from numb lips. "You may return to your duties."

The note was signed with a paw print instead of a name, but she knew a message from Swift when she saw one. The fox didn't send it personally, but they had scribes to take down notes from mental communications.

She read it again to be sure she hadn't hallucinated: *Adrius is heading to Emberglen Village. For you. If you are receiving this, it's been a day and I haven't checked in to stop this message. We need your help.*

"No," she said in a low moan.

She held her head. *If he's charging off for me, then he must be doing this because of yesterday,* she thought. Like she'd given him something to prove. In his own way, she could see how he'd come to that conclusion. But she'd never ask him to take on a threat alone when it'd apparently bested several fae already. It wasn't brave; it was foolhardy.

She went directly into Adrun, calling out to Caladorn mentally. *"It is time we mobilized the guard."*

"Saddling up as we speak, my queen," he responded.

"Is Sorsha with you still?" After he replied to the affirmative, she had the fae Sorceress make her a portal directly to him, which she stepped through and cast a glance around. Caladorn was saddling a regal elk with a mane so dark it was practically purple. Its extended rack was strung with lanterns, and its saddlebags

were heavy for an extended journey. Sorsha was petting its soft nose and murmuring praise to it.

"Caladorn, why does my lifemate know about Emberglen Village?" she asked almost casually, her gaze darting between the two Seelie, daring one of them to offer her a half-truth.

"He came here on a metal monstrosity demanding to help after intercepting a message meant for you," Caladorn said with a shrug. "I gave him a guardsman to help and my only heavenly artifact. They were supposed to scout the area."

"A motorcycle," Sorsha whispered behind her hand.

"What is...never mind, it doesn't matter." She held her head.

"Actually, it does. It means he's traveling faster with modern technology," Sorsha pointed out.

Nyah kneaded her forehead, trying to control her reaction. She could feel her wolf stirring and embraced the rush of ferocity that lent her. "Adrius wouldn't just scout the area."

"Then he doesn't know how to follow orders, just like he doesn't respect a sealed missive." Caladorn's tone was practically freezing.

Her teeth bared, and she stepped closer until she was speaking heated words up at his face. "You have a duty to protect all that come to this land. You more than others should have done everything in your power to stop him!"

He took it like a soldier, his expression unchanging and stony. "Celeste was right there behind him, and he didn't know who she was. What sort of man doesn't know—?"

"I haven't told him," she interrupted, bitterness creeping up her throat at the stark reminder that Adrius wasn't the only one keeping important secrets. If he knew the magnitude of this one, he would have every right to be furious with her. "Do you see the irony in that? You judged him on something he doesn't even know."

Sorsha stepped between them. "Sorry to interrupt," she said, her head turning upward toward the timbers of the stable. "Do you feel that?"

They stepped outside, forcing several fae to jump out of the way from Sorsha's quick bustle. Craning her head skyward, Nyah looked at the glittering barrier above for any sign of something unusual. Night's Howl sensed it first, howling in alarm before anything became visible. A halo of heat lit the magic before a falling star streaked through the sky, followed by a deluge of salt water over Adrun like a junior druid's first attempt at weather-wielding.

Dragonhelm came alive with screaming. Nyah wiped her stinging eyes, soaked to the skin but desperately watching the barrier as it knit itself together and cut off the rush of ocean water into their bubble of safety. "What was *that*?" she demanded.

"It didn't land far from here," Sorsha said, opening a second portal. They all stepped through to the forest before Izell's private home. The scent of burning greenery floated to them from something glowing and...muttering.

Nyah crept to the tree line, blinking away sunspots as she spotted the glowing outline of a man in pristine silver armor stamping at the remains of Izell's prize rosebushes, putting out the embers threatening to consume the last pristine blooms. But she wasn't staring at his boots, not when he had a pair of wings made of pure light on his back.

"Excuse me!" she exclaimed, stepping forward. "Are you an angel?"

The man went rigid, and his wings disappeared with a bright burst. Working the buckles securing his helmet, the stranger only turned to her when it was free and rolling aside.

Their gazes met, and time slowed. She knew that face, with all its little scars and the cleft in its jaw. Smile lines had overcome the battle with their more strict counterparts some time ago, leaving his blue eyes to crinkle at the corners naturally. While she couldn't remember if his hair was ever that pristine shade of straw-yellow, she assumed there had to be some perks to being an angel.

Back straight from his prime and holding his arms open as she rushed for him was her father, the legendary Gabriel Legion.

Chapter 22
Neala

Neala arrived to find Coven Rehnquist's meeting room changed, the antique wooden table turned and chairs crammed in on the far side. There was one high-backed seat in the center, probably hers, even though it was currently occupied by the young Sorceress, Violet, chatting quietly with Alex with their hands twined. Her shoulders were drawn, nervous and perhaps fearful.

Several semi-familiar faces filled in the rest of the panel, all scowling. It made for an intimidating first sight. They weren't here for their health; they were leaders of allied covens who'd all come together under one banner to stop the menace of Lucia. Behind them was a space filled in with a standing audience. She recognized Coven Rehnquist's leadership in the deputy and his wife, Sam and Melanie, along with feral-eyed Luke Tsosie, who seemed particularly pleased with this moment. Julian and Olivia stood just behind Alex, and for once, he was smiling and she was not.

"Welcome, Neala," Alex said, pushing to his feet and dragging Violet with him. Murmurs of greeting and a few half-bows passed through the leaders, which she wondered at. Did they really see her as some kind of royalty? Modern vampires didn't have much respect in them, so even this token amount seemed noteworthy.

She dipped her head and sat in the high-backed chair, flanked by Alex and the little seer girl, the Ancient Cossette. She felt no pity for the woman stuck in the body of a girl, just as she asked for none of the same with her lack of a voice. They all carried their own burdens.

As much as Neala dreaded the bureaucracy inherent in this trial, she was glad to have a distraction from her past. *"As I understand it, the man you will bring before me is unequivocally guilty,"* she said, fiddling with the wooden gavel before her.

"Maybe," said Cossette, her voice as serious as it got. "But you are here to pass the sentence. The most neutral person we could find."

"Let us get this over with," she sighed.

Someone flung the door open and marched in, a scowl on her face. She was unfamiliar, but her voice was not. "Why wasn't I invited to this?" Izell asked in a new glamor, this time wearing a sequined gown and a trim of fine fur around her neck.

The coven masters glanced amongst themselves and murmured in confusion while Alex stifled a sigh. "Hello, Izell," he said, gesturing down the row to an empty seat at the end with Coven Master Taylor. She adjusted her power suit, made eye contact with him, and flashed a nervous expression. "We saved you a seat."

Izell sat with a huff. *"Are we ready now?"* Neala asked, resisting the urge to roll her eyes. She didn't know how Nyah stood her dramatics.

There was a general agreement, and thus, a pair of burly vampires brought in a chained man and forced him to his knees before them. Neala knew him from her last confrontation with Lucia, where his unconscious body was taken from the underground stronghold with Lucia's. *"Bryant Collins, you are charged with ten counts of breaking the Deveaux Accords. How do you plead?"* Neala asked. One count per coven before him now.

"Not guilty," Collins said.

"Of course you do," Alex muttered.

The man before her didn't look like anything special. His Ancient status was nothing with a set of nephilim chains on his wrists. If he had wealth, a plain gray jumpsuit had erased it. He wore no finery except for a tarnished wedding ring and looked like he hadn't slept or had a drink of blood in weeks. His lips were chapped, and his skin was stretched too far over a skeletal face. A patchy red beard and mustache covered many of his freckles.

He had no allies, especially in this room. Neala had personally killed many of the Fell Mad that'd fought as a last-ditch effort to keep the joint army from reaching Lucia's stronghold. Later, they'd learned that most of those men and women had been Haveners, Collins's followers, strategically placed so that when they ran out of the golden cure for the Madness, the fanatics were the ones to go.

"Because of your unique situation, you will be allowed to state your case. Speak until you have no more breath if you must," Neala said, lacing her hands. She expected this to be the longest part of the trial.

Collins took in the hostile stares of his audience, coven masters and otherwise. His green gaze fell between Neala and Cossette, who were at least neutral. "Before you condemn me, listen." She picked up a piece of her homeland in the hint of his Irish brogue.

The sudden tension in her shoulders had nothing to do with him, though he drew himself up as well. She heard another man's brogue screaming a world's worth of time away, though the words were already blurring to a furious slurry along with the sounds of breaking things and a woman choking.

"...under the influence of foul witchcraft," Collins was saying as Neala gave herself a mental shake. "Lucia is your true enemy here. As you saw for yourself, she exploited all of her would-be allies, myself included."

"Which hardly excuses your other crimes," Alex said, his hands flexing into fists.

"Your previous associations with me aren't why we're all here, Rehnquist," he said without fire, his head bowing.

He's already defeated, Neala thought, strumming her fingers against the back of her hands.

"What can you recall from your time with Lucia?" she asked.

"Lucia put me under her thrall almost immediately. I was made to send my people to her one at a time for a kind of meet-and-greet. We made it very *special*," he said bitterly. "What I didn't know was that she'd already attacked and in some cases killed several of my men saving her." He jerked his chin toward Violet standing just behind her lifemate, causing attention to shift toward her.

Violet flushed from the sudden scrutiny but nodded in agreement. "At the time, I didn't know why she'd bitten Kim Cox before turning me into a Sorceress."

"She did it to kill her later and harvest my tears to make a portal to Hell," Collins said, his lip splitting along with its disgusted curl. "Anyone who knows me knows I founded Haven on Christian principles. I would never willingly work with a demon."

"I believe him." Attention shifted to Izell. She stared at him intently. "That ring on your finger, where is it from?"

Collins glanced toward it in confusion. "My wedding band?"

"Don't play coy with me, boy."

"Boy," he repeated, shaking his head. "If you must know, I found it during the Crusades as a young vampire. It is a token of God's favor."

"Uh-huh," Izell said heavily.

Collins's eyes narrowed, his tone heating. "With it, I can walk in the daytime, free of harm when the sun kills all other men. I've even summoned deadly light from it. If you could see its holy power for yourself, you would not laugh."

Neala nearly interrupted there, seeing why the fae was so keenly interested. But Izell spoke the truth aloud first. "Then you are wearing a Fell Key, not a token from the High Heavens. But it may be your faith that saves your life."

A few vampires gasped along the table, those who knew what a Fell Key was. *"You there. Take the ring from him,"* Neala ordered one of the two men who flanked Collins. The Irishman held up his cuffed hands, the beginnings of hope lighting in his eyes.

Because when both men took turns trying to pull off the ring, it stayed put. Now it was Neala leaning forward to make eye contact with Izell, speaking to her privately instead of broadcasting her mental voice through the room. *"The ring is bound to his soul. How is it possible?"* She'd only seen the phenomena with Adrius and Nyah, who'd both had their Keys magically attached to them as a sign of devotion at their wedding. Adrius had later tried everything in his power to remove the Shield Key from his person to no avail.

"Faith is funny that way. He believes in its power, and thus, the ring stays with him," Izell answered in kind.

"Point made. Don't yank off his finger," Alex ordered, his lips pressing to a grim line.

"Guess you can't kill me after all," Collins said, starting to smile as the room erupted into shouts of anger or dismay.

Neala knew that wasn't quite true. Technically, anyone but Adrius would surrender their soul bound Keys in death, with no soul to tether the ring and its power to them. It was the conclusion this audience wanted, to see him dead and the Key on his finger passed to another. But...she knew Lucia, and she believed his tale of betrayal. He had nothing now, with his wife's heart powering a portal and his men slain.

She smacked the gavel on its stand. *"Order,"* she said sternly, and all but the most stubborn quieted. *"I've come to a decision. He is guilty."*

This wiped the smirk from Collins's face. *"I give him to Izell and the fae for training in proper use of his Key. If he does not conform, he dies."* Neala swung around to Izell. The fae had the only happy expression in the room, grinning with all eight fangs and rubbing her palms together in glee.

"I'll take *great* care of him," the fae said.

Alex's lip was curled in outrage. "For ten counts of breaking our laws?" he demanded. Agreement sounded from all around, threatening the tenuous authority Neala had over this group. So much for the respect she'd gotten upon entering.

A small hand reached over and tapped the gavel for Neala. "She made the right decision," Cossette said soberly. "I'm the one who wrote the Accords, and I agree with Prince Wraith. We can't make Mister Collins our scapegoat. Not when Lucia's trial is next."

The shift in the audience was obvious. Neala saw bloodlust cross the faces of the coven masters. *"We will punish her properly,"* she agreed.

"I will do everything in my power to help," Collins said, making eye contact with her. "Your mercy will be rewarded. I will use God's light for good this time. From this moment, I am a changed man."

Izell stood and approached him. "Let's go, changed man, before they *change* their minds and decide to kill you after all."

The two guards glanced to Alex, who gave a strained nod. "Make the most of your second chance, Collins," he sneered. "It's the only one you'll get."

The Irishman didn't make eye contact as Izell led him out. As Neala got to her feet, so did many of the coven leadership. It was a briefer show than she'd expected and not nearly bloody enough for those present. Cossette slipped her hand into Neala's, tugging like a child leading her to something of interest. "Let's be in the right place at the right time." She was giggly again, which Neala understood meant she was no longer a serious adult for the moment.

She was just glad to leave the room and the disappointment and anger hanging heavy in the air. She hated politics and how truth and reason were twisted to fit a narrative. *"What are we going to see?"* she asked to get her mind off it.

Cossette took her to the infirmary before releasing her hand. An exasperated sigh escaped her lips as a haggard whisper of sound. *"Jaromir!"* The man had resumed his place on the bed he'd claimed, sitting there with his nose in one of the glossy-covered books by his bedside. He shot her a resigned look over the top of it.

"Am I not allowed to read?" he asked defensively.

He had, at least, dressed himself properly. But she still pinched the bridge of her nose. *"That's not the point. Why are you still convalescing?"*

"My Gift is still gone," he muttered.

Voices and boots approached the room. Neala turned to realize she really was in the right place at the right time as her jaw dropped. Nyah burst into the room first, leading in the last man Neala thought she'd ever see again. Her old commander, Gabriel Legion, so famed for killing his namesake's amount of Fell. He looked younger but just as fit as the man she remembered. His eyes seemed to sparkle with otherworldly power as they made eye contact.

Out of old habit, she saluted and felt the tickle of air on her cheek as Jaromir rushed to stand with her and do the same. "At ease," Gabriel said before clapping Jaromir on the shoulder. "Nice to see you, old friend. And Neala, daughter, word gets around in Heaven. Gwendolyn adopted you. Long overdue." He took her into a hug.

Surprise crossed Nyah's face over his shoulder. *I should've said something earlier,* Neala thought. The adoption happened when she was an adult and was more of an afterthought to give Keegan and Sorsha familial ties to Gwendolyn, the only person at the time, other than Lucia, with any capability to teach them magic.

"Heaven?" she asked, pulling back enough to look him over. He smiled and lifted a palm, which glowed with light. The plain armor over his person lit up with dozens of runes, many of which looked like twisting flames. She stumbled away, but the light didn't burn her.

"It's a miracle," Jaromir said in awe.

She nodded in agreement. *"How are you back?"*

"I am but a visitor. The story is too long to share at this hour." Gabriel gave them an apologetic smile. "I'm here for my wife, and then I must finish the task I came for." He glanced to Nyah, who led him to the only curtained-off bed while Neala and Jaromir trailed behind them.

Jaromir nodded in understanding. "He's going to burn out the demon magic in her," he shared behind his hand. They watched from the foot of the bed as Gabriel took Gwendolyn's hand then shifted his hold down to her wrist.

Neala remembered the wounds there and the corruption

Gwendolyn had burned from them upon unleashing her nephilim light. She nodded in understanding.

"Jaromir, can I count on you to keep her comfortable in my stead?" Gabriel asked.

There was no hint of hesitation on Jaromir's face now. It was the moment he needed to step back into his old role. "Of course."

"You may want to glance away." That was the only warning they had before he clenched his fingers and unleashed a flash of radiance that sent a wave of heat over Neala's skin.

She unclenched her eyes slowly to a sunspot shaped like an arc. Gwendolyn inhaled sharply in her sleep. "Gabriel? Is that... you?" she whispered.

"Yes, my love. Rest for now," he murmured back, brushing her temples. The older woman fell back asleep with a smile on her face.

Chapter 23
Adrius

Adrius wasn't surprised to "wake up" seated in a rocking chair next to Soren, his guardian angel, but the sight of Zerenth's hulking, dark form a stone's throw away gave him pause. He hadn't considered what would happen to the dragon if they died. Apparently, they were still linked, even in death.

Soren had one of his brilliant smiles on full display. His words slurred on the edge of Adrius's consciousness as he regained his bearings. "When I said I thought we'd see each other again, I didn't think it would be so soon."

"Sorry," he muttered. "Hopefully I'll be out of your hair soon."

"Nonsense! But you must tell me where you found your, ah, friend." Soren flinched as Zerenth's massive claws slashed a furrow into the ground, sending a clump of flowers into the abyss off the side of his island home.

Adrius crossed his arms. "We aren't friends." For once, his head wasn't full of the dragon's concentrated bitterness. It was perhaps the only good news about this whole situation.

"Right, my mistake. I'm going to go save my begonias. Make yourself at home!" The angel managed to sound cheerful even as he rushed over to stop Zerenth from uprooting more of his plants.

Adrius stood and walked to the other side of the garden, as far from both of them as he could get. He sat with his legs dangling over the endless blue sky below, wondering what would happen if he were to slip. Could one die while they were dead? Or would he just fall forever?

He chewed on those thoughts as he replayed his death in his mind's eye, over and over. It was a hazy memory, tainted by the last tendrils of a persistent nightmare. He could more clearly see that fae asshole's lips on his wife's neck than the sword stab from Vistral that killed him. When he began muttering about male anatomy, it was a tossup which fae he was actually referring to.

"Hoo boy! What did you do to make that dragon so angry?" called Soren.

Adrius scowled out into the sky. It seemed he couldn't get a moment alone. "He just came that way," he muttered.

The angel sat next to him, leaning his weight back on his palms. "What happened while you were away? Did you get to apologize to your brother?"

"Of a sort." The mention of Sirius didn't do much for his spirits, not when it reminded him of how he hadn't even seen his brother since his angry outburst.

"I must imagine your dragon got an apology 'of a sort' as well," Soren remarked.

He felt his scowl deepen. "What's that supposed to mean?"

"Well, no one starts off hating someone so deeply."

"He's an exception." With nothing else to do and sure Soren would continue bothering him until he told the story, he did, from the soul trial to the realization that Zerenth hated him for killing the Fell Emperor. "...And I cannot separate from him, because that will kill him and upset Nyah's people," he said to finish his tale. The sun was setting at he spoke, turning the sky pink and orange on the cusp of night.

"I see," Soren said, nodding slowly. "Would you like some dinner?"

Adrius raised a brow. All that, and he had nothing to say? "No, thanks."

"Did you want some advice?" The angel finally looked serious, even though his resting face still bore hints of a smile.

"Why not?" he sighed.

"I didn't hear an actual apology in any of that," Soren said, proving that Adrius should've never invited his criticism. When he didn't reply, the angel pushed to his feet. "Give it a try. What could it hurt?"

Adrius frowned up at him. "I have nothing to apologize for."

"An apology is sympathy, swallowing your pride and admitting you didn't mean harm to another, even accidentally. Couldn't you offer that to someone who now shares your body and fate?" Soren paused for a moment before brightening. "I bet my roast is done. Sure you don't want to join me?"

"I'm sure." He turned back to the skyline and waited for the sound of Soren walking away.

Apologize. What a joke. The dragon was the one who attacked him, over and over. If Adrius had known visiting Zerenth would end this way, he'd have chosen a different animal spirit. Anything but the bitter old creature whose voice was at times indistinguishable from the demon whispers that'd broken him.

But haven't you caused him harm, too? It niggled at him as the stars winked into existence in the fabric of the night sky. He cursed Soren for planting that thought. It was true he hadn't meant to hurt the dragon, but he obviously had. He was the man who'd put Zerenth's last master to the sword, the one to draw him out of his long grief vigil just to immediately want to declare them a bad match, no matter that it would kill him for good.

In a way, he was the villain of Zerenth's story.

And that was the realization that had him on his feet at last, crossing to the shape observing the same sky on the other side of Soren's island. Zerenth lay in a bare patch of earth, his scales shining brilliantly under the stars like an astral fae's skin. Adrius had quickly forgotten just how large the dragon was, even while lounging. He stopped short when his arrow-shaped head turned, red eyes blazing.

"What do you want?" Zerenth demanded.

All the moisture evaporated from Adrius's mouth. How had he really expected this to go except poorly? He doubted he could fix the gulf between them with an ocean of apologies, but he pushed the words from his throat anyway. "I'm sorry."

Zerenth blew a sulfurous gust over him and turned his head back to the sky. "I mean it." It was easier to speak without that angry stare fixed on him. "I'm sorry for getting you in this situation."

"The angel put you up to saying that," the dragon rumbled.

Silence stretched between them, and he shuffled awkwardly. Mission accomplished, he'd apologized, for what good it'd done. He prepared to leave when Zerenth said, "Why don't you do me a favor?"

"Leave you alone?" That, at least, was a favor he was used to fulfilling.

"Sit down."

Adrius did, his nerves jumping to his throat when Zerenth carefully placed his head by his knee. The dragon's slitted eye was tilted toward his face. "There, now you'll stop yelling up at me," he grumbled. "I'm a dragon, not deaf."

"I've noticed," Adrius sighed. "Look, I never meant to tie you to me like this. So you would die when I die. That's my personal Hell, not yours."

"Heaven. Not Hell. I never thought I'd visit such a place, yet here we are."

"Here we are," he agreed, unsure what to do from there, but now Zerenth was watching him. "What I mean is...I just wanted to visit you during the spirit trial. I didn't know your way of testing people was picking a fight with them."

"I know. You were perfect, my match in all respects. I wanted you to beat me." Now he had Adrius's undivided attention, his eyebrows drifting to his hairline. "You're not the only one with a death wish."

"You..." He replayed several moments between them in his mind's eye. "I don't understand."

"Of course you don't." The dragon sighed. "Let me spell it out to you, then: I've waited a long time to find someone who can best me, because at the beginning of my life as a spirit, I decided the only one worthy of me was someone who could do so. I was ready for all of this to end."

The rest clicked into place for him, and he scrubbed his face. "You wanted me to kill you for good."

"I did. I thought it would be poetic to destroy the man who killed the one fae I ever loved. I know how the fae feel about my presence." Zerenth's teeth clicked as his muzzle scrunched in some foreign expression in the face of Adrius's shock turning to hardened anger. How dare he play Adrius's feelings that way purposefully! "But then I put the pieces together and changed my mind."

"Oh, you've decided against ruining me, hmm?" He sneered. Really, he shouldn't have expected anything else. This creature that'd seen every moment of his suffering and despair had chosen to use it against him. Just like Lucia. Just like the demon.

"You didn't kill Calinhes. Not really." Zerenth's hushed voice was barely more than a hum in the night. "And because of that, we are not enemies."

Adrius forced his fists to unclench, thinking this was going somewhere important if he could just keep his mouth shut and listen. "You may have swung the sword and gathered his blood like some barbarian, but the one who killed him was the demon Jazrach."

"What do you mean?" he whispered.

"The spark. Think about it."

Adrius did. The spark...the piece of demon magic in Lucia, now Izell. The true curse that had driven his old enemy mad. His mouth formed a silent "o" as he realized what the dragon was getting at. "Calinhes gave her the spark out of spite. How long did he have it?"

"Long enough that you knew an entirely different man than I did. Calinhes was a *good* person. And by the time he met his end, he was just a monster." Grief laced every word as fire seemed to burn in Zerenth's eyes. "I'm not ready to die while my true enemy breathes freely."

And he was telling Adrius this *now*? He could hardly believe his ears. Yet it explained another comment: *I mean to see it for myself.* Along with Zerenth's moments of deep thought. "You're ready for an alliance with me?" he asked.

"Help me hunt Jazrach, and I will complete the merge with you." His claws dug a new furrow in the ground in anticipation.

"You have a de—"

"And I expect our merge to be fifty-fifty. I will not hide under your skin," he continued. "You will wear my scales proudly as a dragon shifter."

He only hesitated because he wondered what Nyah would think. Footsteps approached, waylaying his response ahead of the smell of cooked meat. Zerenth raised his head, and both of them turned to Soren approaching with a sliced side of ham. "Ah, hello again, Adrius," he said, tossing a piece of meat to Zerenth, who ate it in one mighty snap of his jaws. "In my youth, I enjoyed feeding bread to the pigeons. Thank you for giving me a more thrilling version of the experience, Zerenth."

"Thank you for the ham." The dragon was practically cordial as he waited for another slice.

Adrius watched this exchange with a bemused smile. It gave him a few extra minutes to think. Of course Nyah would approve of him being any kind of dragon on the surface—it was better than Zerenth's spirit dying and sending her entire nation into distress.

He whispered to the dragon, "You have a deal." Zerenth's acknowledgement was the gleam in his eyes.

Chapter 24
Adrius

He woke in a patch of flowers to the sun baking his skin. The unfamiliar sensation was the kind of pleasantness that he meant to explain to Vistral when he asked about the burning orb. He wished he could have this kind of wake-up every day, maybe with a hammock and a scantily clad Nyah to sweeten the deal. His eyes closed to view the fantasy behind his lids.

"Good morning!" Soren's voice cut into his drifting. Adrius glanced around to see the angel kneeling on the edge of a Zerenth-sized furrow in the earth a few yards away, his hands patiently adding and kneading in new dirt as he hummed a cheerful tune. The dragon himself was nowhere to be seen.

Adrius greeted him in a mumble as he stood and stretched his back. "Care to join me?" Soren offered.

"I would rather return to my body," he said, wondering if Soren had a say in that kind of decision this time. He still went over and knelt next to the angel.

"Understandable." Soren hummed louder as his hands cupped a seed. Light haloed his fingers as he buried it deep. "Your body will dictate when that will be, and I fear you will return to great danger."

He thought of Vistral again, how...strangely he'd acted moments before Adrius's most recent death. "I agree."

"There's quite the stir in the Council right now. A demon as powerful as Jazrach hasn't been let loose on Earth since the old days," Soren continued. When a new green shoot broke from the ground, he brushed its first leaf in approval.

"Does your Council plan to do something about it?" Adrius paused to watch the plant grow further into a hardy little sprout. He debated asking whether it was Heaven that caused accelerated growth or some magic of Soren's doing but decided it had to be some of both.

"We do, yes." Soren shook his head, his expression threatening a frown. "We have a problem locating the demon. It's somewhere in Faerie, which means a political nightmare. The fae have their own gods and laws, and angels aren't entirely welcome. But..." He took a deep breath, and his cheer returned. "The good news is that I think it will be resolved soon."

"You could always send the angel to my temporary home. Coven Rehnquist's headquarters in New York," he offered. "We have portals."

"I'll remember that," Soren said with a nod.

They worked in silence for a while. "Do you know where Zerenth is?" he asked, needing some distraction from his thoughts as they played out every possibility for what he might encounter when he woke from death.

"Off visiting some other angel, I presume. No harm in it." Soren shrugged as he encouraged another new plant with a pulse of warm light from his palm.

He hadn't known that was possible. But then again, this was only the second time he'd even realized that he went to Heaven upon his deaths. "Do all angels live on their own island in the sky?"

"My dear fellow, no. But you are a living man. You need not know all the secrets of what comes next. What if you told another?" He scuffed the sweat from his brow. "I have a certain status to have a home to myself."

Adrius's brow furrowed. "You're on the Council, aren't you? You said 'we' when referring to them."

Though he feared some thought him slow, he knew he'd hit the mark when Soren stilled and considered him anew. "That is correct. I've upheld my grace long enough to ascend." He picked his words carefully, leaving Adrius with more questions than answers, but his tone implied there wouldn't be much more explanation than that.

Still, he had to try to ask more. Gwendolyn would eat all of this up, when—not if—she woke up. "Your grace?"

"Yes, what I represent." Soren gestured to the expanse of his garden, full and carefully tended. "Life! In all its beautiful forms. Who better to be your guardian angel?" For once, his dark eyes were sober as he turned to Adrius. "You, who walks through the valley of the shadow of death?"

He opened his mouth to continue the verse when an icy flush covered him crown to toes. "Adrius?" Soren's voice seemed far away as he blinked awake.

Alive.

He had the impression of Soren calling his name again, echoing in his head as he took his first breath of fetid air. He'd come back to life so fast that he was still cold and stiff. A deluge of water fell from the sky, filling his gasping mouth with a salty taste. Ironically, he was still on his knees but this time, in the middle of a dead zone. The grass in front of him was brown. He caught the sight of a line of bushes in his periphery, reduced to sticks with their leaves curled husks below.

His nose was assaulted by the stench of rotting meat as he continued getting his bearings. The world seemed tilted on its axis, and that was likely because he was swaying to one side, held from falling by something firm and cool around his wrists. It didn't feel like chains but definitely some sort of restriction, as he couldn't move his arms or ankles. No matter how he twisted and pulled, the bindings held tightly.

Think, he told himself. Whatever had caused him to wake from death early wouldn't wait for him to reorient. There had to be some danger he wasn't seeing.

His gaze focused on something white protruding from the sodden grass. A bone. And a foot away, another one. He recognized the stripped skull of a cow with a sick lurch. Its eye sockets had familiar grooves and nicks that suggested something with sharp teeth had scraped it completely clean.

Fell, screamed his instincts.

More stripped bones suggested he was in the middle of a slaughterhouse. His mind put the pieces together like a horror show's jigsaw before realizing the big picture was before him, waiting patiently. Bones were piled up like a throne, and seated upon it was a creature straight from the darkest imagination.

A whisper drifted into one of his ears. *"Hello again, Adrius."*

"Did you miss me?" And this second came from another direction. Adrius's brow drew as he wondered how it was possible.

The creature before him still whispered in his own voice, trying to blend with his thoughts as if it belonged there. "Jazrach," he gritted out.

It was worse now that it had a physical form, because it wore Elandros's face. Well, half of it. The other half was nearly obliterated from a blackened burn that spanned from its temple to a torn and bloodstained cravat. Its mouth opened like on a hinge, revealing two rows of jagged fangs. Unlike a real Fell, its teeth crammed every available space on its gums to bristle with menace as it took a bloody tear of meat from a dripping bone.

It chewed as it replied, *"Your soul goes to Heaven."*

He was too busy staring at its arms, which looked like they'd been grafted in from a much larger beast. Purple-red skinned like a fresh bruise, they were studded with the occasional gash. Blessedly, the rest of its body appeared unmodified.

Don't cry out. Don't show it any fear, he told himself as he stared at it in defiance.

A few of those gashes opened like wet mouths as it whispered, *"Consider me shocked."*

"So much blood on your hands."

"Fell. Human. A lake of it." It was like every whisper came from a different mouth, converging on him from multiple directions.

Adrius screamed, shutting his eyes tight as if doing so would make the demon go away.

Jazrach laughed at him in a chorus of voices. *"I forgot. Under all that muscle, you're still just a child."*

"Let me go," he said, testing his bindings with a jerk.

"Oh, I think not."

Its voices prowled around him. *"Didn't you want to find me?"*

He quested in his mouth with the tip of his tongue, feeling for the bead to ward of demonic corruption.

"Are you looking for this?"

Reluctantly, he opened his eyes to see Caladorn's artifact glimmering between two black claws. *"A bauble,"* the demon chuckled, crushing it and snuffing out the only hint of light in the circle of decay.

He blew out a sigh. The tiny thing was his one lifeline, and now he was to be lost in the dark. He searched his head instead, trying to feel out the empty space where he used to sense Zerenth. So, the dragon hadn't returned with him. It would be his luck that Zerenth wouldn't be able to—that somehow, Jazrach had cut their connection right after they'd finally forged an alliance.

The demon stripped the bone of its flesh before poking it at random into its throne. *"I have a modicum of pity for you,"* it said.

Its second whisper stroked the back of his neck. *"A man who cannot die."* He whipped his head around, but there was nothing there. Only Jazrach.

It gestured, and out of the shadowed tree line stumbled a bent over form that offered it another uncooked slab of meat. Adrius recognized it as a Fell, a real Fell, with skin marked in patchy blotches. *Vistral?* he thought in shock.

But the shifters were supposed to be immune to corruption. The people here had first merged with animal spirits to overcome their Fell afflictions, or so he understood.

As if reading his mind, Jazrach laughed. *"I can corrupt anything."*

"If it has flesh, corruption lives in its veins. It is its legacy."

Cold sweat dripped down his back, saturating the material of his undershirt. This situation was so much worse than he'd ever expected and word *still* wasn't going to return to Dragonhelm unless he broke free of his bindings and ran. Unless...Swift had escaped. He didn't dare try to count the shadows, fearing he'd see a flash of red fur.

"Nothing to say, Adrius?"

It waited a few seconds before shrugging. *"Very well, then."*

Jazrach left the rest of its meal on its macabre throne and lurched closer to him. It moved in jerky jolts, as if every limb responded at its own pace. "If you wish to wear a man's skin, at least fight me like one," Adrius said, finding his tongue as the demon drew closer. He had a feeling he could defeat it in a heartbeat if it came to armed combat.

That's why he captured you this way, he thought to himself as it simply laughed. Playing it straight wasn't in a demon's rulebook.

"What a magnificent creation you will be."

It reached out like it wanted to stroke him. *"Unable to die. Unable to be stopped."*

It lashed out with darkness, which he felt invading his mouth and nose. He gagged, his mind's eye dragging him back to his earlier nightmare. Nyah in another's arms. This time, he could feel himself believing it happened in a change of conviction dripping through his consciousness. It was slow enough that he recognized what the demon was doing now. Dark tendrils dug deeper in his head, searching for more memories to twist.

The ground rumbled, sending vibrations up Adrius's arms. He barely registered it, his mind's eye consumed with memories.

"You there, stop that noise. I will be undisturbed."

That thought didn't belong to him. The idea of Caladorn and Nyah kissing splintered with the sound of a revving motor.

The world exploded with light. The motorcycle's headlight, aimed straight at Jazrach. Straddling the vehicle was the screaming silhouette of a human woman. It wobbled at her hand, but there wasn't enough time for it to veer off course before it caused Jazrach to jump out of the way.

A *crash* followed, and light shone right across the clearing as the motorcycle spun its front wheel in futility. It illuminated a miracle in motion; the grass brightened, and new growth erupted from the soil in a chaotic mass of nature. This wasn't Soren's tame garden; it was the wrath of the earth.

Adrius felt his bindings loosen. Glancing over his shoulder, he saw that he had four tendrils of shadow connecting wrists and ankles to a stake in the ground. The piece of metal shot free, and he stumbled to his feet. He swung a fist toward Jazrach, who dodged the clumsy strike. Adrius cursed his newly alive reflexes.

Several Fell flooded the area, just to be tied down by thick roots. The woman who'd saved him was on her feet as well, her hands glowing as she made fae gestures to summon magic.

"Oh, you take me for a weakling, hmm?" Jazrach laughed as dark tendrils erupted from its many mouths, ensnaring the woman's wrists and neck and dragging her into the motorcycle's beam of light. More shadows wrapped around Adrius, banding down his arms as if they were made of steel rather than smoke. He struggled and strained, feeling the tension build in his neck until something popped in a surge of agony.

"How delicious. I get two of you." It flashed a gruesome smile.

Adrius's would-be savior turned and screamed at him, "You have to merge!" More shadows plugged her mouth, and she choked on anything else she would've said.

There was still no sense of Zerenth in his head. He didn't want to make her sacrifice one in vain, but it seemed it would be so. "You should've left it alone, Swift," he murmured. Though he didn't recognize her, there was only one person he assumed would try to save him.

Swift met his gaze, her eyes desperate and beseeching as Jazrach's laughter echoed around them. *"So touching. So tragic."*

"Shall you watch as I corrupt your daughter first, Adrius?" It turned to savor his expression.

She made a muffled scream as the shadows flooded her nose. Her legs kicked out as she tried to pull away. "W-what?" Adrius whispered.

Swift's screaming sounded like, "Merge! Merge!"

Despair seized Adrius's chest. How could he merge with a dragon that wasn't there? Swift was quickly going limp as the shadows assaulted her. In moments, it would be too late for her.

"Zerenth!" He screamed it mentally, tilting his head to the sky. He had no illusions that he was shouting to empty air as his senses filled with Jazrach's laughter.

"Zerenth!" he tried again. *"I...need you."* He was ready to beg, to plead, to pray. But a sense of surety filled his chest.

Someone else made a connection with him. All he knew was a feeling of cheer, an impression of a smile. *Soren.*

And then, the fury followed as Zerenth's voice echoed in his head with reverberations of power. *"I claim this man, two souls in one, from this night to the death of the sun."*

"I claim this spirit—" Jazrach turned toward him, those terrible red eyes flaming wide as it seemed to realize what Adrius was doing. Shadows tried to choke his lungs as the spirit within him whispered the right words. Zerenth had taught him the simplified ritual only hours ago in Heaven. "—two souls in... one..."

He couldn't breathe; his last gasp was frozen in his chest. He turned his gaze from the monster before him to Swift, whose limp body suggested the worst.

Strain built and pulled at his dislocated shoulder. Jazrach tightened the shadows around his arms and ribs, trying to crush him. On a sound of pain, Adrius warbled until he mouthed the words on a wisp of sound, "a merge that breaks for no one."

"Remember, I take half," Zerenth rumbled.

Wings erupted from Adrius's back, straining the shadows until they broke. Adrius landed on his feet, jabbing himself with new claws as he grabbed his elbow and pushed his arm back into place. He shifted so rapidly that he had no idea what was him and what was Zerenth, but his whole body was aflame as he bared his teeth with a dragon's roar.

He belched a sulfurous ball of fire, setting Jazrach's borrowed body alight. The demon's laughter turned to a chorus of screams as it burned like a corpse. Swift's body collapsed, and Jazrach transformed into a twisting column of shadow, retreating into the trees.

Zerenth roared obscenities while Adrius turned away, stumbling to one knee next to Swift. He pushed her on her back, ignoring the gnashing of Fell trying to claw and bite their way free of their root prisons.

Adrius pressed shaking fingertips to Swift's neck, breathing a ragged sigh when a weak pulse beat back at him. She was unconscious with her eyes open, glazed in a look of horror, and he couldn't imagine what terrible things Jazrach had shoved into her mind. His...daughter. What nonsense was that?

"The truth used as a weapon. If we are not giving chase, let us be off," Zerenth growled.

He scooped Swift up delicately and carried her from the clearing, feeling the wings on his back as heavy and awkward bulk. He was dragging a tail, too, he realized. "Can we fly?" he asked, coughing hard from a flash of pain in his throat. Right now, he didn't care if the scales he wore were rainbow if they could just get to safety.

"Allow me the honors." Zerenth took control of their shared form and flared those wings, clearing the ground in a heavy leap. They headed for an arc of light on the horizon, a beacon in the night.

Chapter 25
Nyah

Nyah and Gabriel emerged from a portal on the outskirts of the Sanctum. It was the closest place to Emberglen Village that Sorsha could send them to. "I'll take care of this," Gabriel insisted as she knelt down and coaxed a new growth from the ground.

"Sorry, Father. You may be an angel, but he is still my lifemate," she said, a furrow appearing between her brows. She grew a type of fae-bred vine with an unpronounceable name. The shifters had taken to calling it "vanity vine," as it offered a temporary fix for shifting without clothing.

"I'll end up outpacing you." His light-and-flame wings flared as he spoke, giving him a halo behind his head.

Night's Howl stirred as Nyah looped the newly grown vanity vine around her neck. Their fierceness was one being, both woman and wolf in concert. She shifted and trotted past him, turning her muzzle to the sky for a hard howl.

"Outpace this." She took off at a run, hearing echoes return to her from a wolf pack picking up her song. Thundering through the forest, she relied on instinct and enhanced senses for every place to set down her paws. If there was a demon, it was about to be at the end of her claws.

She'd hold it down for her father to kill permanently, as such a dire threat to her kingdom and people had to be handled personally. The underbrush swished from a bright form flying overhead. Nyah pushed harder, refusing to be left behind.

As the tree line gave into wide plains, another form joined Nyah, racing to her side. The other wolf was smaller than her shapeshifted form, but its pelt gleamed, and muscles bunched underneath as it moved nearly as fast. Night's Howl barked a gruff warning from their shared muzzle.

More furry shapes joined the first, all young and fit. *"Upstarts,"* grumbled the wolf within her.

"Let them run with us." Nyah had to laugh. *"We are all one pack. Or so you say."*

Night's Howl didn't dignify the mirror of her wisdom with a response. They led their little pack, sure that the young wolves would tire as they ate up ground that separated them from Adrius and whatever danger lay ahead.

What lost them the other wolves was not fatigue but spotting something foreboding on the horizon. With a flurry of frightened barks, they scattered. Nyah smelled it before she could see it, a scent of decay and sulfur that threatened to turn her stomach. And under it, something more familiar...

She stopped short and watched a winged shape cut across the sky on night-dark wings, carrying with it the smell of her daughter. Fur spiking with aggression, she watched Jazrach fly straight for Gabriel. *"We won't be able to help,"* she grunted.

"That's not Jazrach," Night's Howl said.

"Then who...?" Gabriel was motioning downward, and the unfamiliar flier followed as he swooped into the tall grass.

Following him and landing heavily, the other man lay Celeste down like a porcelain vase that was already cracking. She padded forward and nuzzled her cheek with a soft whine, smelling the halo of decay over her face.

"Why didn't you tell me?" the rumbling voice held a note she recognized.

"Step aside. She is corrupted." A firm hand pushed her head out of the way. Gabriel pressed glowing hands to her cheeks.

Nyah padded a safe distance away, activating the vanity vine around her neck with a tug of a claw. She shifted and felt it wrap around her torso, covering her adequately. "Adrius...you shifted?" she asked, gazing up at him in delight until she realized he wasn't smiling.

Dragon-like eyes burned as he seemed to stare through her. "When were you going to say something?" he demanded.

"I was waiting for the right moment. I didn't realize it would end up this way..." She took a hard swallow, understanding now how he'd felt when she'd uncovered his most touchy secret in the worst way.

"You didn't think I would find out?" Embers drifted from his mouth on a puff of smoke.

Her shoulders drew in. "I figured it would be a happy secret once we were mated again."

"You thought I'd be happy that you'd turned to Caladorn for pleasure and *lied* about it?" he hissed. With a blink, she realized they were talking about two different things.

"What are you going on about?" she asked with a disbelieving laugh. "Caladorn lost his mate and wed duty in her stead. You think he and I...how preposterous." But as his fists clenched, she realized he was serious. He truly believed it, and now he was a full-fledged dragon shifter, his rage strengthened by the presence of another being known for its temper.

A glowing hand shot out and covered Adrius's face. He sputtered in surprise but held still as black fumes escaped from between Gabriel's fingers. "There's not much," the angel assured. "He changed a few of your memories, but you should feel your senses return in a few seconds."

Adrius took a deep breath. So did Nyah, watching this happen with her heart in her throat. Her gaze strayed to Celeste lying in the grass with her arms folded neatly. Smoke was leaking from her nose on each exhale. If altering a few memories had turned Adrius so hostile...what had happened to her daughter?

"I can feel it now. Thank you," Adrius said, turning and beholding Gabriel with a shocked expression. "Lord Gabriel. You are...back?"

"For now, son. Excuse me from a long story." He clapped

Adrius on the shoulder and crouched down next to Celeste, his form radiant as he wrapped her in glowing wings.

Nyah felt Adrius's attention shift to her, and she cautiously met his eye. "I didn't mean it," he said, his massive shoulders drawing in sheepishly. Now that was the Adrius she knew, yet all she could muster was a halfhearted grunt.

"What happened?" she asked.

"Swift saved me. Our daughter?" He seemed to search her face for answers.

"I was waiting for the right moment to tell you." They'd gone full circle, it seemed, but now she saw the understanding in him. "She needs to return to the Sanctum. The spirits will help heal her," she continued to Gabriel.

"Can you do it without me? I have a demon to hunt." His glowing gaze was fixed on the horizon.

"And Fell to cure." Adrius took up an explanation of where to find a group of Fell that Celeste had captured in twisted roots. His chest heaved with exhaustion, while Nyah could feel the hair on the back of her neck stand on end.

Fell. Jazrach had corrupted the incorruptible, just as Lucia warned. "And Fell to cure." Gabriel nodded, "I've purged her of corruption. Now she just needs to rest it off. Will you send in reinforcements to gather up the Fell I cure?"

"The guard is coming," Nyah said. "Caladorn implied it would take a day of hard riding."

"I can make due. Please," he beseeched her with her hands in his, "take these two to safety. I can handle the rest."

"Okay, Father," she said, relenting in the face of her unconscious girl and Adrius looking like a breeze could topple him. Gabriel flew away with haste, leaving Adrius to scoop up Celeste and carry her close to his chest.

"We can be back at the Sanctum quickly if you want to fly there," she offered. "I can run underneath you as a wolf, show you the way."

He shook his head. "I want to walk."

"You...do?" she asked uncertainly. "It will take us hours..."

"As long as Swift is stable. Do you think she is?" He glanced down at her with a frown.

Nyah took her hand and inspected her with her Keys. Nothing seemed amiss or in need of further healing. "She's just sleeping off her trauma."

He nodded. "Then let us walk. We have much to discuss."

So they did, she thought. She led him back the way she'd come, adjusting the vines over her hips where they'd curled in too tightly. "This is long overdue," she agreed.

"Won't you tell me about her? Our...daughter?" He hesitated like it wasn't real. Sadness haloed him along with his fatigue as he gave her the kind of betrayed look that made her want to explain until her face was blue. "The one you didn't tell me about."

It hadn't seemed like reality to her when she'd started having morning sickness only days after being parted from him. She'd thought it was a side-effect of her heartache at first. "She was born eight months after I came here. I named her Celeste, after the stars. At the time...the only nice thing about the Fell Lands."

"Celeste," he repeated quietly. Heartbreak etched over his features, coming to her empathy in a punch of emotion she couldn't help but echo. Her virtue was apparently back just to twist her insides to knots. "I never imagined you could've been pregnant. I wish I was there for her."

"You were in spirit. I told her all about you." She smiled sadly. "How proud you would've been of her when she decided to be a druid rather than a Sorceress." A decision to follow her spirit rather than her training and bonds to those around her, even her mother. "That was the day she decided she was happier as a fox. She rarely shifts back."

"I'm glad she made an exception in my case," he murmured.

"I am as well."

Silence passed between them, punctuated by the rasp of Adrius's breathing. They had time to talk out their problems, yet she found her tongue stuck to the roof of her mouth. His false memory hadn't let up its grip on her quick heartbeat.

He, too, seemed lost in thought. Yet he spoke up first. "Am I unattractive?" he asked.

Of all the things to dwell on.

She'd gotten a good look at him in the light of Gabriel's wings, yet they walked in shadows now. She was used to navigating the forest without light. It just made his expression inscrutable as his scales blended in with the night.

Adrius had sacrificed a good portion of his human side in the merge. His arms were scaled, taloned, and spined up to the elbow, much like Izell's. Scales replaced sideburns and teased at his hairline. But what was striking were the wings and tail, even if the wings weren't quite folded and the tail dragged behind him. With eyes like a dragon and new fangs in his mouth...was he attractive?

"A handsome man doesn't dim when he's paired with a fearsome beast," she said. "In fact, I believe I like the look of fearsome and handsome together."

He breathed a relieved sigh. "You're not just saying that?"

"Why would I? Now we both have our quirks. You'll have to put up with me on my hairy days. Sometimes a lady needs a fine pelt." She spoke more lightly as they both smiled.

"Sometimes a man needs to bury his face in something soft." He laughed as she bounced a playful punch off his shoulder. Then he winced and rotated it. "My regeneration's not what it used to be."

Her fingers flew to her face, because of course he was injured. She made him stop and pushed life energy into him with her Keys. It wasn't as effective as a Gifted healing, but it would keep him going with less pain. Adrius didn't scowl again for the rest of their walk.

She decided it was time to breach another subject while they were still alone. "Do you wish to be mated with me again?" Her breath stilled in her lungs as she thought of everything they'd been through since their reunion.

"Maybe I need to fight another demon if there's any doubt of that," he said with a sigh.

"You didn't need to," she murmured.

"Swift said the same thing. I wondered how she knew you so well." He nearly tripped over a root as his voice faded with fatigue.

Maybe she was being silly, embracing too much doubt. Adrius had always thought good deeds were the way into her heart, and in that way, he hadn't changed. She loved him for who he was.

That was also still true. As she guided him carefully in the last leg toward the Sanctum, she embraced the feeling in her heart. Distance had erased the fire of it, but now it lay kindled in her chest as she beheld her man and the tender way he carried their daughter. Her little family was whole at last.

He would be hers again. They had nothing else to hide.

Chapter 26
Adrius

After leaving Celeste to the care of a team of druids, Adrius insisted on a bath and nearly drowned himself in the druids' hot springs as the water soothed his lingering aches. Nyah fished him out and helped him to a bed of vines much like the one still clinging to her and obscuring all but a hint of skin here and there on her belly.

"Relax," Zerenth sighed when Nyah laid him out and the bed contoured to the shape of his body.

"Why is it moving?" he asked Nyah aloud as he shifted to his side, letting his heavy wings rest atop one another.

She winked as she drew a sheet over them both. "It's a druid thing. You'll get used to it."

Upon waking and realizing the vines were now holding him down with thin creepers, he fell from the side of it with a yell. Nyah peered over the side with a sleepy blink, seeing him holding a fistful of vine strands and poking their sticky tips.

"Is this a druid thing too?" He wiggled them up at her.

"Actually, yes. Smell them." She took a few and held them to her nose with a happy sigh. Cautiously, he did the same, scenting something floral. "That's to help you sleep."

"I would sleep better if the bed wasn't trying to eat me," he said matter-of-factly.

She rolled her eyes and hooked a thumb into the vine still covering her modesty. "How about a distraction, then?"

They were distracted for quite a while. The first time, they fumbled like virgins. She didn't know what to do with his wings, and frankly, neither did he. When the flowery creeper vines pinned them gently to the bed, she called it a sign and took over.

He *really* liked this new dominant, alpha-female attitude she had.

Their mating bond returned in the heat of passion. One moment pleasure, the next an explosion of sensation as she became his once more, sharing feelings and thoughts in the most intimate of ways. The distance didn't matter, not anymore. For the moment, neither did the world, which could've crashed and burnt around him for all he cared.

As they were resting, a semi-familiar voice followed a knock at the door. "Brought you clothes!"

"Thanks, Chandra," Nyah called back.

It turned out "clothes" was a loose sense of the word. He'd never seen anything like it, but Nyah forwent her vine wrap for a dress made entirely of flowers and leaves. The pollen stung his nose, and he sneezed a few times.

"The height of druidic fashion." She did a proud twirl, showing only hints of creamy skin under buds and blossoms from collar to knees. The stems were braided in such a way that they naturally stretched with her motions.

"It's...quite something." His gaze lingered on her curves, even as she presented his newly fashioned clothing for him too. "I'm not wearing that."

"I'll show you how to take this dress off if you at least try it on."

"Deal."

He had his doubts upon seeing the tunic and shorts, but they were made of enough leaves to cover him. Someone had weaved a flower in here or there. "It is...functional." There was a full-length mirror in their room, and he knew he needed something less girlish the moment he could find it. "What if I move too fast? Do I moon the druids?"

"They're held together with magic. They're not going to rip," she said, muffling her giggles behind a hand.

"I need leather!" He grinned as he felt her mirth. "I can't be-*leaf* this situation!" Her laughter included a cringe, her nose crinkling up just like he remembered.

He hadn't told a pun in years. The mental block for that bit of creativity was finally gone.

"Our druids don't believe in killing animals, so this is the best we've got. Why don't I show you around the Sanctum?" she suggested.

"Sure. But...you were going to show me how to take off that dress."

It turned out to be pretty easy.

ADRIUS PUT OFF SEEING THE SANCTUM BECAUSE OF THE leaf clothing if he were honest about it. But eventually, Nyah pulled him out the door to see the heart of Adrun and say hello to a ghost from his past. All druids wore similar natural clothing to them, but Chandra sailed over in a magnificent leafy sari, looking like the perfect model for the fashion.

"It's so good to see you again," she said, pulling him into a fierce hug. "And so...dragon-like. I'm glad someone finally tamed that old beast."

Were Zerenth not currently asleep, Adrius feared his spirit would have something quite biting to say to that.

"I'm just glad he accepted me," he said honestly.

Chandra accompanied them on a walk around her patch of land, explaining its spiritual significance. Adrius treaded more carefully when he learned that the place was festooned with fae spirits. They were in the plants, the puddles, the air, and in the center chamber, burning in the sconces.

"We keep Adrun alive here as its beating heart. The spirits give back to the land, and we continue to thrive," Chandra said by way of finishing the tour. "The fae speak of an even larger, more powerful Sanctum in Faerie that does the same for them."

"Incredible." Adrius could barely wrap his mind around it. It was a completely new way of looking at life and souls.

As they walked into the dining area, a sight caused Adrius to stop in his tracks. It was Taryn, laughing as a druid half his size guided him to the kitchen while he carried a laden box. He turned to Nyah, a question in his gaze. "He got a new start too," she said, gesturing for him to go inside.

Taryn turned to him as he approached, seeming no different, except...the range of emotion on his face was a miracle. They clasped forearms like old friends. "I see you got the leaf treatment as well," Taryn remarked. Someone had at least done him the favor of dark, leafy fronds. "And you are...different."

"So are you," he said, trying not to stare as he felt the warmth of Taryn's natural regard. It was like someone had turned back the hands of time. It had to be Nyah's doing, her kind intervention. "But are you well?"

He smiled as if he had no worries here. "Never better. I just wish there was more to eat than..." He bent and retrieved a root vegetable from the box, still crusted with soil. He'd carried in a mixed harvest of fruits and vegetables in a medley of colors.

"You're kidding."

"No meat, no eggs. Bread's good, though. Don't drink the wine like a druid. They can heal off the sickness afterward for themselves, but not for you," Taryn advised.

They turned to see Chandra popping the cork off a new bottle while Nyah studiously looked away. "It must be good," Adrius said.

"Too good," he agreed. They turned back to each other at the same time. "So, what happened? How did you get wings?"

"Long story. How about we sit down?" he suggested. Adrius shared his trial, and Taryn spoke of training a new power of his own. He cautiously held his hand away from anything flammable as he summoned a hot blue flame to his palm that danced over his fingertips on command.

Taryn extinguished it in his fist with a shrug. "My life is different now. But these people are pleasant, and someday, I may leave in search of adventure. For now, I live like a druid."

Adrius could feel the concern rolling in Nyah's gut as she glanced out the window here and there. The mating bond made him share that feeling, and he gave her knee a squeeze under the table. She had to be worried about her father and people as they continued the hunt for Jazrach.

"And what a nice thing it is to have some muscle around here." Chandra laughed, well and truly tipsy as the spirits flushed her dusky skin.

A girl came up to their table, curtsying with a little pinch of her flower dress. She was not an astral fae, Adrius noted, taking in her striated skin the color of bark and mop of hair that was a deep emerald. Her doe-like eyes glowed with swirls of green and yellow under a coronet of daintily woven daises.

"Pardon the interruption," she said, turning to gaze at him a few moments too long. "Um, Swift is awake. She's asking for you."

Nyah pushed to her feet. "Is she all right?" she gasped.

"Yes, Queen. But...she specifically asked for her father." The fae drew in her shoulders nervously at sharing that detail. Adrius could feel Nyah's heart jolt over their mating bond, but she sat and folded her hands primly.

They shared a look and a nod. His nerves made his palms hot, which was silly. Swift was a friend, and Celeste, a daughter. He gave himself a shake as he followed the young druid.

She stepped aside and gestured for him to go into a secluded room on his own. The scent of herbs and fresh plant life tickled his nose, but it was far better than the stink of Jazrach that'd hovered over her while he'd carried her here. A few fae lights hovered around the room, giving him his first good look at her as a human.

Celeste had rearranged her vine bed until she was sitting up with a pillow behind her. She had Nyah's heart-shaped face and his dark hair flowing freely around her head in an unruly mass that hadn't seen clippers in years. When she saw him, she smiled, and an inkling of her fox's cunning came with it. "Hello...Father," she said. Her shoulders drew in, uncertain, as her gaze dropped to her hands.

He couldn't stand her doubt for a moment longer. Since she

seemed healed, he leaned over her bed and pulled her into a warm hug. She chirped in surprise, just like she had when he'd embraced her before facing Zerenth for the first time.

He pulled back to take a closer look at her. Her eyes gleamed silvery-green in the light, glimmering with emotion. She had the windows to the soul of an accomplished druid with Sorceress magic. "How are you feeling?" he asked quietly, dragging a wicker chair over to sit by her bedside. It creaked in complaint at his weight.

"Fine. Like it never happened," she assured. Her voice was still hoarse from the encounter, but he heard hints of the sweet tone Nyah hit with ease.

He helped her drink from a glass of water at her bedside. "How long have you known?" he asked.

"That your plan was reckless? From the moment you told me," she said lightly.

He rubbed his forehead. "No, I mean, about me being your father."

"Oh! Right away. It was an honor to lead your trial." Her mischievous look was back. "Most entertaining one in ages. It's the talk of all my spirit guide friends."

Mortified heat rose to his face. Not because of the gossip...he expected tale of a man challenging a dragon and winning would be the stuff of whispers and speculation. In that moment, he realized... "You saw everything about me, as my guide." Zerenth had been kind enough to pull *everything* out to lay it bare between the three of them.

If she'd been paying attention, she knew him better than his wife.

"True," she said, tilting her head. "It wasn't a problem then. Is it one now?"

Is it? He hadn't thought she had a personal stake in his life at the time. Just another trial-goer, even if it had ended in a most extraordinary fashion.

"Everyone has moments they regret," she said, reaching over to take his hand. "I wouldn't have been able to guide you if you tried to hide part of yourself. But I must admit, I knew you'd walk away with Zerenth."

"You...did?"

"I said to myself, if you're really Adrius, the man from my mother's stories, it was your destiny to wear dragon scales." She gestured to him. "And I was right. All you needed was one glimpse of him in his usual hunting grounds, and you were on the hook."

Realization sank in a few moments later. "You took me there on purpose."

She hummed agreement. "Guides are neutral. It's not like I could just tell you about Zerenth right off."

"But you made me talk to three spirits beforehand."

"So him taking everything out of you wouldn't be so traumatic. You would've been paralyzed by all your forgotten memories at once." She nodded as if she'd seen it before. "If you were even a tiny bit weaker, Zerenth would've killed you. He almost did anyway. Good thing I know how to heal."

He held his head, if only to prop his jaw closed. "I don't know how I'll ever repay—"

"Well, don't go thanking me yet. We've got to face the music on something first." She released a sad huff. "Jazrach beat us."

"Easily," he said, sighing.

"You need to get stronger so it won't happen again." Her shining gaze flashed to his wings. "I know who can help you."

"Who?"

"You're not going to like it."

His brow creased, and he gave her a more leery look.

"The best shapeshifter you've ever met. Master of many forms. Someone really in tune with his inner beast." He saw where this was going and swallowed his nerves. "My uncle, of course! Prince Sirius, the Dawn."

"Nyah told you about him?" He didn't even know where to *find* Sirius.

"Well, sure." She smiled wider. "But your memories did too."

Chapter 27
Neala

Neala found herself in the Fell Lands—Adrun, whatever it was called now—moments after she and Jaromir put their heads together over what would happen when Gwendolyn woke up. Between Gabriel, Nyah, and a demon, she knew Gwendolyn would rush into this strange world the moment she was able. Despite the dubious chance she would wake with the strength to do anything about the threats her family was facing.

She meant to contact Sorsha right away, knowing the fae was spending most of her time here getting to know the father she never had, but as she emerged from the portal between worlds and grew accustomed to the gloom, she wandered. The land was quiet, dark, and peaceful, like the embrace of her beloved Honfleur forest. It reminded her of a simpler time, with her at the head of a small coven that made her exile feel more like home.

Of course Sorsha liked this place. Honfleur was where she and Keegan had grown up, secluded from those who would take advantage of odd children with stars in their skin. Neala walked with her memories until she found a white-brick road heading for the only glimmer of light on the horizon.

Her time dream walking had given her too much to think about. A whole different life to pine for. A husband, a coven, a family of her own. She knew it was a mistake to crack open her past. What set her apart from Adrius when she wished for another chance with Marcus?

For one thing, you know he's dead, she thought. The only closure their marriage would have was his last living son. Julian was awfully tired of being compared to everyone's memories of her husband.

She sighed at the irony. As much as she harped on her peers for their angst, here she was in a dark world, contemplating what she'd lost. She put it behind her as she realized her legs had taken her to a city of vaulted white stone, a beautiful echo of Nyixa. Shining fae leading elk steeds streamed from the open front gates, moving quickly to a bellowing set of men and women calling for them to fall into formation.

Neala stopped short and watched, wondering if she would see any semi-familiar faces amongst those here. Nyah wasn't the only human-born to be banished to the Fell Lands, yet she only saw a couple mixed in with the fae.

But there was someone familiar weaving around the waiting men and women, testing, prodding, and inspecting. He'd been gaunt and hollow-cheeked when she'd met him, but now, he was just another graceful fae. She wondered if he would even remember her, when his starry gaze fixed upon her.

Caladorn beckoned to one of his lieutenants, who took up the inspection in his stead, and started walking her way.

Neala hadn't placed a glamor over herself, but that helped, because she obviously had a face this fae hadn't forgotten. The scar on her mouth stretched as she tried to smile for him, this stranger whose child she'd raised.

"Lady Neala, we meet again." He saluted with a fist over his heart.

She paused for a split second, torn between a salute back or a regal nod, when he began to walk past her. "I'm afraid I have little time, but I wanted you to have a gift."

The wave of guardsmen parted for Caladorn, and she followed him, eager to have a look inside the city. But a gift? *"There is no need."* She could already tell this was about Sorsha.

"There is every need. Because you took her in, my daughter

never had to grow up knowing the pain and hunger of this nation's early years," he said, slowing to keep one pace ahead of her. His stern face was marked with an earnest intensity. "Allow me to give you a token of appreciation."

She would've argued more but decided to bite her mental tongue. This man probably knew the details she'd originally come here to learn. *"Do you know where Nyah is?"* she asked.

His lips pinched to a thin line. "Last I heard, she was in our druidic Sanctum. Sorsha has visited it, so she can give you a portal there."

"Outstanding." Though she doubted it would be as easy as grabbing Nyah for an easy in-and-out when there were other concerns in motion. *"What of the angel Gabriel and the demon he hunts?"*

"We are mobilizing to offer assistance. Last word we received was that the demon has gone into hiding with an accompaniment of Fell minions." He glanced over in time to see the shock set in at his words. "He's figured out how to corrupt us anew."

"And no word was sent to the Blood Princes?" she demanded.

"No offense meant, Lady Neala, but the Blood Princes are an elusive concept here. We have been at our own devices for the better part of three thousand years," he said. "Do you believe you can be ready to march with us in an hour's time?"

She thought of Gwendolyn and shook her head. *"I have other duties that require immediate attention. However, if I can get a nephilim on her feet, I may be back in time to join you."*

"Ah, is she awake?" Caladorn stopped at a crossroads and flicked a small white coin into a fountain molded in the likeness of a black dragon. He murmured under his breath as the coin landed in the water with a *plop.*

"Almost."

"That must be a comfort for Queen Nyah," he remarked, taking her to an unremarkable home in the shadow of the palace. Inside, she noted a duster moving of its own volition, currently sweeping across his mantle with care for a smattering of knick-knacks. "Be right back."

Feeling like she was intruding, she beheld the simple setup of a fae bachelor, all straight lines except for the items on that mantle above a cold fireplace. She drifted over to inspect them. A tarnished medal lay next to a jeweled locket, its chain draped over the polished leather of a sheathed dagger with a dark handle. Feathers assaulted her face a moment later, and she sneezed as she batted the enchanted duster from her. It returned to insistently tickle her nose, chasing her as she took a few steps back.

She knew Caladorn was back as he laughed at her expense. "My apologies. I've been meaning to get a new one," he said, grabbing it and giving it a sound shake. It floated off to his kitchen, starting to sweep the cabinets.

"*That is quite all right,*" she said, watching it go about its task efficiently. "*It must be convenient to have.*"

"When it's not enchanted by Izell, yes. It's always liked to attack faces." He shook his head as he offered her a lacquered ebony box etched with fae runes.

It opened soundlessly on oiled hinges, revealing a glass bottle embedded in a velvet setting. It looked like a fine perfume, except it was capped by a heavy glass stopper. "*Thank you,*" she said automatically. Something so fragile and frivolous didn't belong in her calloused hands, but it would be rude to hand it back to him.

"I thought long and hard about what you might like and came up with this potion. Queen Nyah and Izell helped, and I won't bore you with the specifics of its arduous brewing." Judging by the wry twist of his lips, it must've been quite the task. "It's missing one ingredient, though. We are unable to acquire it here in Adrun, but if you ever find yourself in Faerie…"

"*What does it do?*" Unlike most Alchemyst-created potions, it wasn't glowing. The liquid within was an inert yellow-orange.

"It's called a second song potion, said to give the imbiber a new voice with perfect pitch."

Her skin prickled as she turned the little glass over in her hand. She placed it back in its box before her fingers could start trembling. "*A…new voice,*" she repeated.

"Queen Nyah shared what she'd tried with returning your voice. It sounded like you needed a more extreme intervention."

He gestured to the box. "I wish it were complete, but it needs a tear from a siren first. We have no sirens here."

"Then I will find one," she murmured, clutching his gift to her chest. *"Thank you."*

She believed it might work. Despite trying every foul-tasting tonic and nearly every medical treatment Jaromir could think of, her voice had remained stubbornly mute. She'd lost it as a babe, and unfortunately, she remembered every detail of the night it'd happened.

But this was something different, and it deserved a chance.

"No, thank *you.*" He clapped her on the shoulder. "Visit me again when things are less busy. I would like to know my daughter's mother."

The wording gave her pause, but she nodded in agreement. *"Will you let Sorsha know I need that portal?"*

They parted ways on a promise, and she followed his instructions toward the guardsman's barracks while he returned to his urgent duties. She cradled the box and its precious contents close, staying more than a safe distance away from the few fae she'd passed.

She'd safely avoided more than a few curious glances when she noticed a fae man stumble from a tavern. The open door spilled upbeat music into the street. With a glance at the sky, she wondered what time it was in this place of eternal night. Did this establishment operate at all hours, or was it a weekend to enjoy with spirits and song?

"Excuse me!"

She glanced far down at a bird waving long tail feathers for her attention. She could've squashed it with one errant step. "Excuse me," it twittered, glancing over its shoulder. "You seem like a strong and capable woman. Would you mind...hiding me?"

How bizarre. But she scooped it up with a free hand and laid a simple illusion over it, making it disappear against the fabric of her shirt.

Three burly fae men burst from the tavern a heartbeat later. One had his hands balled into fists, breathing like a charging bull. His two companions were a shade less angry, their gazes panning the road and all landing on her. "Have you seen a bird?" one asked, mimicking the general shape of the one she held.

She drew her brows together in her best estimation of confusion and shook her head.

"He has to be close," the leader snapped, the three of them brushing past her.

Continuing on her own path, she wondered what'd just happened in bemusement. The bird spoke up despite the illusion over him. "You have magic, huh? This is amazing!"

"I only saved you because you are the first talking chicken I've ever met," she remarked.

"Chicken!" He made a human-sounding gasp of shock. "I'll have you know that I am a *superior* lyrebird, capable of memorizing and repeating any sound I've heard."

"So, you've memorized speech?"

"No, I'm a shifter! You know, part fae, part animal, all fun?" he exclaimed.

She shook her head slowly. Of course he was a shifter, just like Nyah. *"How unfortunate for you, to be paired with a small bird."*

The guardsman's barracks were up ahead, and she could see Sorsha's familiar outline casting spells over fae and elk alike as they passed her. She removed her illusion over the bird and set him on his feet, heading for her destination. Sorsha gave her a quick hug and a portal to the fae's Sanctum with a promise to visit there soon.

"Hey neat, I love this place," said the lyrebird as the portal closed behind them.

Neala turned to him in disbelief. *"Why are you following me?"*

He lifted his wings in an approximation of a shrug. "Sorry. You seem interesting. You wouldn't leave a poor lyrebird out in the forest, would you? So many *bigger* animals out here that could eat me!"

She sighed and picked him up again. She'd hand him off to some druid at the first opportunity.

"What was your name again?"

"Why were you running from those men?" she retorted.

"Oh, you know." He waved a wing. "Some people have no sense of humor. Would you mind going back, actually? I had to leave my lute behind."

She kept walking toward what she assumed was the Sanctum, seeing the outline of a stone fence. *"You seem like trouble, chicken."*

Chapter 28
Nyah

It was later in the evening when Nyah and Adrius braced their daughter and walked her out to get fresh air. Celeste didn't need much help, but there was a glint in her eyes when she'd asked for them *both* to assist her.

Whatever had passed between her and Adrius had put new fire in her mate. "I need to go back to Earth and find my brother," he finally told her after they'd enjoyed the evening air as it breezed through the flowers. There was humidity hanging over the Sanctum, promising a druid-born storm to wash away the salt water of Gabriel's unexpected entrance.

As they went back inside to snag a bite to eat, Nyah stopped short at a familiar figure hunched over a table with Chandra and Taryn. Draining a glass of wine and frowning at its empty insides as if taking personal offense was Neala. The hollows under her eyes were growing more pronounced every time their paths crossed.

She looked up and did a double take. *"What are you wearing? What...happened?"* she asked Adrius, her brows drifting toward her hairline as her gaze flashed to his wings.

"Leaves," he deadpanned. "And I'm half dragon now."

Standing, she came over to tug on his tunic and touch his scaled arm. "I don't see why this is so..." He started to snicker. "Unbe*leaf*able."

Neala's nostrils flared. *"Why? Violet is bad enough."*

She took hold of his wing, manipulating it to open and close and rotating it in its joint. She seemed fascinated.

"Do you mind?" Adrius asked.

Shrugging, she turned to Nyah. *"Gwendolyn needs you. Can you come back?"*

Concern hit her immediately. "Is she awake?"

"Not yet. But you charged off, and she needs to see you when she does wake." Judging by the line of Neala's frown, she didn't approve of Nyah's absence.

"I absolutely agree. Now that Adrius is safe, we can both see her. And prepare to house her here so she can reunite with my father." She relaxed when Neala's expression smoothed and she nodded, mollified with that.

Nyah could feel a cloud of negativity hanging over Neala like a looming shadow. "In the meantime, why don't you enjoy more of our wine and turn in for the night here?" she suggested.

"I think I shall. By the way…I accidentally brought a chicken along with me." She pointed to a dark-feathered bird perched on a different table, chatting casually with a few druids.

Celeste perked up with a laugh. "Oh, it's Cedric!" She parted with her parents to go over too, joining the other ladies.

"He's an entertainer," Nyah explained as a flurry of feminine laughter drifted from that table. Her gaze rested on a lacquered box Neala rested an elbow on, and a smile crossed her face. "With a voice that could make a siren cry."

"Is that so?" Her attention sharpened.

"Theoretically."

"Interesting," she said in a neutral tone.

She cleared her throat awkwardly. "So, we are sisters now? Officially?"

The wave Neala gave was dismissive, but her expression was genuine. *"We've always been sisters."*

Though she acted like it wasn't a big deal, Nyah could feel the thread of happiness in her as she hugged her tight and whispered for her ears alone, "Our family's coming back together at last." Now they all just needed to get along.

Celeste made a portal back to the rift between Adrun and Earth, where they parted ways. Adrius and Nyah went through, while she and Cedric doubled back to Dragonhelm to retrieve the latter's clothes and lute.

"Do you know where he might be?" she asked Adrius when she felt his nerves spike.

"I'll have to find him. Say hello to Gwendolyn for me?" he offered with a hesitant smile. They took the second portal to Coven Rehnquist's mansion and emerged to find it late evening, the sun starting to set. Fatigue tickled her to see the warm rays of fading light, since they'd already been up for a day's worth of time.

She took Adrius's hand in both of hers. "Good luck. I'm sure he'll be happy to see you."

He didn't seem as sure but still leaned down to kiss her. "Maybe he will." He then glanced down at himself, flexing a scaled hand. She talked him through how to shift back into a fully human form, which was sure to annoy his dragon spirit were Zerenth awake to notice.

Nyah went up to her borrowed room to comb out her hair and slip into a soft dress that was flattering for her hips. She looped her hair into an immaculate chignon and balanced her crown atop her head. It wasn't the silver and moonstones Lucia had claimed from her but her own thing with gold and citrines. Hopefully her mother approved when she woke.

As Nyah went back down to the infirmary and Adrius left the mansion, she wondered how long it would take and how much time she could spend sitting there without helping Gabriel and her army handle Jazrach and its Fell. She was a queen. She was meant to stay away while her men got their hands dirty on her behalf, but it still didn't sit right with her to be inactive during the height of danger.

She found the infirmary nearly empty. Jaromir was nowhere to be seen—she hoped he was actually getting rest elsewhere—

and the curtains were drawn around Gwendolyn's bed. After checking with her mother, who smacked her lips in the middle of a deep dream, she drew up a chair to wait.

And wait...

Voices drifted in as the sun set and vampires went about their nights. The first person to come into the infirmary was Izell. She took her human glamor off the moment the door was shut behind her. "I thought I might find you here," Izell said.

"Where have you been?" Nyah wanted it to be a mild question, but with a demon loose in Adrun, it came across more confrontational than she meant.

The fae shrugged, her tail lashing irritably. "Too many fires to put out. Someone has to look for the remaining Fell Keys before midwinter."

Nyah glanced down at her hand, where her emerald and ruby rings glinted together. "It slipped my mind," she admitted.

"You, and everyone else," Izell sighed.

"I understand they cannot be scried, too."

"That's true. I put a spell over them so no one would be able to reunite them easily. Except..." She inspected her sharp nails as she let the sentence dangle.

"Except?" Nyah prompted.

"I made sure I could still scry them, of course. I'm not stupid."

She jumped to her feet and grabbed Izell's shoulders. "You can find them? With magic?" she demanded.

"Didn't I just imply that?" The fae waved her away. "We have a problem."

Of course there was a problem. Nyah growled and started to pace as she waited to hear it. "We have seven Keys. Eight if you count Lucia, though hers is bound to her soul. That leaves five unaccounted for," Izell continued.

"So, our problem is getting Lucia to use hers to help us?"

"No." Izell scoffed at the thought. "Our problem is that my people have reclaimed what they could of the Keys. The five remaining ones are all in Faerie."

Nyah went numb all over. "What?" she asked quietly.

Izell licked her lips, tasting the words before speaking them aloud. "I'm going there. And I need a team to come with me."

"I wish I could go—"

"Not you. You have two Keys already," Izell said briskly. "I wanted you to know first, though. We will be gone for months."

"Hopefully not too long." All Nyah knew on the topic was that they had until midwinter before the veil between worlds weakened enough that demons and Unseelie fae would have free passage to Earth. It would be doomsday for millions of innocent people.

Izell's expression lightened. "We will be gone and back in just enough time. I mean to take a Blood Prince with me to act as a Blade—any suggestions?"

Her thoughts immediately went to the lacquered box and Neala's shadowed eyes. The potion she'd help brew in the mouse's hair of a chance it would pass her sister's lips one day needed the last, impossible-to-obtain ingredient. "Neala. You have to get her a siren's tear. She'd be a perfect Blade. She was one of the best at swordplay in her time, and her bloodline specializes in illusions."

"Then it's decided. She'll come with me." She bared her teeth in a confident grin.

"How, exactly, do you intend to get to Faerie? It's not like the miracle that got us to Earth," Nyah pointed out.

Izell exuded confidence as she got to her feet. "There's always a way. Trust a Seelie to know." She left at a rapid clip, calling out to Armando as she entered the hall.

Sitting back, Nyah pinched the bridge of her nose. She was just grateful Izell was on their side and thinking ahead while the rest of them didn't see the forest for the trees.

Lost in thought, it wasn't her that noticed movement behind the curtain first. Night's Howl flushed a wolf's hearing into her ears so she picked up the subtle rasping of sheets. Nyah's heart leapt to her throat as the bed creaked.

Gwendolyn grumbled as she swung her weight around. "Could've at least placed my cane—"

"Mother!" Nyah exclaimed. There was no playing coy here.

The curtain drew aside sharply as her mother peered out with wide-eyed shock. Her body had accepted some of Nyah's life magic after all, leaving her posture ramrod straight and erasing most of the wrinkles lining her face. She still resembled an older woman, but between the magic and her nephilim glow, she could've been a spry sixty.

They embraced, and Gwendolyn sobbed, holding her tight. "My baby. My little girl."

"I'm back, Mother. I'm here now," she murmured, feeling her eyes sting. She was so grateful to Neala for making sure she didn't miss this moment.

"So, this is Heaven? It looks so...realistic." The other woman shot a glance around the infirmary with a puzzled hum.

Nyah had to laugh. They had a lot of catching up to do. "It's not! You're alive—and so am I."

Chapter 29
Adrius

He found Sirius. That was probably the easy part.

Seated at a bar with his back to Adrius, his brother was recognizable from the crowd due to his size and that of his companion. Korin had taken pity on Adrius and given him directions to this place after a mental inquiry.

"He misses you," was how he'd ended their conversation.

Queasy with nerves, he struggled through the undulating dance floor. *Stop it,* he told himself. *You've fought both a demon and a dragon since you last saw him.* He should be able to have a conversation with his brother and not lump it in the same category.

"Is this seat taken?" He slid in on Sirius's free side.

The other man had lain a glamor over his eyes so that they glinted brown rather than red as they flashed his way. His grip tightened on a nearly empty glass. They spoke up at the same time.

"You cut your beard."

Sirius was clean-shaven. All the better to see him frown.

"I was tired of being called a viking," Sirius muttered.

"And I wanted a new start." His heart was in his throat as his brother swirled the dregs of his drink.

"How is that going for you?" he asked at last.

He held back the urge to tell him everything in one long, incoherent explanation. Instead, he picked out the most important bits to share first. "Nyah and I are mated once more."

Korin lifted his drink. "Cheers to that," he said, downing it with a grin.

Sirius lifted a brow instead. "So, you remembered her?"

"Down to every last freckle. Though lack of sun has taken most of those away," he said.

A chuff passed his brother's lips. He inspected Adrius over the rim of his drink as he knocked back the last swallow. "What do you want, then?" he asked in a low voice. "You didn't track me down just to share that."

Adrius swallowed hard under his stare. "No. I miss you. And I need your help."

"With what?" Sirius sighed.

"I have acquired an inner beast of my own." In the shadows between their bodies, he allowed dragon scales to creep up his arm. Sirius's eyes widened in shock, and he made a quick dismissing gesture to keep it hidden. "And I can think of no one better to help me master it."

Sirius raised his hand for a refill as he remarked, "You seem to have it under control if you can demi-shift." A technique for him, as a shapeshifting vampire, that showed true mastery of his abilities.

But for Adrius, it wasn't so simple. "I need combat training," he said, seeing the shift in interest immediately.

It was permission to beat on him after all. And his little brother never turned that down.

"I WOULD ASK WHAT YOU DID TO DESERVE THIS, BUT I *already know,*" snarked Zerenth as Adrius was knocked on his ass yet again. The point of a sword touched the underside of his chin.

Sirius turned the blade so the flat of it tapped Adrius's wings. "These are making you clumsy. Let your dragon control them while you focus on me." While initially impressed with Adrius's dragon side, Sirius had found their joint weaknesses without much effort.

The druids had cleared out a circle of spirits, letting the two of them tromp all over their delicate flowers in the Sanctum. This was in exchange for letting the whole druidic order sit in the grass a safe distance away and watch their extended duel. He wondered when they'd get bored and get back to work. So far, not yet.

In the front of the group were Nyah, Celeste, Neala, and Taryn, with Chandra notably absent because she was showing Gwendolyn the Sanctum and how its magic worked.

"I'm trying," Adrius grumbled, getting back to his feet.

Sirius placed an arm behind his back, the other thrusting his sword forward. "Then try to scratch me this time."

They'd stripped to their shorts, both bearing bloody lines where they'd hurt each other. Sirius's regeneration had him fully mended, while Adrius had to be more careful. He let scales cover his exposed skin—one of the only things he and Zerenth could agree on. They were like armor, which he needed because his brother was not holding back.

His sword screeched in complaint as their blades collided. The force was many times what the original forger of the weapons had expected them to take.

"Talk to your beast. What am I going to do next?" Sirius prompted. "Let him read my body language."

"*Left,*" Zerenth sighed, bored. Adrius parried the next strike with a split second to spare.

"Good. Now do it again without him saying anything," he said.

Adrius blinked in surprise and earned a scrape against his scales. He knew what Sirius was going to say...the same thing he'd been repeating.

"Shifters are hardly any different from shapeshifting vampires." Sirius reset to the same starting pose. "You're one person with extra instincts. Start listening to them."

"*Yes, start listening to me.*" If his ears weren't deceiving him, Zerenth was amused by this advice.

If anything, the dragon talked too much. He'd heard most shifters barely heard from their spirits once merged. There was a sense of *knowing* and an integration of instincts, so what Sirius tried to teach him was second nature to them. Lucky him to have such a powerful, willful spirit.

They went another round, to the same results. "It's not that hard," Sirius sighed.

"As entertaining as this has been, if I may offer some advice?"

"Please do." Adrius was ready to try anything to feel like he wasn't a boy with a practice sword again.

"The only way we flew earlier was when you gave me control of our body. It's an our now. So, let me have a bit of control." When he hesitated, the dragon breathed an irritated hiss. *"I'm not going to do anything except help you fight."*

Well, he'd just thought he was ready to try anything. He squared off with Sirius again and let the dragon do what he wanted. This time, they didn't communicate, but he found himself not falling for a feint. Sirius could move like a viper if he wanted to, his movements transitioning to boneless fluidity as he realized that Adrius had caught on to this lesson.

The druids cooed over their show as sparks flew between the brothers. Adrius was finally matching Sirius like he used to, going for brute force verses lithe showmanship. He'd never believed in fancy footwork when he was usually the strongest man on the field. Sirius danced around him, but he was finally felled with one well-placed strike.

Nyah cheered loudest as the watching crowd showed appreciation. "See? Not so hard," Sirius said, accepting his hand up and brushing himself off.

"I do now, thank you." That being said, they drilled until Adrius felt fatigue really start to creep up on him. The druids left one at a time until, at some point, he looked up to see Gwendolyn standing with Chandra and Nyah. The women whispered together urgently, and he met the nephilim's fiery gaze. He nearly took a step back, having forgotten how intensely the light burned within her to reflect through her face at full power.

And she was only *half* angel, so who knew what level of holy fire Gabriel could call on now? Jazrach really stood little chance, but Adrius pushed himself hard for the small chance he'd face the demon again. He was sure things would be different if they had a rematch.

Nyah came over after a few minutes and stepped between them. "Time to have dinner," she said. "You'll have another chance to cut each other to ribbons tomorrow."

"Looking forward to it," Sirius muttered. And just like that, they had a hard time looking at each other.

"We're about to have visitors anyway," Chandra said, stopping short and turning toward one of the gates that separated the Sanctum from the forest. Adrius turned too, smiling at first when he saw Sorsha pass through the magical doorway with her occultarus lighting her path like a personal sun. Next came Ash, who, unlike Sorsha, was still wearing her human glamor. Neither fae woman looked victorious.

Caladorn and Gabriel followed. The general was disheveled, his cloak torn and starry gaze dull. Gabriel's armor bore a set of claw marks down the breastplate. "You found him," Adrius said as they approached.

"No," Sorsha said, rubbing her temples. "All we've found are Fell. Jazrach's hunkering down somewhere and letting his minions do the rest."

In teams, soldiers and guardsmen started streaming through the gates, carrying the wounded and unconscious as the druids ushered them to safety. Adrius was heartened briefly to see Vistral again on a stretcher, looking like a fae instead of a Fell. There were severe bite marks on many.

"The Fell haven't passed their infections back to us," Caladorn said as he watched the grim parade. "But we've let this fester for too long. We need a better plan."

Chapter 30
Nyah

Despite the circumstances, Nyah was glad to have a table full of friends and family. She hadn't been surrounded by a more capable group in three thousand years. Some faces, she'd never expected to see again, such as Gabriel at the head of the table and Gwendolyn farther down, studiously avoiding eye contact with him.

The chefs had pulled together a hearty meal of soup and bread for the unexpected influx of visitors, many of whom would have to camp outside for the night amongst the flowers and spirits. This impromptu council was crammed in the inner room with a table and chairs moved in for the purpose of privacy. It was just them and many of the silent spirits that helped keep Adrun alive.

Gabriel and Caladorn took turns narrating the warzone they'd marched into and confirmed Nyah's worst fears. Despite having a tough old Blade in charge of her army, it was more of an "army" that had spent the years growing softer with no major conflicts on the horizon. They'd forgotten the Fell's ferocity and had no way to change the monsters back except with Gabriel's light.

They'd been overrun. And she'd just sat in the grass all day while it happened outside of the Sanctum's peace.

"It's not your fault." Adrius gave her hand a squeeze under the table as he picked up on her mood.

"Isn't it, though? I could've brewed purification potions..." She pinched her lips together. "I should've been there."

Caladorn glanced her way and shook his head. "One does not field their queen out front. However, now that we know what we're up against..."

"You will drown in potions to help out," she promised.

Adrius slammed his fist on the table. "The Fell are just the symptom of the disease. Where is Jazrach?" he demanded.

"Only one person at this table has seen him," Gabriel said, gazing pointedly at him. The attention naturally shifted to Adrius as fae and Blood Princes alike murmured in speculation. "What, exactly, did you see?"

Adrius recited everything he remembered upon waking from death just to find himself before Jazrach and at its mercy. Questions came from everyone, but mostly Gabriel and Gwendolyn. Both of them dissected even the smallest mannerisms. When Adrius mentioned the demon's jerky steps, they exchanged a glance.

"His body is damaged," Gwendolyn said, stroking the column of her throat.

"That was very helpful, Adrius. Thank you." Sitting back, Gabriel steepled his fingers and thought. The room was quiet, waiting for him to chew on the information.

Nyah leaned in as his expression grew troubled. "I believe I know what happened," he said at last. "He and Gwendolyn damaged each other, actually. He possessed Elandros's body and immediately sustained a blast of light from her. Without another demon to purge him with darkness, he's weak."

"So, he won't attack us directly," Caladorn grumbled.

Neala gave her head a shake. *"He never has. He came for us as whispers when he didn't have a body. Under his guidance, Lucia established the Fell Mad to shield him from us. It's the same thing again. He's corrupted innocents into minions for us to fight."*

"That's just what corruption demons do." Gabriel's grim mood was contagious, leaving Nyah to fret with the ends of her hair. "However, Adrius said he was eating raw meat. So, he's building up to something."

"What is the significance of that?" Nyah asked.

"Demons have to first consume to have any power for their magic. Their main sustenance is souls, but blood and meat are a substitute," he explained. "It also gains power being around what it represents—corruption. We cleared out its encampment and burned the bones it's been sucking on, but..."

"There were a lot of bones," Caladorn finished for him, lips twisted in disgust.

"With enough power, it could purge itself of Gwendolyn's light or transform its borrowed body into a full demon's form, but not both with us on its trail. Not without a sudden and significant feast of souls." His gaze drifted to the pool of water where most of the fae spirits rested, clusters of light dancing and sending off rainbow shards.

Nyah felt a thought skitter across his emotions like a flash of inspiration and discomfort. *If Jazrach wants souls, here they are,* she thought, shifting in her seat with every hair on her body standing up straight.

"There are wards, Father. The druids are our most powerful spell casters, and our only Sorceress counts herself amongst those ranks," she said. "There's no way Jazrach can come in here, to our most sacred shrine."

"Actually..." Chandra ducked her head as she moved to contradict Nyah's assurance. "There's one flaw to our defenses. Jazrach could come here...if a druid invited him in."

Adrius muttered a colorful litany of curses under his breath as murmurs broke out amongst the group once more.

"Are you missing any druids?" Nyah asked, clasping her hands to keep them from shaking.

Please say no. But the druids didn't sit on their laurels in the Sanctum. They patrolled, guided trials, and fostered new growth while charting patterns of land in need of rainfall.

"At least two," Chandra admitted.

Standing sharply, Caladorn saluted with a fist over his heart. "I will ready the army to guard us overnight. Stars be with you."

"And you," Nyah answered, nodding to him in approval. "The rest of us need to rest. If the demon is anywhere as clever as he seems, he'll wait for us to exhaust ourselves first in anxiety."

"He'll have my sword through his heart before that happens," Gabriel assured.

She met his gaze and looked him over more closely. He'd been going for days, she realized, seeing the fatigue hiding just under his glowing façade. "But first, you need to rest too," she insisted. And she had a vat of potions to make.

POTION MAKING WAS AN INTERESTING AFFAIR WITH HER mother by her side. Three thousand years after they'd brewed their last potion together, now it was Nyah guiding Gwendolyn's selection of ingredients and mixing techniques. They'd relocated to the dining hall, sitting across from Sorsha and Ash, making more exotic fae tonics while druids and medics tended to the wounded lining the room where there was space.

"And what does this one do?" Gwendolyn murmured as she swished a purplish concoction in concentric circles as instructed.

"Tornado in a bottle. The harder you spin it, the longer it lasts."

Gwendolyn flicked it more, getting her wrist into the motion.

Though they had no sun to inform them, Nyah could sense they were working toward the twilight hours. Night's Howl was ready to howl at the moon. Despite their predicament, the wolf seemed to be the source of Nyah's contentment. Finally, she spoke up about it. *"Our pack is here."*

Their pack. Nyah hummed in agreement, because she felt it too. Their family, working together at last toward a common purpose. Just one thing was bothering her in that moment.

"Why haven't you spoken with Father?" she asked, watching Gwendolyn's glowing fingertips still.

So, it wasn't her imagination. She *was* avoiding Gabriel. "You don't understand. We are not worthy of an angel's presence, no matter who he is," Gwendolyn murmured. "Me more than anyone. I've made some terrible decisions in my time."

If her father wasn't currently sleeping outside amongst a section of the army, she'd drag him in here personally to refute that statement.

"If you were unworthy, you wouldn't burn anew with a nephilim's light." She took up her hand with a little smile. "There was an opportunity to send one angel to us. Someone had to decide Father was the angel for the job. What if the opportunity was granted because you are still here?"

The light within her wasn't the only reason Gwendolyn's eyes shimmered.

Chapter 31
Adrius

He was only able to sleep when Nyah laid out with him, sharing a good night kiss and a little rub of their noses. When he finally closed his eyes, he went under the dark tide of rest quickly, ebbing into scattered dreams that had his heart pounding as he lived out his anxieties behind the curtain of certainty that they hadn't happened...yet.

In one such wandering, his mind had him waking up to a familiar sound. His name. Echoing out from the corridors of the Sanctum, through the open door to his room. He was eerily alone, sitting up without Nyah by his side or anyone crammed into the corridor. Someone was screaming his name outside.

"Elandros?" he murmured, wandering down the hall like a sleepwalker. Dark mist swirled at his feet, leaking in from the windows and skylights.

Outside, the meadow and its abundant flowers were empty of the army camping amongst it. Instead, there was a single figure, his form glowing with the same ghostly light he'd seen with the animal spirits during his trial. Elandros beckoned him closer. "I was hoping you would be here," he said.

He approached the ghost with a head full of a dream's calming fog. He didn't even question somehow seeing him here, alone. "You died before I could thank you. Taryn is healed because of your actions."

Elandros smiled sadly. "I'm glad to hear it. Maybe...you can help me too?"

"I'm not sure how much help I could be to a dead man," he remarked.

"He took my body, and now he's eating my soul, one nibble at a time. It hurts...it hurts so much!" Elandros clasped his hands in supplication as he screamed. "Adrius! Help! Don't let him take everything from me!"

Boldly, he approached and laid a calming hand on his shoulder. Some part of him knew it was a dream and that his worst fears were playing out in the ghost's pleas. It made sense that the demon would hold on to the soul within the vessel.

Elandros morphed at his touch, becoming solid. Alarm rippled through him as he felt Zerenth wake as well. *"You're not dreaming!"* the dragon exclaimed a moment before Jazrach's grotesque form took the place of Elandros's ghost.

There was something different about it, though. It'd donned Adrius's dark armor and now wielded his lost sword against him. As the sound of fighting and screams echoed into being around him, Adrius realized he'd sleepwalked from bed with little more than his fists and a light undershirt and shorts.

As he dodged a thrust of the demon's weapon, he and Zerenth agreed. They would kill this thing with their bare hands if they had to.

He swiped with his claws, scoring against the breastplate and earning a grunt of pain despite that. "Foul creature," he muttered. His throat heated as he prepared a gout of flame, remembering how it burned during their last encounter.

"I do not suffer a monster to live," it hissed, striking at him at the maximum range the sword would allow.

"Monster?" he sputtered. "You're one to talk."

"Quit bantering. We can't breathe fire if you're busy talking," Zerenth growled.

They barely dodged the thrusting sword as Jazrach wielded it against them in a furious flurry. *"The only monster I see is right in front of me. How many innocents have you slaughtered?"*

This time, he didn't reply, not letting it needle him as the heat mounted in his throat. *"That's right, I thought so. Murderer. I'll be glad to send you back to where you came from,"* it taunted.

Adrius took a deep breath and unleashed a white-hot arc of flames. The demon barely jerked out of the way in time, beating on its shoulder and side with a hiss of pain.

"You cannot defeat me that easily."

It left the sword on the ground and split the air with a fast punch. Its knuckles grazed the scales Adrius swiftly put in place to absorb most of the impact. He swiped back, catching its burned cheek and opening a flap of skin that exposed bone.

Jazrach roared and jumped at him, taking him to the ground, where they grappled, evenly matched. Claws punched into his skin, threatening to tear apart the fibers of his hands, yet Adrius persisted. He had the wings, so he had the advantage in balance as he flipped the demon onto its back and charged a new burst of flame sure to douse his target.

He'd forgotten about Gabriel in this melee. But the thought hit him just as Jazrach broke from his hold and punched him in the face jaw, rattling teeth. *"Nasty beast,"* it spat.

"Am I getting a rise from you at last?" he asked with a humorless chuckle. Jazrach had never spoken above a whisper, but now it seemed downright furious. Maybe it was realizing it had threatened him one too many times. He was ready to destroy it before it could despoil the heart of his mate's beautiful home.

This time, he didn't see the strike coming before the force of it had him lying flat. It felt like he'd been hit with every ounce of the demon's might, and his vision swam on impact with the ground. Jazrach straddled him as its oversized fists pummeled his face and chest.

"Is this enough of a rise for you?" it screamed, every word punctuated with a punch. *"This is for all the suffering you've caused! This. Is. For. Fucking. With. My. Brother!"*

Adrius lifted his arms defensively as the words sank in along with the bruises. Because suddenly, the demon's rage made sense to him, the words setting off a reaction in his brain and washing away the last of Jazrach's magic. Pummeling him to death wasn't that monster, but instead Sirius, who'd called on a demi-form to pump his arms with extra muscle as he bore down on Adrius with feverish intent.

"Sirius, stop!" he yelled. "It's me. It's Adrius!"

He watched as reason set in and his brother sat up, horror taking over his expression. "W-what?"

Adrius felt his eyes start to swell closed as his regeneration worked to mend internal damage first. "Thank you. For, um, dedicating that to me," he murmured awkwardly.

"Save it. Get up." Strong arms pulled him to his feet, and he got his bearings as the world stopped spinning and coalesced from double vision into one single, horrific one. He had a moment to exchange a glance with Sirius before they launched into motion, piling into a melee of soldiers attacking one another.

"It's not real!" Sirius cried, shaking the first fae he grabbed until she looked at him and down at herself with a gasp.

While he had been lucky enough to survive the duel with his brother, Adrius grimly realized many in their number weren't so fortunate. He looked for Gabriel, sure if there was any sanity to be found, it would surround the angel in their midst.

When he spotted Gabriel's blazing form, it was when he unleashed a wave of light over the fighters. Dark mist evaporated from the halo of his presence. Shouts of rage dwindled to silence as everyone was forced to take a look around. A woman's wail came next, calling a name. There was a scramble as their situation set in.

Adrius and Gabriel met each other halfway. "The demon prepared all its magic for something like this," Gabriel said, his fists clenched as his wings burned white-hot. "We have to find it."

As he turned away, before he could start counting their losses, a spike of fear coursed along his mating bond. He tore across the meadow, screaming, "Nyah!"

Chapter 32
Nyah

SHE WOKE TO SHOUTING AND THE BED STILL WARM WHERE Adrius had rested. How had he gotten past her without waking her?

Sitting up fast enough for whiplash, she grabbed a fistful of potions by her bedside and peered out into the hallway. Night's Howl jumped to high alert in her mind, guiding her gaze downward to where there was evidence of a struggle and then a trail in the dust. A bleeding Chandra was dragging herself toward the inner sanctum. She lifted her gaze to Nyah, pushing her away when she tried to heal her. "The spirits. The demon," she said weakly. "Go. Now."

She left a potion by her friend's side as her expression drew grimly and braced herself for what she might face beyond the stone doors that guarded the most sacred of sacred spaces. One was ajar, showing the outline of Jazrach as it knelt before the seething pool of fae spirits. It swiped its hand into the water and stuffed a sip of souls into its mouth as she broke her way inside.

Shadowy mist leaked from the gashes on its arms, eddying around her feet. It didn't bother turning around as a host of voices whispered in her ears. *"Queen Nyah."*

The next whisper caressed her from behind. *"I've heard so much about you."*

She didn't hesitate to bolt down one of her potions. "Step

away from the water," she said, her voice transitioning to a growl as fur erupted from her skin all over. The potion helped her quickly shift into a perfect form somewhere between a wolf and a woman. It would give her minutes in a state of heightened abilities, both physical and magical, past what she could accomplish shifting without it.

As she changed, so did it. It turned to grin at her as everything human in it twisted with a series of impossible contortions. Elandros's burned face turned into a slit-nostriled visage absent of any hair. Bat-like wings burst from its back, erupting with multiple mouths. It stretched the limits of Adrius's old armor as it hulked up to eight feet high, resting on its fists as its legs gained hooves and a double joint.

"I chose to show you the truth." Still, its main mouth didn't move as it whispered to her.

"Behold my true form."

She launched herself at it, fangs snapping millimeters from its neck as it pulled to the side just in time. Sailing over the pool of souls, she twisted around as she landed.

Nyah took another jump toward it, interrupting a second attempt to swallow more souls as it staggered from the impact. As soon as her feet hit the ground, she grabbed it by the arm and flung it out of the inner room, snapping her jaws in rage. It would take even one more spirit from this place over her dead body.

"That can be arranged."

Black claws swiped down her front as it recovered within a blink. Her pelt split with a rip of pain.

"The next soul I want is yours anyway."

Its second whisper sounded furious as it snarled. *"Shift into a dog, die like a mongrel."*

She bit its arm as it came in for another strike, just to spit out a mouthful of putrid blood. Its stink wormed its way into her senses, and she gagged.

The demon's massive hand closed around her throat, lifting her to kick uselessly at the air. Its blood clogged the rest of her airways as its purplish face swam in her vision with a smile of crooked fish teeth.

"Look at you, the gilded queen of a great nation." It spoke at last from its own vocal cords as a slimy tongue snaked out to lap at her cheek. "I will savor your soul, but your body deserves to be strung up like a trophy. How do you think Adrius will react when he sees you hanging?" It tilted its head thoughtfully as she struggled harder, kicking ineffectively at its iron-hard body.

She couldn't die here, not like this. Not when she'd finally gotten her heart's desire—her family back. Mocking laughter trickled into the fog of her consciousness as it seeped away with the last of her breath.

"Your family," it practically giggled. "I'll string up the fox next to your corpse. Your sister will hang too, stubborn wench."

It filled her dying mind with each image. Her beautiful family gone, with the last fractured piece remaining in Adrius, whom it intended to spare.

"The perfect minion. Unstoppable."

All it needed was her death to set it in motion.

Helpless anger built in her chest, looking for an outlet as her struggles reduced to weak twitches. How dare it try to violate her dreams in such a way! Even as numbness drifted up her limbs, she seethed. She regretted. Years and years of allowing her empathy to fade, keeping to herself rather than embracing those around her. It wouldn't kill *just* her and her family, but everyone here, down to the last druid. It would slurp up all the souls it could and come for the rest once it razed Adrun to the ground.

Just because Nyah had died like the snuffing of a candle.

No!

"It cannot have our pack," Night's Howl agreed. The wolf spirit seemed to stoke that kernel of anger in her until it roared up into a bonfire. Behind her eyelids, the darkness flared with an explosion of light. Jazrach dropped her with a pained growl.

She dropped to her hands and knees, coughing and opening her eyes to the sight of her silhouette glowing and Jazrach backing away with its mouths gaping. Burns marred the front of its body.

"It cannot be!" Its whisper was more a cry.

It hissed from its mouth, "Another nephilim!"

Nyah didn't stop to marvel at the miracle of her own self. She loosed a strangled howl and gave chase as the demon turned to fly out of the Sanctum. "No one threatens my family!" she yelled after it, throwing a ball of light at its retreating form and shaking her fist. "Do you hear me? No one!"

Her chest was seized by a wracking cough as her lungs spasmed in complaint.

"Nyah!" It was Adrius, rushing to her side and pulling her from her doubled-over position. He was bruised on every exposed patch of skin, but his full concern was on her as her fur retracted back to skin. The potion wore off just in time for her to collapse into him.

"It's gone," she murmured into his chest.

"That light...was that you?" he asked, eyeing her still-glowing skin with undisguised awe. She lifted a hand, allowing herself to admire for a moment.

"I found my grace at last." And it'd been hanging just out of her reach all these years. Her *family*. Her strong yearning for those she loved was why Night's Howl had chosen her in the first place.

She didn't allow herself to rest long, as she heard the sounds of mourning around her. "Chandra," she gasped, turning to rush back to her side. Spirits clustered over Chandra's wound, which was half-sealed as Nyah's potion did its work. The spirits were keeping it stable from there.

"Thank you," she murmured to them as she called on her Keys to pulse life magic through her fingertips. What came from her instead was a burst of light, sealing the rip in the druid's side.

Spirits clustered over her in Chandra's stead, tugging on her clothes and ghosting over her fingers. She stood, wobbling past Adrius as a mass of souls clung to every available space on her. Though she wasn't a druid, she knew they were tugging her along for a purpose.

The meadow was a battlefield, and the living clustered over the dead to mourn. Tearstained eyes turned toward her glow as she cast light over the broken meadow and countless fae who'd died so senselessly fighting each other.

Nyah took a knee next to a druid's motionless body. The fae

had died from a stab wound to the chest, and above her body floated a single spirit. "What do you want?" she whispered to the spirits on her clothing as they tugged downward. "Do want me to help her?"

The tugging stopped.

Healing a corpse was technically impossible. She'd seen the diagrams and knew the science behind the magic. Once a body was dead, there was no way to speed up the natural mending response to achieve healing. But this was the Sanctum, where the power of thousands of deceased fae communed with the living. If a miracle could happen, it would be here.

Nyah pressed her hands to the druid's chest, breathing out as she called on her magic and tried to heal her. As her palms rested there, she felt a heartbeat stutter to life. The druid breathed anew with a gasp, her eyes flying open as her spirit returned to her body.

"T-thank you," she said, giving Nyah a grateful look as she took her queen's hands with her cool, quivering ones.

"If you can help, let's do the same for others," Nyah replied, glancing up from her to the few fae who'd witnessed what she'd done. "Spread the word! Heal those you can!"

The field became a flurry of motion. Druids and medics took control, and Nyah stumbled her way from body to body with Adrius's support, healing those she could and closing the eyes of those too far gone to save.

The Sanctum's spirits left her to return to their haven when she was done. As they disappeared, so faded her light, and she fell...straight into Adrius's arms as he caught her.

A soldier lifted his fist. "Nyah! Nyah!"

Soon they were all chanting her name, man and fae, druids and shifters. Adrius held her upright against him, and she lifted her arms to them, her people.

"*Our pack*," Night's Howl said approvingly.

In a ripple, her people knelt, her family amongst them. Sirius nodded to her, close to Gabriel, whose face could've split with his proud smile. They seemed expectant, and she gave it her best attempt despite the exhaustion threatening to take her at any moment. "We survived. Let us tend to our wounded. But first, we must send our fallen to the next life."

A small bird stepped hesitantly out of the group. Cedric the lyrebird trembled and glanced around, obviously traumatized. The frivolous little man must've come back expecting the usual, peaceful Sanctum. "I-I could perform a song?" he offered.

Nyah flashed a smile and beckoned him over. Adrius was the one to bend down and carry him to Nyah's lips as she whispered, "Did you bring your enchanted instrument?"

"Yes, of course. It was almost pawned, but I got it in time."

"I could use a song to ease the sights of this night along after the ritual," she confided, knowing he could perform some magic on that lute of his. She was one of many who needed it.

The bird bobbed as he stammered out promises for a great performance, just as soon as he caught his breath. He raced back into the Sanctum.

"Let's find a place to sit before I fall over," she whispered to Adrius before kissing him shamelessly in front of her people.

Chapter 33
Neala

THE BATTLEGROUND WAS SILENT AS THE DEAD WERE SET OUT in rows. The fae solemnly linked arms, catching Neala in the chain, until they'd formed a circle around their fallen.

Chanting as one, the fae performed a ritual she watched with the fascination of an outsider. She understood as the bodies faded away, becoming orbs of light like the spirits guiding Nyah earlier. All they left behind was their earthly possessions, which the exhausted army left where they rested.

Neala lingered outside as wine was poured liberally. She was on her second glass, toasting Sirius with the first and Taryn with the next. A druid came by to cure the burns he'd inflicted while hallucinating that she was Jazrach. No hard feelings, because she'd thought the same about him. *"It seems that it can change perceptions as well as memories,"* she remarked as they waited.

She wanted to hear the voice that could make sirens cry, according to Nyah. She also knew she wouldn't be able to sleep after the incredible adrenaline rush of fighting what she'd thought was a demon, as well as the sight of the bloodstained meadow that followed. Even with all evidence of it erased, it was still a memory that would stay with her forever.

"It is gone but not defeated," Taryn answered, frowning. "We had best remember that."

Draining her glass, she hailed someone with an open bottle and started in on her third serving. *"Not my problem right now."*

"Someone, somewhere, sees it as their problem at this moment," he said, sober as a heart attack.

"It's licking its wounds somewhere," she scoffed. Gwendolyn and a handful of druids had left to track it, if they could.

She went to take another sip of wine, just for him to swat the glass out of her hand. It shattered beside her. *"What the—"*

"You've had enough." He gave her a stern look as she raised a fist. That expression practically dared her to take a swing at him. "Besides, I thought you hated wine."

"Certain events have taught me to always drink deeply of it," she muttered bitterly, folding her fist and crossing her arms instead.

The druids were coaxing out a ring of floating glass balls to serve as a stage as she looked away from him. She fumed while waiting for something to happen. The chicken was sure taking his time getting ready for this.

When he stepped into the light, he wasn't a bird but instead a man she only recognized because a lute was strapped to him. Its face glinted with copper as he strummed it, mimicking its thrum with his vocal cords as a smattering of applause followed. Side conversations hushed as attention turned his way.

Dressed straight from the past in a tunic and breeches with foppish, bright colors, he doffed his hat and bowed to those present in one fluid motion. It felt like her eyes were about to pop right from her head, and he hadn't even begun to sing.

He must've been some sort of half-fae, she thought, as his bright smile was set in a Spaniard's bronzed complexion from which only a scattering of stars shone. The long hair he tamed with his cap was dark rather than the white or gray of the astral fae surrounding her. But that wasn't why she was staring.

No, the little man starting to strum and sing woke a feeling in her that she hadn't had in years.

Since Marcus.

"Impossible," she muttered mostly to herself. It had to be the drink—the druids had made that wine awfully strong. It blended

well with the notes from the lute, mingling together to fill her chest with a heady sense of peace. He sang of a girl he'd left behind in his village, drawing sighs from more than one lady present.

Neala rolled her eyes. She could see the charm in his smile and the twinkle in his eyes, but he would have only one lifemate out there...and apparently, she had two. Just like Alex Rehnquist, lightning had struck her twice.

But why now? And why a fop of a boy instead of a warrior like her first husband?

"What's wrong?" Taryn whispered. He was visibly relaxing next to her, his shoulders sagging with the fatigue she felt creeping in too. There was something about this performance that made it feel like she could go back to bed to finish her rest.

"*Nothing*," she muttered, wondering if it would be gone by the time she woke up in the morning. Maybe she was hallucinating again.

Cedric was perched on a table in the dining room by the time she woke from a deep, dreamless rest. If there was magic at work there, she didn't begrudge it. She wasn't even hungover, proving she hadn't drunk as much as she thought she had. So, she took a long, hard look at the boyish fae strumming his lute and accepting a grape a druid dressed in literal daisies fed him. He had a nice retinue of female admirers, which only grew as she muscled into their midst.

Sure, she elbowed out a petite fae who shot her a dirty look, but she needed to get a closer inspection of the man. Their eyes met. Butterflies danced in her belly, as if she were just admiring, when she felt that nascent tug toward him as a perfect match.

Cedric's fingers strummed too quickly, sending off a discordant twang. "Oh, hello there. If it isn't the lady who saved me earlier. I must say, you are quite large." A hint of color rose to his cheeks as she raised a brow. "I mean, I find that attractive. It's nice that you are...uh, large. Actually, I don't know what I meant. Please don't hurt me."

"You have a nice voice," she said, realizing she was staring and glancing down at his lute instead. *"Is there magic in that?"*

He stopped playing and waited. It didn't take long before his retinue of admirers moved on, leaving them alone. Flashing a wink, he said, "Maybe so. Or maybe I'm just that good."

She considered asking if fae felt the possibility of lifemates the same way vampires do. Or if it was different because he was only half fae. He kept talking as she puzzled over it. "Actually, if you want to know a secret, it's my grandfather's. It can do a lot of fancy things, but I only know a smidge of the spells." He held his thumb and forefinger approximately a smidge apart. "He was from an order of fancy bards on Faerie. But I don't have his training. I just found it gathering dust in my mother's basement and went from there."

"Are you always such an open book?" she asked.

"Only with pretty ladies." Now she figured he was patronizing her, because without a glamor, she was hardly anyone's definition of pretty. "I'm also really curious about you. Spare a bard some gossip, would you?"

"Do you mean that you're curious about the company I keep?" She knew how this particular song and dance went all too well.

He shook his head quickly. "No, I mean you. Like, where did you come from? What is your name? How did you get to be so, um...?"

"Large?" she asked with a sigh.

"I really need a better word for it. Muscular. Let's go with that. How did you get to be so muscular you look like you could snap me in half?" He started strumming an upbeat tune with a cheerful smile. "Which I imagine you would do if I wasn't so stunningly handsome."

She had to shake her head. Such an ego on this one. *"My name is Neala, and I'm one of the original Fell Hunters."*

"Oh, I know the story of the Fell Hunters. Everyone here knows about..." He drifted off as a flash of red moved in the corner of her eye.

Conversations turned to whispers around the dining hall as a dragon strode in by Keegan's side. Her adopted son went straight to her, and they clasped forearms formally. He'd dropped his glamor, just another astral fae in this place where he wouldn't stand out. "Hello, Mother. Izell sent me."

"You missed it," she remarked.

"You say this like Ash hasn't been chewing on my hide the whole flight here." His starry gaze roved the room for her, and he lifted a hesitant hand as he made eye contact with an irritable-looking Ash. "This is my dragon, Vidia."

The dragon came over to give her a sniff and chuffed in approval. "Keegan has told me all about you," she said.

"He had better. I raised him." She felt her lips lift as a chuckle left them.

Vidia nudged his side. "Well? Give her the letters."

Keegan produced three sealed envelopes. "From Izell. I don't know what's in them, but she says you'll find them of intense interest."

"And she couldn't deliver them herself?"

"She's apparently in Faerie," he admitted. He nodded to her and crossed the room to Sorsha and Ash. Instead of tearing into the letter addressed to her, as she burned to do, she watched them interact, waiting for a candid moment. Her children hadn't admitted to any relationships, but she had her guesses.

Unfortunately, Keegan's back was to her as he greeted both women.

She shrugged to herself and broke the seal on the envelope marked with her name. Speed reading through it, her eyebrows rose to her hairline.

It was as brief and blunt as she'd expected of Izell, a formal invitation to join her at a date a couple weeks out to head into Faerie to act as the fae's Blade at court. In return, she would help Neala find a siren for her second voice.

Oh, and Cedric was invited too.

She thrust one of the other letters toward him so he could read his own invitation. "Oh yes, she didn't forget about me," he said, taking it gleefully.

The last was made out to Sirius, she realized. Because, apparently, no Fell Key hunting team was complete without at least five members to carry the artifacts back to where they were needed.

"You know her, hmm?"

"She's my patron." And Neala was completely unsurprised.

He jumped off his table with a gasp as he clutched the letter close to his face. "No way, we're going to..." He dropped his voice to a conspiratorial whisper. "Faerie. I'm going to go pack my stuff."

She lifted a hand in farewell and scoured Izell's letter for any sign of how this would go and how long it would take. Instead, she found she'd missed a PS on the back.

Three seconds after you read this sentence, look at Keegan.

She did, to find him holding Ash and pressing a kiss to her crown.

"I knew it," she said to herself.

Chapter 34
Adrius

Adrius spent his first waking hours as a pillow, with Nyah snuggled on top of him. She was out cold and partially shifting in her sleep, growing and losing wolf features at will. Considering the potion she'd taken earlier had left her a little... furry, he wouldn't be surprised if this was some sort of side effect. It made their cozy bed warmer, and that satisfied the dragon in him, which was also passed out.

Really, he should've slept in too.

But she was awake before he could act on that thought. Her fingertip traced the pattern of a scale where his shoulders transitioned to wings. "Good evening, sunshine," he said, finding the statement had never been truer.

Her light had caused a miracle, and even if her glow had faded, it had created a moment no one present would soon forget. But now, she was disheveled and licking dry lips as she caught her bearings. He thought she was adorable when she wasn't expected to be her perfect, queenly self.

"Hi. So, that wasn't a dream?" she asked.

"Unfortunately not."

She buried her face in his chest. "It was *awful*. And we had a bard present, so you know there's going to be songs about it."

He stroked the smooth line of her back with a sigh. "I don't disagree. But...why wouldn't you want to hear someone singing of your prowess?"

"Songs are never forgotten," she remarked. "And I would very much like to forget what Jazrach showed me." She spoke hesitantly of it at his coaxing, of a plan to murder and hang their family. To shape *him* with it, unable to join them.

"It won't happen. You prevented it," he said, deeply shaken that she'd endured such a thing with Jazrach's hallucinations to tell the tale to him later without a tear staining her fair face.

"Do you think I'm still an Alchemyst?" she asked quietly, looking him in the eye. Hers sparkled like molten gold.

He held out one of his claws. "There's an easy way to find out."

It was odd to watch a bead of golden blood well to the surface of her skin and not have an urge to lick it up. His belly rumbled faintly for more solid sustenance. "Well, there's your answer," he said, smoothing her hair. "Alchemyst, queen, shifter, *and* nephilim."

"Add it to the list of my titles," she said with a long-suffering look and a weariness over their bond that drew a laugh from him.

"I know one title I'm glad you have," he offered, his touch drifting lower to cup her hip.

"Oh?" She leaned in when he did, their lips meeting in an unhurried exploration.

He took his time to show her that was the title of being his mate.

They emerged when it became apparent the Sanctum was moving with activity. The army was forming up again, with Caladorn and a few of his officers speaking to Gwendolyn by one of the gates. Adrius reached over to help Nyah adjust her crown, seating it amongst her flaxen hair like anyone could mistake who she was.

Fae saluted them both as they made to join the conversation. "—No rest for the wicked," Gwendolyn was saying.

"Never," Caladorn agreed.

Gwendolyn's poise was tossed aside as she pulled Nyah into a long, hard hug. "I saw your light, my dear. What is your grace?"

"It's been hanging just out of my reach for so long. It's family, Mother."

As they drew to the side to talk privately, Caladorn met Adrius's eye. "The army is about to march. Jazrach's Fell have been spotted heading for a township not far from here, but I would speak with you before we go."

With little space not taken by a soldier or druid, they passed through the gate to a private copse within sight of the Sanctum's walls. "What is it?" Adrius checked the sharpness of his question. They were allies, but he hadn't forgotten the general's cold reception.

"We have something in common," he said, clasping his hands behind his back. "And I have made the mistake of comparing you to myself unfairly."

Adrius frowned. "Oh?"

"We have both experienced something unprecedented, being reunited with our daughters after such a long absence. When we met, I didn't realize you were kept in the dark about Swift." *Oh.* Now he understood where the fae was coming from. Most of the time, if he saw Caladorn, there was Sorsha in his shadow, acting as if they'd never been parted.

"You thought I didn't care about her?" he asked, scoffing at the thought.

Caladorn's lips twisted. "That's what it looked like. I had the opportunity to share more resources with you or even foil your first attempt to apprehend Jazrach. After seeing what it can do, I recognize that I did poorly by you for even pointing you in the right direction."

He chewed on the words, it dawning on him what was about to happen. For the first time in his recent memory, someone else was apologizing to *him* for their behavior. "I don't think you could've done much to dissuade me. I thought I could do it," he said.

He waved the words away. "Still, I behaved poorly and wish

to make amends. You are on the path to coronation as Adrun's king, and thus, my duty will soon be to you. I do not want bad blood between us."

"Nor do I," he answered.

"It is a popular story that the man to merge with our dragon spirit would be our fated king." Amusement pulled at his lips. "And here you are. You've caught the imagination of countless fae crafters and artisans. They all imagined you as a fae rather than a man. But there is one work you may find of interest now..."

He described the shop of a leatherworker who displayed a centerpiece of an "enchanted" set of armor embossed and detailed to look like dragon scales. "I imagine he would be honored to see you wear his work."

"That sounds like a work of art, not something I should be fighting in," he said with a frown.

The fae raised a brow. "That's why it's enchanted."

"I don't know what that means," he admitted.

"Just...go talk to him." Apparently, this was too big a knowledge gap to simply explain. "Our trackers have reason to believe Jazrach has returned to Earth, by the way."

Adrius inhaled sharply. "What?" If it had wormed through the portal back to Earth, it could easily follow the next one and attack the heart of Coven Rehnquist.

"Talk to the angel-kin. They have an idea of what it wants." He jerked his head back toward the Sanctum.

Before he went back in, he held out his hand for a shake. "Good luck to you."

Caladorn took the offer with a firm grip. "Stars be with us both."

"If I may ask..." They headed through the gate together as he earned a curious glance. "Are you a shifter? What is your spirit?"

He flexed his hand, producing tawny feathers. "Falcon. Self-control."

"Very nice." They parted on that note, with Caladorn rejoining his officers. Adrius marveled to himself at how much he'd almost had in common with the fae general. Self-control was a much better look on Caladorn, he decided.

He glanced around for any sign of Gwendolyn or his mate, finding them both sitting cross-legged amongst the flowers, balancing light in their palms. It looked like something he shouldn't disturb, but time was slipping away with a demon at large. Gwendolyn glanced up first as he tromped toward them.

"I need some time with her," she said. "Go find Gabriel."

Nyah blew him a kiss, her breath sending up a cloud of light. Well, if some training already had her doing that, he could give them a moment. He waited until Gwendolyn turned away and gave Nyah a warm and meaningful look.

"Flirt later," Gwendolyn grumbled.

Laughing, he went into the druids' home in search of his former commander. Only for someone else to find him instead, rushing to intercept him. "You have a moment?" Sirius asked.

He supposed that he did, so he nodded. "Listen, about last night..." Sirius began. Looking distinctly uncomfortable as he spoke, there could only be a handful of things his brother was about to say. "I didn't realize how powerful and *real* Jazrach's magic was. When he was just whispers and suggestions, I thought he was some kind of joke. What kind of creature fights that way?"

"A very intelligent one," Adrius ventured. As little as he liked it, that was the bitter truth.

"Yes. Unfortunately. The only one who got the full brunt of his abilities was you, which I didn't realize until it happened to me and..." He took a deep, steeling breath. "I apologize for doubting you. You are strong as ever to come back from what he did to you."

Shock stole through him. Sirius waited with obvious nerves until Adrius grabbed him for a deep, backslapping hug. Relief was like a weight lifted from his shoulders. "It's all right. I'm just glad to have you back."

"It's good to be back. You've turned a lot around, huh? Got Nyah back, and a surprise daughter..."

"Have you met her?"

"I am quite fond of my fox niece already," he said with a chuckle.

He couldn't help but laugh with him. "She looks a lot like Nyah in her human form."

"Well, good." Sirius slugged his shoulder. "Wouldn't want her looking like your ugly mug."

"No kidding. Have you seen Gabriel, by the way?" He regretted having to change the subject but knew he couldn't put off the looming threat for much longer.

Sirius's expression sobered too. "Through here."

They found him sitting in the dining hall with three fae in close conversation. Sorsha and Keegan were immediately recognizable by their bearings, while Ash's fae form gave him pause until he noted the telltale bandolier around her torso. He'd never seen her with her human glamor down, thinking, as an Unseelie, she probably wanted to hide her true face. But she was as lovely as any other fae he'd met.

Her wings smoldered with live embers, putting off her namesake as they twitched. In her eyes resided the true flames, burning as she glanced their way. "So, you're some kind of fire fae," he commented, drawing the whole table's attention.

"Seems that way," she replied archly.

Her skin seemed to glow as he drew closer and sat with the group. It was an unnatural shade of pewter, combining with her snowy cap of hair to render her mostly monochromatic. "Don't be too alarmed," she continued. "I'm a nice destruction fae, unlike my kin."

Considering her relationship with the truth, he wasn't sure how to take that. She nudged Keegan, who added, "The Sanctum's magic allows her to tell the truth."

"I don't want to leave. This is nice, actually," she said.

"Does that mean you can tell a lie?" he asked the two Seelie by her.

They exchanged a glance. "Do you want to do it?" Sorsha asked.

"No. You do it."

She took a deep breath and screwed up her eyes. "I am telling a lie."

Adrius's brow crinkled in confusion as she relaxed again and smiled brightly. "That paradox is a guaranteed way to put a Seelie in a lot of pain unless they *can* lie," she explained.

"All right, back to business," Gabriel cut in with a sigh. "We were debating strategies."

Sirius raised a finger with a hum. "The army is gone. What strategies remain?"

"The demon," Adrius muttered over to him.

"Jazrach has returned to Earth and abandoned its pet Fell. To what end?" Gabriel said. "We are reasoning that it's searching for a better source of souls. Fae spirits are heavily defended here at the Sanctum, and it must've been badly injured when my daughter caused it to flee. Humans make for easier hunting."

"So, a simple bait and switch. We go for the Fell problem while it builds itself back up." Sirius caught on with a grim expression.

Gabriel nodded, mirroring that look. "Worse, it knows we will want to save the fae it infected. That means at least myself or one of the nephilim stay behind to help. Fewer threats if a team does go to track it before it's ready."

"I believe it's tracking down its spark," said Ash. "If our theory is correct, it's been festering within Lucia this whole time, gathering power. Reclaiming it would make it too strong to defeat."

Adrius was struck dumb for a moment. *Theory?*

Then he realized Izell must not have shared her deeds with them. Already a step ahead of the younger fae. "Well, good thing that's not possible."

"What do you mean? If it disabled the protections on Lucia's prison, it would be an easy venture." Sorsha had her occultarus in hand, spinning it with nervous twitches of her fingers. "The people guarding her expect trouble from within."

Adrius started to laugh despite the dirty looks it earned around the table. "It's not a problem because Izell has the spark."

Sorsha's starry eyes widened. "What!"

He told them of the elder fae's deal with Lucia while Sorsha and Keegan exchanged alarmed looks and likely some mental conversation. "I'll be damned," Keegan said finally. "The old bat's still got it. She's in Faerie right now 'on personal business.'"

"And while the demon was here in Adrun, she stayed on Earth." Sorsha shook her head in quiet awe. "It will have no idea its spark is elsewhere. With Lucia in a magical dead zone, it more than likely didn't notice the original change in ownership."

Ash rested her chin on her fist, watching them with her lips quirked. "When you're done patting her metaphorical back, remember that means she's next to be corrupted when it *does* figure out what happened."

The other two fae sobered immediately. "Can you burn it out of her?" Sorsha asked Gabriel.

He was smiling as he nodded. "So, we have some good news here. It is my duty to hunt Jazrach, but I am also bound by an agreement the High Council made with one of the fae gods to ensure it does as little damage here as possible."

Sorsha perked up. "Which god?"

"I believe her name was Raenith."

The three of them nodded in approval.

"Therefore, I believe it would be best if I stayed to help with the Fell while Gwendolyn and Nyah handle the demon," he continued with a sigh. "With one alternative." He stood and drew his sword, laying it on the table before them.

Glimmering like glass shards, it was the prettiest weapon Adrius had ever seen. A plain sheath and unadorned pommel understated the blade itself, which seemed to be forged of diamonds rather than steel. "This blade has the ability to slay a demon, no matter who handles it. I believe..." Gabriel turned it until the pommel pointed toward Adrius. "...you should take it."

"Me?" he murmured, taking it up to inspect it reverently. It was sharp enough to split the scale on the pad of his thumb with little pressure.

"My wife and I have always been a team," Gabriel said. "She can help me with the Fell, and you can assist Nyah in killing the demon."

Ash spoke up before he could. "And it would basically be your fourth encounter with Jazrach. The height of good luck."

"I would be honored," he said honestly. He couldn't wait to put this blade through his tormentor and end it for good.

Chapter 35
Nyah

There was far more to being a nephilim than Nyah could learn within the few short hours she had with her mother. However, they went over the basics at a breakneck pace. Now that she'd awoken the light within her, much of the control aspects were like second nature.

Nephilim could wield their powers in only one of two ways. For Gwendolyn, she'd always had the ability to invoke wrath and harm, making her light something to be feared amongst photosensitive vampire kind. At the height of her powers, she could smite a Fell to dust with a flick of her fingers.

They could already tell that Nyah had the other half, where her light was a gentle glow. She was a nephilim healer capable of incredible feats once trained, but Nyah asked for what she could use right away. Her new light could help her sense demonic taint and thus assist in tracking Jazrach, and she could utilize proper Latin cantrips that, if used correctly, could do a number of things. She memorized one to ward off demon magic so she couldn't be taken by a hallucination and a second one to cause pain to any demon who heard it.

That was about all they had time for. She kept muttering those phrases under her breath to commit them to memory as she stood to help Gwendolyn up. "Now we have to go see my father," she said, linking their arms and dragging the other woman along with her.

Gwendolyn protested weakly as Nyah followed Adrius's scent to find him. "You haven't talked to him, and you need to," she said firmly.

Instead of arguing, a sigh left her lips. "It is in your grace, I suppose."

And the last link for us to have a whole family, Nyah thought. She went straight into the dining hall and only stopped when her parents were face-to-face. Gwendolyn bowed her head, and Gabriel stopped the motion with his fingers under her chin.

"I've missed you," he murmured.

"And I, you." She took a step closer. "What is Heaven like?"

"Beautiful. And lonely without you." He closed the gap, and Nyah glanced away, allowing them some privacy.

Adrius beckoned her over and showed her a glimmering sword with reverence. "Are you ready to kill a demon?" he asked.

"You're not going without me," Sirius put in beside him.

"Or me!" Celeste's fox form popped up from under the table.

The brothers exchanged a glance. "Did you know she was there?" Adrius whispered.

"Nope."

Sorsha offered a portal for them as Celeste slunk off to change into clothing rather than fur. "I'm sorry, but our services would be of better use here," the fae said, palms up.

Adrius accepted it graciously without an excuse from her, as long as she redirected their portal to Dragonhelm. Once Celeste was ready, he led their little band past the portal and into the city, where he followed a path while murmuring under his breath. With single-minded focus, he took them directly to a store she recognized.

"Caladorn told me about it," he explained as they walked into an artisan's shop full of the scent of fresh leather and polish. She took a deep breath on a happy sigh, waving to the leatherworker currently tending to his wares. Gere had once been an armorer in Faerie before his time as a Fell but had retired from that business to let his muse take him. His shop was full of goods as varied from purses to decorations.

The only armor that remained was behind its own display case, its polish gleaming in the fae lamps floating above. Gere had slaved over the hide, etching in symbols of magic amongst hand-tooled scales top to bottom. The helm hung on a hook above it, marked with the visage of a roaring dragon.

His mouth hung open as he beheld Adrius by her side. "Gere, I would like you to meet my mate, Adrius. He has recently finished his spirit trial." She wished she'd brought him here sooner as the fae clasped his hands with starry eyes shimmering.

"It is a pleasure to meet you, sir. I see with my own eyes that you are the Dragon of Adrun. Did you come for the armor?" he asked, heading for the display case.

"It is a work of art," Adrius said appreciatively. "But...I need something I can fight in."

"So you can with this. It is real armor." Gere hadn't taken his eyes off of Adrius's scales. He fumbled with his keys and missed the lock on the case.

"I wouldn't want to damage it," he said, putting his hands up. "Besides, you deserve a king's ransom for work this fine."

Gere shook his head. "It would be an honor if you wore it, sir," he insisted, laying out each individual piece on the counter between them.

"Besides, it's enchanted. I put the two enchantments I thought you'd need the most in them. Granted...I thought you would be a fae too." He held up the tunic, shaped for a fae man's trim torso. "Nothing more magic can't fix."

Adrius licked his lips. "Enchantments?"

"Indeed."

"I...am not from around here," he said hesitantly.

Amusement lit up Gere's face, causing Adrius to relax. "An enchantment is magic woven into the material, sir. Most objects made by a fae will have one at most. I was able to put in two—fire-proofing and mending. So, you shouldn't be worried to use it, because it'll restore itself to new unless completely destroyed."

"That's incredible," he murmured, glancing to her in awe. She smiled back, more used to the idea of fae artisans' capabilities.

"If you want to come into the back, we can mold this on you," Gere offered, carrying the leather and leading him into a private portion of his shop.

Sirius came to her side as they waited, looking disappointed. "I want special armor too," he sighed. He pulled on his shirt collar. "Or, well, any armor."

"But you shapeshift?" she said.

"It's the principle of the thing, Nyah. And won't he be shifting as well?"

She patted his shoulder. "I'll commission you a set after this is all over. Okay?"

Some of his coveting feelings faded from her empathy as he accepted the offer heartily.

Celeste came up on her other side. "Me too?" she asked with a laugh.

"Druids don't wear leather, though!" Nyah giggled.

"We don't? Darn." She plucked at her flowery dress. "Well, this is nicer anyway."

Sirius hooked an arm around her shoulders and mussed her hair. "Silly fox."

Nyah watched them out the corner of her eye as they waited. Maybe recent events would coax her daughter to spend more time as a woman amongst civilization rather than being a rare sighting out in the woods. She just hoped Celeste wouldn't spook on seeing how built up New York City was, since her druidic powers relied on a connection to nature.

As she was occupied with those thoughts, Adrius returned dressed in the armor. The material had been magically stretched to fit his frame, making the scale pattern broader, especially in the chest. "I will craft extensions when you can return it," Gere was saying, admiring his work as it walked away. The dark leather flowed seamlessly into the real dragon scales.

Adrius donned the helm, and Nyah nodded immediately in approval. He looked exactly like the mythical Dragon of Adrun as depicted by artists and crafters as they posited in creative efforts on the person who would someday tame Zerenth the Fury. Most of the time, the person was a man with a blade and dark armor.

And here he stood before her, an angel-forged sword on his hip. They were ready.

Chapter 36
Nyah

Nyah's glowing hand made their path apparent. Once they picked up on Jazrach's trail in the forest, heading straight for the portal in Izell's home, Nyah's light made it appear as an inky stain on the ground. Not that she needed it once her wolf's nose picked up on the sulfurous stink of the creature.

They headed back to Earth, and her heart was in her throat as she picked up on a thicker trail. "It must've idled here," she remarked, seeing it head closer to the second portal to Coven Rehnquist's mansion. Yet it stopped short with a thin loop.

She released a relieved breath but kept moving at the head of their group, realizing quickly that her light was needed when Jazrach's scent mingled with the aroma of humanity that she'd only started getting used to. If she hunkered down as a wolf, she could continue to track it by scent, but then she'd leave her clothes behind.

They emerged from the underground bunker as Celeste started drawing her shoulders in, rubbing an arm in discomfort. "What happened here?" she whispered.

The bodies were gone, but other hints of an old battle still remained. Fell Mad had a particular stench, and that was what Nyah noticed most as she led them away from several choke-points that protected the bunker. "Great evil. But it will be resolved when we are finished tonight," Nyah answered.

Except when Jazrach's trail finally headed topside, she realized they had a different problem. Sunlight.

She and Adrius exchanged a glance as Sirius climbed outside without fear. He was one of the rare few vampires who could still withstand the sun, which had given him his Blood Prince title, Dawn. But Adrius wasn't so fortunate, and neither Nyah nor Celeste had seen the sun in an eternity.

"You're not a vampire anymore. You should go first," she told him.

"And you're a *nephilim*. Ladies first." He offered her the ladder with a dramatic flourish.

She tilted her head back and forth before finally scaling it and holding her hand up to the buttery afternoon light. It was warm... hot, rather. But her skin didn't start blackening like meat thrown in a fire, so she took it as a good sign. Sirius helped her up, emerging into an alleyway away from prying eyes.

Adrius followed, apparently winning some internal war with his dragon, as he'd retracted his draconic features. "I missed the sun," he murmured. Between him and Sirius, they hauled Celeste to her feet and replaced the metal cover to the ladder downward.

As Nyah feared, Celeste was putting off heavy feelings of distress at this unfamiliar place. "Be strong for me, baby girl," she murmured. "Find a connection where you can."

Celeste huffed, putting on a brave face. "I'll be fine, Mother." At least she didn't roll her eyes.

Turning back to the trail, Nyah's glow was nearly invisible with the sun overhead. She soaked in its warmth as she tried to uncover Jazrach's trail, to find the last wisps of shadow burning up in the light. She muttered an unladylike curse.

"I've lost it," she sighed to Adrius.

"Well, we know where it's going right?" He glanced up and down the street. People were gathering around a street vendor whose wares smelled deliciously of cooked pork.

The prison, but where was it? "If we can get there," she said.

After a few moments, Sirius brushed past her. "This way."

"You sure?" she asked.

He glanced over his shoulder. "Apparently, I'm the only one

here who's spent any time on these streets. Yes, I'm sure. It's not that far away."

As they walked, Nyah felt the hair on her nape rise from attention shifting to them. Despite losing the dragon features, Adrius was hard to miss, and the rest of them were little better when they looked like they'd walked out of one age and into the streets. She hoped they weren't far from their destination.

"I've visited this place too many times," Sirius muttered to her. "Nothing better to do than rattle Lucia's chains."

"Then you might remember how many people protect it during the day?" she asked.

"About two dozen, night or day. I'm still worried..." He glanced up at the sky. "When better to attack a group of vampires?"

Her lips pressed together grimly. Yet when they arrived at the prison, they found it untouched. The same oppressive magic hung over it, so they huddled together outside. "It could be waiting for night," Nyah said, thinking that was the most likely answer.

"Weakness to sunlight does seem to be a defining trait of its creations," Celeste agreed, rubbing her arm as goosebumps rose to the surface of her skin.

Nyah turned to head inside despite the displeasure Night's Howl emanated at the wards. Something dark swooped in at the corner of her vision, followed by the smack of flesh hitting stone. She whipped around in time to inhale a mouthful of smoke from Jazrach, looming over a fallen Sirius, whose body had broken a section of brick and the ward etched into it.

The world warped while she bared her teeth in outrage. The demon's form turned into wisps of darkness, swirling inside the prison as the oppressive aura over it dimmed in intensity.

She muttered the cantrip to ward off corruption, her vision clearing of fog to show Sirius crumpled on the ground and the rest of her family gone. She went to him first, pressing her fingers to his forehead for a quick and sloppy burst of healing. It was unlikely he would wake right away, and screaming was starting to rise from the building.

Standing, she took a potion off her belt and swallowed it in one gulp. The world narrowed as she and Night's Howl merged perfectly into a combination of woman and wolf for combat. She relied on those heightened senses as she barreled into the prison, only to find it full to the brim with shadowy smoke.

Wards were scratched, warped, or painted over with blood as she took the twists and turns of the maze of pallets. She discovered bodies as she chanted her cantrip, all vampires as caught off guard as they had been.

When she emerged before Lucia's inner prison, she feared the worst. Instead, she felt the last vestiges of suppression and saw the Sorceress was unharmed.

There had to be more wards somewhere. Jazrach was attacking them first, making sure there was no place to hide from its hallucinations. Its darkness eddied before an invisible wall in an oval around Lucia.

"Did you expect anything else?" Lucia asked as Nyah stalked through, her head whipping around as she looked for wards, or Jazrach, or any sign of her mate and daughter. She made eye contact with the Sorceress. Lucia looked her over stoically. "Are you what is to kill me?"

"I'm here to save you," Nyah replied.

Shock etched over her features before it was quickly schooled away. "A new look for you, Nyah. You know what you have to do. Release me."

She hesitated.

"Release me!" Lucia hollered. "Do you think I work for him anymore? I won't go without a fight!"

She hated this woman. But logically, without Jazrach's spark, she was as keen to kill it as the rest of them. She went over to open every nephilim chain keeping Lucia tethered to the wall, catching her when the Sorceress tottered upon bearing her own weight.

"You have made the right decision." Lucia flexed her fingers.

Though Nyah wasn't so sure, she had little time to worry. A form burst from the darkness hovering above them, followed by another swinging a diamond-bright sword. Adrius's blade struck a pallet, and down the tower of them went with a shattering crash.

Lucia noticed the last ward fail before she did and hurriedly flashed her hands through a complicated spell. The approaching smoke blew away from a hard breeze.

"Don't breathe in the smoke," Nyah said, focusing on finding the creature with any of her senses. She could smell it lingering in its darkness, dampening her wolf's best asset.

"Got it." Lucia extended her arm, shooting out a crack of lightning. Jazrach went tumbling down from its perch behind another tower of pallets.

"Hello again, Lucia."

"I've come to set you free."

Its whispers surrounded them as it lurked back into its shadows. Nyah's nape itched, feelings its hostile attention closing in. A cantrip was halfway off her lips when it burst from the side, eight feet of menace and bristling teeth in ill-fitting armor. Its left hand came down, embedding black talons in the concrete where she'd stood.

Lucia had a split second to cast a spell. Her lips pursed with determination as her hands lifted. Nyah lunged, claws extended for its neck.

As she sailed toward it, she noticed Lucia take a reflexive breath before her spell cast. Her face went slack with awe at what she saw. "Marcus?"

Jazrach batted Nyah aside as his sword pierced the Sorceress's chest. She died with a smile in a growing puddle of quicksilver blood.

The demon turned a vicious grin on Nyah as it cupped a hand, drawing the air over Lucia into its mouth. *"Finally, the power to defeat you."*

"My spark."

She coated her claws in light as it paused, turning to inspect Lucia more closely. "What spark?" she growled.

The demon's many whispering voices rose to an eardrum-shattering shriek.

Chapter 37
Adrius

"ADRIUS! HELP ME!"

It was Elandros again, which meant he was hallucinating. Adrius flew in tight circles amongst the top of the pallet maze, swiping at shadows and hints of mocking laughter.

"He's going to eat me. He's going to destroy my soul!"

He angled his wings toward the voice, finding a shadow amongst many.

"*I have an idea,*" Zerenth ventured before having him breathe a gout of fire. They had a few seconds of clear air, enough to see Nyah's glowing figure below. That's all he needed, tucking his wings to swoop to the ground, his sword out to skewer Jazrach a few feet from her.

The bulky figure of Jazrach glanced over its shoulder, turning to smoke and coalescing a few yards away so all Adrius stabbed was the unforgiving ground.

"Save me," crooned Elandros from Jazrach's spiked maw.

"*What delicious coincidence.*"

"*Two souls I would—*"

It cut off with a hiss as Nyah shouted a phrase in Latin. While it cringed away, it started laughing, passing its sword through its massive fingers before lunging for her.

Adrius was there, knocking the sword aside with his bulk.

The demon spat a glob of darkness in his face, choking off his senses on impact.

Whispers surrounded him in susurrations as he was enveloped in thick black night. He couldn't hear; he couldn't see. Stumbling backward, he thought he might be clawing at his face, trying to dislodge the magic.

Pain scored over his chest in a jagged three-pronged tear. He was helpless to stop it, until Nyah's voice came in, cleansing him in a flash of brilliance. They jumped apart as the demon spat again, the discarded glob hissing on the ground like acid.

It glanced between them and grinned, taking to the sky in one flap of its wings. As he made to do the same, something caught his eye.

Lucia's body. Shock rippled through him.

She'd been his enemy for as long as the vampire nation existed. The usurper who'd worn his wife's crown while faking both of their deaths. Who'd menaced him and the Blood Princes in modern times, down to allying with the demon who'd dealt the final blow. In death, rendered small. A drop of pity evaporated in his futile anger. *He* wanted to be the one to send her on to the end for everything she'd done.

"Go!" Nyah shouted, startling him from his thoughts.

He glanced up, where the warehouse was full of eddying darkness. A gush of flame preceded him as he scythed through it, setting several pallets alight and revealing the outline of the demon amongst them.

"Adrius! Help me!" shouted Elandros, followed by an agonizing scream.

Setting his teeth, he tried to ignore the taunts. He failed the fallen Blood Prince every moment he let the demon live. All Jazrach wanted was to push him into making a fatal mistake.

He spotted a different figure leaping from the flames, heading into a pocket of clean air. *Celeste,* he thought, recognizing her svelte build. She started waving her hands about with her spellcasting, but he had his focus on the demon now that he knew she was safe.

Jazrach lunged for him, their swords colliding and hooking

them into a dizzying midair spin. It was still grinning. "I'll consume him here and now. Just because you all stole away my spark," it hissed.

He spat flames at it, but this time, it didn't get set alight. Laughter echoed on all sides in the warehouse's acoustics. "Corpses burn, demons don't." Its whisper lingered in his ears as Jazrach twisted away on a column of darkness.

It solidified behind Adrius, claws aiming for his wings. Zerenth's instincts pulled them into a short freefall, and he felt the wind where those lethal points nearly scraped his scales.

He realized he was still outmatched by this thing if dragon's fire didn't affect it. The moment it crippled him with its poisoned spit, he was done. *"Then we must ground it before we are its victims,"* Zerenth growled. *"Use your allies."*

Nyah was down below, but somewhere amongst the fires was Celeste, maybe still casting. He hoped she had something for him soon as he and Jazrach circled each other. Going for a feint, he realized the demon wasn't flinching. If it could still read his mind, it would know his plans.

No, that was *exactly* what it was doing. It knew every feint and avenue he considered as they circled, because it always had its thumb on his thoughts. *"Zerenth, take control,"* he said, hoping his dragon was more inscrutable. If he didn't know what the dragon was thinking, perhaps Jazrach wouldn't either.

His heart lurched as his body moved without his accord. Zerenth had them charging right for Jazrach, who was already drawing breath for another glob of black acid. But instead of engaging, they angled to fly past it as it spat. Zerenth reversed their course to attack it from behind, their sword swinging down in a glittering arc. The shout of outrage that followed deafened him as Jazrach listed to the side, plummeting to the ground behind its severed wing.

"Why didn't I think of that?" Adrius muttered.

Zerenth rumbled as he tucked their body into a dive. They caught a glimpse of Celeste sitting cross-legged on an intact pallet, her fingers hooked and trembling as she worked some sort of spell.

It didn't matter when Jazrach was getting to his feet, shaking an arc of steaming blood from its wound. Nyah's half-wolf form flitted across its flanks, scoring needling wounds over its exposed arms. As Adrius landed, its talons mauled her side, sending her sprawling.

He roared in fury, ignoring reason as he charged directly for it. It sidestepped his sword, its own blade biting into his shoulder. "Think I killed her?" it mused, following this up with a flurry of blows that drove him a step backward. "Why don't I check?" Turning away, it rushed for where Nyah was pulling herself to a sitting position, her hands resting over her side.

It stumbled as the whole warehouse shook. Pallets tumbled, and wood shattered around them, much of it eaten up by new embers. Adrius grounded himself, arms and wings out to prevent a fall of his own.

The moment he regained his balance, he grabbed onto Jazrach's wing stump, pitching the demon away from his mate. A second quake rocked the building, strong enough that he thought the whole structure would collapse. It went on and on, the foundation beneath his feet crumbling to reveal a flash of greenery.

A tangle of thick vines exploded from the ground all over as he gaped in shock. They slithered like living things, pushing aside ruined chunks of concrete as they attacked Jazrach from all sides. It swiped sword and claws alike, tripping as it backed over one positioned like a root. They twisted around its limbs, trapping it spread-eagled as it thrashed.

Adrius leapt over what remained of the ground, surprised when a vine twisted around to offer him a bridge to the captive demon. He glanced up to make eye contact with Celeste, who nodded to him from her precarious perch, her hands fisted full of glowing green magic.

He nodded back, taking a flying leap from the vine to land sword-first. It pierced the demon's breastplate as gravity took hold.

"No," the demon whispered, black blood trickling from between its teeth as it gave one last thrash.

Light spider webbed through its veins, glowing from within

and spreading rapidly as every mouth in its skin gaped with agony. "*NO!*" it screamed in a chorus. It went limp beneath him, its flesh scattering away into dust. Sword and armor alike hit the ground with a clatter.

Adrius breathed a soft laugh of relief. He'd done it. Not alone, but with the help of his family. The demon Jazrach was dead!

"Celeste, that was brilliant," he called. She smiled and patted herself on the back, the mass of tentacle-like vines sucking back into the ground as she relaxed.

He didn't notice someone else stirring as he turned to go back to Nyah's side. The wolf features were fading from his wife's face, leaving her looking pained but alive. Her eyes widened as she lifted a hand to point behind him, screaming his name.

He heard a whistle before impact. A sharp stake of wood impaled him through the back, its jagged tip thrusting three inches out of his chest. His limbs turned to jelly as his punctured heart failed.

Chapter 38
Nyah

"How could you?" she breathed, their victory shattering the moment Adrius's body hit the ground with a thick makeshift javelin thrust through his chest.

Lucia climbed out of a crack between two bolder-sized slabs of concrete. She was a perverse miracle, her bones twisting out of alignment and cracking back into place as shadows coalesced behind her. Darkness flooded her eyes as her head lolled before spinning upright with a *snap*. Only the silver iris was left amongst the pits of black. Eerily similar to Jazrach's stare.

"Nothing personal." Lucia's voice was hoarse, like she'd just walked out of a burning building.

That seemed exactly what she did as Nyah said the cantrip for causing demons pain and watched Lucia cringe. Nyah pushed to her feet, holding her side and the tender new skin where she'd healed her grievous wound. The potion that'd pushed her and Night's Howl into a perfect merge was faded by now, but her hands glowed as she prepared to fight a new demon.

"How dare you!" Nyah demanded, balling her fists. "Nothing *personal*, after I let you go?"

Lucia tilted her head unnaturally far. "I wasn't about to burn. Not for you, and especially not for him."

Nyah tossed a ball of light at her, splashing over her arm with a sizzle of blackening skin. Glancing down at it in detachment,

Lucia then turned to inspect Nyah anew. "No wonder he wants you." And then she struck with a bolt of lightning.

Electricity danced over Nyah's nerves. She saw Celeste casting another spell out the corner of her eye and prayed it would be faster than her vines. Somehow, Lucia had returned with her Sorceress magic intact, making her dangerous indeed.

Nyah edged away from the wall, growing her claws and allowing her wolf to dictate their reflexes. "He, hmm?" she said from a numb jaw. "Someone down there chew you up and spit you back out?"

Flames danced to life in Lucia's hands as she gestured, setting her face into a play of shadow. "You'll see soon enough," she replied, throwing the spell to the ground and flooding the cavities between concrete blocks with flame, incinerating the new growth Celeste was fostering. "In truth, he never saw a soul as strong as mine. Perfect for demon-hood."

"Perfectly corrupted," Nyah hissed.

"I promised your life, and I intend to follow through. This is my second chance to be free," she said, pointing to Nyah. The air around her head grew thin, and she ducked, taking a gasp to rein-flate her lungs.

She thought fast. Celeste was casting with Sorceress magic now, building two glowing fists of warm light magic. If she could just distract Lucia a little longer, they could work together to send her back to where she came from.

Nyah lunged, her claws glimmering as she took a swipe at Lucia, catching her jaw and whipping her head to the side. She fell, her neck cracking as she righted herself in a quick jerk. "Such an animal. What happened to the sweet little girl?" she asked. The wound on her jaw did not close, but it also didn't bleed.

"She died the moment you sealed her in the Fell Lands," Nyah growled, sidestepping another bolt as Lucia snapped her hand out. She backed up with purpose now, glad Lucia's focus was on her as Celeste launched a whip of light to crack over the new demon's back. The cloud of darkness behind her parted as she screamed.

"I grow tired of you both," she said on a pained breath,

turning to launch lightning at Celeste instead. The pallet she'd perched on exploded as she leapt aside.

Nyah took that moment to crouch next to Adrius, pulling the shard of wood from his body as she took up the angel-forged sword lying below his hand. She'd never learned to wield one, which she regretted as she faced off with Lucia once more. The other woman scoffed, lifting her hands as Nyah lunged.

How hard could it be to use a sharp length of metal? She thrust it toward Lucia's chest, causing her to scramble to avoid it. The tip pierced cloth and ripped. Nyah pressed her advantage, realizing that being up close and personal with a deadly demon-killing weapon meant Lucia couldn't cast anything complicated for fear of losing a hand.

"You made the wrong decision," she gritted out as they danced around in awkward, shuffling steps, neither making much headway.

"You don't understand. You've never had a demon in your head!" Lucia snapped. "I only wish to be free of it all! And if you are the price I must pay, then so be it. I've done worse."

Nyah stumbled in her haste to avoid a bolt of lightning and tottered until Lucia pushed her, her head bashing on the side of a concrete slab on the way down. Stars and black spots danced in her vision as the sword went clattering away.

Lucia loomed over her, packing flames between her hands, the heat growing in intensity as the seconds trickled past.

This may be the end for me, Nyah thought as she struggled to scramble out of the way. To die in fire rather than darkness, but an end either way.

She'd forgotten in the moment about Celeste, who arrived with a fox's cry. She barreled into Lucia, taking the brunt of the flames as she forced the other woman to drop the magic. Screams of pain and the smell of burnt flesh ripped from them both.

Nyah fumbled for the hilt of the sword, realizing she was seeing double when she groped at empty air. She leaned over and grabbed it, feeling her side split in a shock of pain. They needed to finish this, and soon.

She climbed out of the hole to find Lucia swatting at a

stinging swarm of sparks, courtesy of Celeste. Her daughter's clothing was burnt, but her mouth was set in determination as she cast with green energy, drawing a small tremor from beneath them. A pair of vines rose on either side of her, lashing at Lucia like punches.

Nyah lifted the sword. It seemed so much heavier now, its tip quivering as she rushed forward to try and skewer the demon. Lucia batted a vine into her instead, sending her crashing into the prison wall. "That's enough," Lucia intoned, raising a fist. It was like a great force closed around her wrist and arm, snapping it. A whimper escaped Nyah's lips as she realized this made it impossible for her to use the sword. She could barely handle it with two hands, let alone one.

"I agree," rumbled a new voice from behind Lucia.

Chapter 39
Adrius

Adrius blinked and he was dead. He remembered the stake and the blood on his hands, and then it'd been over. What happened? Jazrach was vanquished, and with it, the last of its influence. He'd died so quickly afterward that his head still spun with the whiplash of being thrown back onto Soren's island.

There'd been someone else in that warehouse that wanted him gone. He clenched his hands into fists at the thought of leaving his mate and daughter to fight that threat without him.

Somewhere on Soren's island rose a furious roar as Zerenth let his opinion be known. Soil scattered into the wind.

"I see you've brought another friend." He whipped to the side to see Soren approaching, a concerned furrow between his brows.

A friend? Adrius gave his head a shake, trying to clear it. Because there was someone else standing beside him, glancing around in awe. His body was not solid like Soren or Zerenth but instead transparent and smoky.

It was Elandros. What remained of him, floating a few inches off the ground as his form faded out in places. "Are you...okay?" Adrius asked quietly, because it didn't seem that way.

The other man lifted a shoulder, his lips twisted in a rueful half-smile. "Thank you. For killing it." He sounded like he was speaking from far away.

"Was that you screaming?" He wondered if this was the

result of a demon eating a soul. But at least there was *something* left behind to save.

"Only the first time...I didn't realize it would use me against you so much." He lifted his palms in apology.

Soren had stopped at a polite distance, only coming over when Adrius gestured urgently. "Can you help him?" he demanded.

The angel eyed Elandros and then gave one of his signature, brilliant smiles. "Can I fix him? My dear man, what do you think you looked like when you got here?"

Adrius's mouth dropped open. Only a soft croak escaped. "Leave him to me. I think you need to know something urgently," Soren said, making a motion to follow as he turned to walk toward Zerenth, who was still ruining a patch of vegetation. Both Adrius and Elandros followed...or floated. He wasn't going to get used to that or the idea of himself damaged in the same way anytime soon.

"You are aware that I see the circumstances of your deaths when you arrive, yes?" Soren asked.

"It's been mentioned," Adrius murmured.

"Well, I need to make a report to the Council, because you unwittingly witnessed a huge breach of contract between Heaven and Hell."

His brows rose. "Oh?" He couldn't imagine what it was he saw. One moment, he was victorious, the next, dead. He hadn't witnessed anything personally.

"You were killed by a second demon. Illegally allowed back into a recently slain body." Soren was as grim as a reaper as they stopped short of being shredded by Zerenth. The dragon turned their way, claws digging into the soil up to his ankles. "You are such a sore sort when defeated, friend."

"I don't consider it a defeat when my opponent won't even look me in the eyes first," he rumbled.

But Adrius's thoughts were far away. A second demon, he'd said, from someone freshly killed. A sick feeling formed at the pit of his stomach, because who else could it be? He seized Soren's collar. "Was it Lucia?" he demanded.

"Don't do anything rash—"

He was ready to shake the truth from him. "Was. It. Lucia?"

Soren eyed him askance, as if he were a bomb about to burst. He let go of the angel, allowing him a moment to regain his composure. "Yes, it was," he said.

"Goddamn it!" He was ready to start destroying cabbages too. Because that meant he was stuck here when he could be defending his family.

The angel's face screwed up somewhere between amusement and horror. "Of all places to say such a thing, you choose here?" he said primly.

Adrius spat out a colorful litany of the woman turned demon —though he wasn't too surprised that of all people, she was the one Hell tossed back out. It seemed the powers that be agreed that she was the worst person alive.

Rocking back on his heels, Soren nodded along almost patiently as Adrius cursed until he felt blue at the face. He finally paused to draw breath.

"Through all this, I'm wondering why you've never used your Key," Soren remarked. Adrius narrowed his gaze, wondering what he meant. "Correct me if I'm wrong, Zerenth, but don't fae cast Shield-school spells to play possum in otherwise deadly situations?"

The dragon tilted his head. "Of a sort. Unique amongst the other schools of magic, Shield has a limited number of uses." He turned to Adrius and blew a hot, sulfurous breath over him. "Unlike you, most fae only have one or two chances to come back to life before they are dead permanently."

"But they do it from the grave?" Soren prompted.

"As I understand it, it is a conscious choice," Zerenth said with a nod. "Calinhes did it once, before we met. He spoke of the moment like he'd had a chance to refuse accepting his death. He sensed his soul's connection with his body and returned."

Adrius was tempted to shake him next for more information. Yet the dragon was much larger than Soren and much more likely to take a bite of him for the audacity. "So, you're saying I can do that too?" He was ready to do it right that moment, if only he knew how.

"I think you've always had the choice," Soren said, walking to the edge of his island home. Adrius did the same, ignoring the vertigo from the expanse of blue beneath them sinking down like an endless abyss. "But perhaps along the way, you've never wanted to return immediately."

He nodded in agreement. He hadn't had a reason to until this death. Somehow, Jazrach had interrupted the last one. Surely he could do the same willfully? "Why don't you close your eyes?" the angel continued. "Meditate a moment, see if you can feel your body."

Adrius did so, trying to slow his breathing and really focus. He flexed his left hand, where the heavy band of the Shield Key felt hot against his skin even now. "I think I have it," he said aloud as a chill drifted over the rest of him.

"Are you sure?" Soren asked.

He focused on that feeling, on the blaze coming from his ring finger. "Yes."

A firm palm pushed him, forcing him off the side of the island. His eyes flew open in surprise as the only solid land in the sky rapidly receded. Zerenth's dark form arrowed off the side after him as Soren called out, "Good luck, friend!"

And if his ears didn't deceive him, the angel's receding echo also added, "I hope you don't return for a long time. Live!"

Zerenth caught up with him midair, reaching out to grab his shoulder. He folded his wings harder, their descent picking up speed. "What are you—?" Adrius shouted against the whipping wind.

The dragon met his eye without fear as they entered a dizzying tailspin. "This is how I rejoined you last."

They passed some threshold together. Adrius slammed back into his body, every muscle spasming at once as he gasped with new breath. His nerve endings were electric with feeling, and he was hyperaware rather than emerging in a slow fog because he'd *chosen* to come back.

His family was in trouble. He heard the magic and the

screams all too clearly, his anger a living thing as it combined with Zerenth's. They agreed to a shift, of the same mind in that moment.

"What if I need to turn into a full dragon?" he'd asked Gere as the fae fitted his fancy armor to his body.

"Try it someday and see," the craftsman had said.

Well, he tried it and felt the armor slip off him as if he'd momentarily become a spirit. His bones cracked the next moment, scales slipping over his form as it elongated into that of a full dragon. It was Adrius that suppressed the urge to roar, as Lucia was otherwise too consumed by neutralizing Nyah to notice him rising to his feet and looming behind her.

"That's enough!" the Sorceress shrieked.

"I agree," he rumbled, seeing red when he heard Nyah's cry of pain. He lunged as Lucia finally turned, her eyes widening a split second before he had her torso in his jaws.

She flailed as he lifted her off her feet, her fists beating against his maw as it closed like a vice. On an exhale, he incinerated her directly with a blast of dragon fire. Her form blew away like smoke amongst the ashes of her body.

Adrius loosed the roar he'd held in, trumpeting his victory to shake what remained of the warehouse.

"Showoff!" Nyah croaked, smiling in a grimace past some obvious pain as she clasped her limp arm with a glowing hand.

He lowered his snout, scenting the blood on her with a soft whine. Though he couldn't do anything to help her, a battered Celeste was soon applying her own magic to the task of mending her wounds.

"Nice work, Father," she said, reaching up to stroke his angular face with a hint of reverence to see a dragon in the flesh.

Nyah folded her arms, letting Celeste have her moment. "But how did you do it?" she murmured.

"I had to take a leap of faith," he rumbled, grateful to the angel who'd helped him take that step, however unwittingly. "I learned how for you both."

"Thank you," his mate said, her golden eyes sparkling as she smiled up at him.

They all looked up when there was a rustling amongst the ruined pallets. Sirius burst out from behind a flaming pile, the side of his head swollen with a nasty welt. "Where is it? Taste steel, foul creature!" he exclaimed. He looked over the three of them and their surroundings before lowering his sword. "I missed it, didn't I?"

Chapter 40
Adrius

THOUGH ADRIUS WOULD'VE BEEN PERFECTLY CONTENT TO parade their group through the streets, they were still in New York during daylight hours. Adrius insisted on finding a skilled healer for Nyah and Celeste alike to make sure they'd patched themselves up well. They put out the fires in the warehouse, and he shifted to human form behind some pallets to put his armor back on.

Celeste made it easier for them, mustering the last of her magic to make a portal back to the bunker, where they could step safely into Coven Rehnquist's mansion and bypass hapless mortals noticing a group of four bloody, bruised people wandering around. They did wake half the coven looking for the Gifted woman, Melanie, though.

And considering that Adrius was ironically the least wounded of them, he was the one left standing before a small and *cold* audience. Violet had pulled a coat on over her pajamas, standing behind Alex and Julian since they'd muscled in front of her. They had thrown on some street clothes, as had Samuel, who was the only one still yawning and rubbing his eyes.

He realized the chilly menace amongst them was coming from Julian. His glowing blue eyes promised a skewering at his earliest convenience. Adrius hurried to address him first. "I apologize for what happened with your mate. I wasn't in my right mind."

When Julian's expression barely changed, he added, "I would apologize to her personally and offer amends?"

Alex glanced up first, before Olivia's voice drifted over them. "C'mon, I believe him." She was on the second floor balcony, and when Adrius spotted her, she waved with a cheery smile. "Hey! You've gotten a little...scaly?"

"I'm half dragon now," he said, unable to help a chuckle as she gasped and rushed downstairs.

"Can you be a full dragon?" She looked like she was going directly for him when Julian shot her a look. She reluctantly stood beside him instead, her golden Alchemyst eyes shimmering like sunlit coins.

He flashed a tired smile. "Yes."

"Hey Olivia, he seems a little *dragon* right now. How about we let him tell his story?" Violet suggested.

He heard the pun there, dragon for "dragging," and appreciated it greatly, though he couldn't think of a good rejoinder at the time. "I missed your puns," he said before launching into his explanation of the battle. Because of Julian's tension, he only pulled the first couple inches of his borrowed sword from its sheath to show off its unique purpose.

Of course, the first thing the Winter Key wanted was to hold it. He admired its diamond-bright surface while Adrius explained that the ash at its tip was what remained of Jazrach.

Julian was aghast. "You didn't clean it?"

"Jazrach is stubborn even in death," he answered.

Their disbelief increased as a unit as he explained what'd happened with Lucia and his death. A few glances were exchanged on her manner of execution—because he knew what they were thinking. He hadn't used the sword, so she was probably not *permanently* gone. But the ladies shared a high-five, and Alex clapped him on the shoulder with an approving nod.

"She deserved it and more," Julian muttered.

Adrius nodded in agreement. "I am throwing a party soon to

celebrate. You are all invited," he said. Hopefully Nyah agreed that this was a party kind of moment when she was in better sorts.

"Great, but I'm going back to bed for now," Sam said to the murmured agreement of the other vampires. He glanced at his phone and snapped his fingers. "Oh, Armando's been talking about his motorcycle. Were you going to bring that back?"

Cold flushed under his scales that the reminder. The motorcycle, the thing he'd promised to keep pristine. The same motorcycle that was abandoned and bent out of shape somewhere in Adrun. "I'll need to talk to him," he said with as much confidence as he could muster. He needed to think of what he could offer in its place. A nice horse would do. Maybe a herd of them.

They parted ways, with Adrius heading up toward Nyah's room. "Oh, I thought of how you can make it up to me," Olivia called. He glanced over his shoulder to find her grinning. "Dragon ride?"

"Fine," he said, amused.

"I'm next," Violet put in.

Alex rolled his eyes as he tugged her along. "Let's not get ahead of ourselves, love."

Her voice drifted to the stairwell, even as they wandered out of sight. "Don't worry, you can be third."

Adrius went to catch some rest with a smile still on his face.

He broached the subject of a party with Nyah after she had her tea and observed her whole evening ritual of waking, bathing, and stretching her body in interesting contortions. Apparently, the fae called the practice "therapeutic."

They sat together on the couch in her room, his arm around her as she leaned against his shoulder. "A party, huh?" She smiled at the idea. It grew wider as her eyes sparkled with some ideas of her own.

He stole a sip of her tea as he waited to hear what she was cooking up.

"We've been through a lot, you know?" she began. "From when we were parted to now." He could've groaned to be going over this again. Hadn't they moved on from rehashing the same story?

"So, I was thinking, why don't we have another wedding?"

She tittered as he nearly spat out another mouthful of tea and thumped him on the back heartily. "When?" he asked.

"As soon as possible," she said, holding up her hand. "I'm already wearing your wedding band!"

He lifted his as well. "As am I. Did you ever think your choice to switch our bands would lead here?" He remembered it like it was yesterday. At the last moment, as they said their vows, Nyah had slipped the Shield Key on his finger. He'd wanted her to have it as a symbol of his protection for her. How differently that had worked out for them.

She'd taken the Autumn Key as her wedding band instead, a symbol of bountiful life. "I'm glad of the change," she said, her finger tracing the rim of his ring. "Because we both put them to good use. You stayed alive, and I..." she drifted off with a blush staining her cheeks.

"Used it and the Spring Key to make butterflies?" he teased, brushing a thumb over her gold-tinged skin.

"I did, when I was young and silly," she agreed. "I've used them both for incredible things and made life of all sorts with the combination. You've seen the results with your own eyes."

He nodded, feeling that there was more she was working up to. She took his hand and rested it over her belly. "I think I accidentally used it right after we were wed," she said.

"Life of *all* sorts," he repeated, smiling wistfully. He still wished he could've been there for his daughter in her younger years.

Nyah licked her lips, pressing her fingers over his. "Do you want another?" she murmured.

He gasped in surprise. "Do *you*?" he asked, a lump in his throat. Because he'd like nothing more than to raise a child properly with his mate.

"I've always wanted a big family," she said meaningfully.

"Kids underfoot, massive holiday gatherings. Let's start our second chance out right."

His heart could've burst just imagining it. He would embrace this ideal of being a family man with his whole self. "I would love that," he murmured, sharing a long, slow kiss with her. "Just like I love you."

She held his jaw as she pulled him in for a second, deeper meeting of their lips. "I love you too. So much." Her nimble fingers started tugging at his beard.

"What are you doing?" he asked, reaching up as she sat back with a satisfied nod.

There was a tiny knot at the tip of his beard. A feat with how short he'd shorn it. "Victory," she proclaimed.

Chapter 41
Nyah

They wed in Adrun's central plaza to a massive crowd of her people who came to see if the rumors of the legendary Dragon of Adrun were true. Adrius played into it without prompting, wearing his scaled armor to the occasion but leaving his head bare. She placed a new crown upon his brow instead to proclaim him her king once and forevermore.

On his side stood the Blood Princes, current and former, with one place symbolically left empty for Elandros. Beside her were Celeste, Caladorn, and a few fae nobles she considered friends. Jaromir officiated after a brief introduction to her people, bringing them full circle to the last time he'd pronounced Adrius and Nyah man and wife.

"You were right," Adrius said as he led her in the first dance.

"I know. But what am I right about this time?" she asked with a giggle. He spun her as a set of minstrels played a slow, sweet number for them. Since she'd foregone an extravagant wedding gown for an ankle-length white dress with a flirty skirt, she felt they could dance all night.

His gaze darted to her skirt, brows lifted in appreciation as the cloth flew around her. "This is much better than a regular party. Though about half your subjects are staring."

"At you." She smiled. His scales were hard to miss.

"Sure," he said. "Don't leave me too fast, all right?"

She winked back, because when the song ended and he finished by bringing her into a dip and a kiss, they traded partners. She danced with her father, who'd finally changed out of the angelic armor for a suit. Adrius took Gwendolyn, dancing with her as delicately as if she were still elderly in build.

"I'm glad we can have this moment." She smiled up to Gabriel. "It hurt that you couldn't be at the first wedding."

"Let's not dwell on it," he said, wearing the proudest expression as they had a moment together. He practically glowed...but then again, so did she.

Another person joined the minstrels, strumming his lute as he joined mid-song with a voice like melting butter. Cedric waved to an admirer somewhere in the crowd and flashed a wink to another. Someone cast a spell over him to amplify his singing over the whole gathering.

"Now it's really a party," she said with a happy laugh, her heart so full to share this night with her father and the rest of her people, which felt like one big family.

Her pack, as Night's Howl would say. The wolf sat at the back of her mind as a content alpha surveying her domain. She even thought to accept ownership of the handful of vampires who'd accepted the invitation to come, too.

Nyah mingled with them since they mostly stayed in one big group. Olivia was trying to pull Julian into the next dance. "C'mon, don't be so stiff," she cooed.

"Yeah," Violet agreed, elbowing Alex from where they were sitting. He was nursing a glass of wine, observing the various kinds of shifter fae as they cavorted with a bemused expression.

"Can't a man take in the...ambiance?" he asked.

"Aren't you a shifter yourself?" Nyah called, beckoning the couple with a laugh.

He glanced to his mate and shrugged languidly, drawing her in to dance. He was a skilled dancer, sweeping Violet off her feet, to her delight.

Olivia planted a fist on her hip. "Are you just going to let him upstage you?" she asked her own mate.

"Do you really want to try keeping up with him?" Julian asked, a surge of confidence crossing Nyah's empathy.

"Well...yeah!"

And off they went too, to Nyah's approving nod. She'd called for dancing before the feast, knowing her people would want to dance their feet off, almost like the literal myths of old that circulated about fae.

She got her fill of it too, mostly with Adrius to save him from being waylaid by too many curious fae gossips who wanted a closer look at his face. He hadn't stopped smiling the whole while.

They parted with another kiss when it came time to toss the bouquet and garter. Several woman jockeyed with each other as Nyah lifted a bundle of white blooms, a generous selection hand-grown by her druid daughter. She glanced over her shoulder after she tossed, watching a sea of hands grabbing for it, just for it to bounce off a woman's fingertips.

It landed square in Neala's chest, who fumbled it in surprise and gave a brief, cross look at a fae who tried to pull it from her.

"*I guess it's a sign,*" she told Nyah privately.

"*Do you have a man in mind?*" she asked.

Neala's gaze drifted toward the minstrels as Cedric crooned on. "*As a matter of fact, I do.*"

She followed where she was looking. "*Cedric? You've sure picked a challenge.*"

"*When have I ever taken the easy road?*" Neala laughed and saluted her with the bouquet. She held it close for the rest of the night, helping Keegan as he hosted dragon rides for little fae on the back of his patient familiar.

Later, Nyah sat alongside Adrius at a high table set up outdoors. The palace had drug out all its spare furniture, fitting in as many people as possible to feast with them. She scooted her chair closer to Adrius's. "Look at our domain," she said, toasting him. They clinked their glasses together. While he drank a sip of fine druidic wine, she instead took a mouthful of rich cranberry juice. The wine was something she'd miss, but it was a small sacrifice in the scheme of things.

"I can barely grasp it. That all of this is ours," he admitted.

"With Nyixa gone and starting to sink, I was thinking myself a king in name only..."

"Now, you are the Dragon King of Adrun." She smiled over at him proudly, with his newly forged crown glinting in the generous smattering of fae lanterns hung above the gathering. He'd chosen a motif of gold and tiger's eye to match the band that'd kept him grounded until they could be reunited.

"A title I intend to uphold with the pride it deserves," he said.

"Can I tell you a secret?" She leaned over as he nodded, whispering in his ear, "You already have."

Chapter 42
Izell

The amplified music hurt her head. Izell perched atop the palace to observe the wedding at a safe, undetectable distance. She grumbled to herself about kids and their music as she tore into a slice of ham.

Thankfully, her favorite chef hadn't seen anything amiss in Izell filching a whole side of meat during the hectic preparations for the night's wedding. When she was the only dragon in Adrun, she'd built up a reputation of consuming like a true carnivore. Except no one expected Izell to be acting like a dragon now as she kept to higher ground.

She reached up to rub at the bandage tied around her forehead. The gauze needed changing over her third eye again, as it stuck to her. One of her last visions of the future had been this chance meeting she was waiting for...and her visitor was late.

Izell had made a quick trip to Faerie to barter with one of the only fae still alive willing to broker her future sight for a favor. Hopefully he put it to good use, because she didn't want it back. Manipulating that virtue was how she knew Jazrach had initially driven Lucia insane. Making her see things that weren't there... making her destroy her own relationships chasing goals that would never come to fruition.

So, she'd seen what she needed to see and let it go. It was her least favorite virtue of the five, so she told herself she wouldn't miss it. The reality was, she'd probably miss it very much in the coming months.

A tendril of smoke rose up next to her, swirling into a vague, coiling shape. Izell couldn't help an amused twist of her lips. "Not used to it yet, are you?" she said.

Lucia couldn't answer except for a dashing of her smoke from side to side. For once, the former queen was the one forced to listen. How the tables had turned. "You are fortunate," Izell continued, practically feeling the disbelief rolling off the nascent demon. "Were you anything else, you would've died instantly in dragon's fire. However, I understand demonic regeneration is quite painful. I do not envy you your position. I just wonder what you bargained your life against. Another person's soul?"

The smoke made its best approximation of a nod. "Bad deal, that." Izell clucked her tongue. "You never bargain another person's life. They're usually quite attached to it."

Resting this close to her, she could sense that Lucia was another corruption demon. Hopefully she never learned just what she was capable of, because anyone with half a brain could be decent at it, but demons with a cunning mind like Jazrach's could be true nightmares. Izell would know. She lived before there was a split between Seelie and Unseelie. Before a good portion of her race pledged their magic to demons in some misguided ideal to keep "balance."

"You may be wondering why I called you here," Izell continued, shaking off those thoughts. Lucia nodded again. "I wanted to talk to someone who understands. You may be the only mortal-born who knows just how frightfully short-sighted humans can be." She gestured out to the wedding. It took Lucia a few moments before she nodded again. She spoke of future sight, knowing Lucia was about to lose that ability, considering that, as a demon, she was no longer virtuous.

Izell retracted the scales over her right arm, revealing an intricate black tattoo on the back of her hand. "Etched into my skin are the terms of our deal. When and if you return to a fleshed form, you will see the same on your hand," she said. "Unfortunately for you, you are a demon and unable to break the terms of a deal. *Even* one you made in life. You owe me one favor without question, as you agreed to when I removed Jazrach's spark from your soul."

Lucia swirled around in apparent alarm. There was no telling what she was protesting—probably that she had to do something for Izell. She had no sympathy for her, of a disposition to hate anything of a demonic persuasion. "However, that means you are still lucky. Because while most believe Jazrach is dead, a little part of it still exists to power the Dark Eye when it is recreated." She slanted her a look askance. "That means *you* will not be trapped in there in its stead."

Lucia's smoke stilled except for a tendril that reached out to touch Izell's tattoo. She let her scales cover it back up. "I do not ask for a favor yet. What would you do for me now anyway?" She shook her head.

The next bite of ham was her last. She savored it before reaching into a satchel at her belt and throwing a handful of leaves in her mouth to chew. Suppressing a gag at the influx of bitter juices, she was content knowing it kept Jazrach's spark dormant until she had use for it.

She rested back on her hands, at ease for the moment, even if her plan was the longest of long shots with so much a stake. She just had to keep the spark at bay until they had the full set of Fell Keys and she had a copy of her grandfather Oberon's fateful Eye of Worlds-creating spell to recreate it. A combination of factors achieved by...no one ever.

Izell and her handpicked group had to be the first, then.

"Choose your next steps carefully," she said to Lucia. "Because you are running out of options, and I need you alive." She drew what used to be a ring from her pocket, the metal melted into a haphazard chunk. But the real power in it was the gemstone, which, thankfully, had survived its brush with dragon fire.

Lucia's shadows stilled. "You wore this for so long, it only responds to you," Izell said, turning over the hunk of metal with a disapproving tisk. "Help me lock Jazrach in a new Dark Eye, and

I can make sure you survive. Is that something you can agree to? Destroying your old master for good?"

There was no hesitation in Lucia's next nod. "Then you must do two things for me. Stay alive. And stay out of my way." Izell was not one to play politics, not when she had a world to save.

Find out more about Izell's plan in...
Court of Illusions: Blood Legacy Series Book 4

Also by Elise Hennessy
Altare World

Are you ready for a high-flying adventure on gryphon-back? Join Sivana as she becomes the first female cadet at the highly competitive Gryphon Rider Academy after the blind gryphon Arimus chooses her as his new rider.

Dragon Riders of Pern meets Song of the Lioness in this YA fantasy series in which a pair of underdogs rewrite what's possible in a formerly all-boys military academy.

- See Gryphon Rider Academy on Amazon -

Join an unlikely crew of five misfits and a mouse as they strive to become one of Altare's newest elite spy teams. Heists and adventures await!

The Gilded Wolves meets Six of Crows in this YA fantasy series in which a former thief uses her skills to become a spy. If you like clever heroines, strong friendships, and found family, then you'll love Royal Spy Institute!

- See Royal Spy Institute on Amazon -

About the Author

Elise Hennessy is an author of young adult fantasy full of adventure and found family. She holds a master's degree in journalism and enjoys crafting unique stories. When Elise is not busy writing, she's trying to reduce her prodigious TBR list. She lives in Texas with her family and is owned by two cats.

Find out more about her books at: www.elisehennessy.com

Glossary

Adrun: A section of Faerie submerged under the ocean and shrouded in magic to make it impenetrable. Formerly a prison for the cursed Fell. Queen Nyah renamed it from "The Fell Lands" when she and her shifters reclaimed it and eliminated the Fell curse. It is a place of complete darkness that sustains life through druidic magic.

Alchemyst: An incredibly rare sub-distinction of vampire with golden blood. They can create powerful tonics and potions with one drop of their life essence. They are immortal, but lack the superhuman aspects of vampirism and the bloodlust.

Angel: A being of pure light and a denizen of Heaven. All angels are called to uphold and spread a grace, or positive emotion/trait. Can only be permanently killed by another angel or demonic magic.

Blade: A fae skilled with martial magic and a weapon of choice, usually a sword. Traditionally they serve as bodyguards to Sorcerers.

Blood Prince: A title given to the few Fell Hunters that survived the Fell Crisis. They are the first vampires and each started their own unique bloodlines.

Coven: A group of three or more vampires, assembled for the protection of its members. Large covens establish territory where they can hunt with reasonable assurance that they are safe. Coven members are sheltered by their coven master, the oldest and strongest vampire in the group. A vampire without a coven is considered a rogue and often live short lives due to vampires' natural territorial tendencies.

The Crossing: Seelie fae can cross The Veil and travel between Earth and Faerie or vice versa during midsummer in a magical process called The Crossing. The only way to otherwise cross between the two worlds is through one of a handful of well-hidden portals.

Demon: A being of pure darkness and a denizen of Hell. The most common demons represent one of the seven sins, though it's possible to find a demon that represents any negative emotion. Can only be permanently killed by another demon or angelic magic.

Deveaux Accords: A set of laws created by the major covens of New York City and enforced by Ancient vampiress Cossette Deveaux. Covens are required to police their members to keep mortals safe.

Dhampir: A half-human, half-vampire by birth.

Druid: A fae or shifter that has manifested the virtue of druidism. They maintain the balance of nature through husbandry and control of the elements. It is possible to be both a Sorcerer and have druidism, but a fae or shifter that has both gifts is considered a druid exclusively. A druid in Faerie serves the four gods and the balance of the elements, while a shifter druid in Adrun keeps the land alive in the absence of sunlight.

Glossary

The Everlasting War: The conflict between angels and demons. The Veil was created to keep this eternal war away from Earth and Faerie.

Eyes of Worlds: A pair of giant tools that anchor The Veil into place. One was created by the willing sacrifice of an Archangel—it is the Light Eye located in Faerie. The other was created from an unwilling greater demon and became its prison—it was destroyed during the events of *Dream Walker*.

Faerie: A separate world magically linked to Earth. The place of origin for all magic and mythical creatures.

Fell: A fae afflicted with a curse of eternal hunger. The curse was spread from Fell to fae via a bite and was considered incurable. Fell are twisted creatures known for squat, frog-like legs, sharp and interconnected teeth like a bear trap, black veins, and pitch-black eyes. All Fell were banished from Faerie to The Fell Lands (see Adrun). The Fell Crisis or Fell War occurred when the Fell learned they could create portals to Earth during the Dark Ages and began consuming man and beast alike like a black tide of locusts. After their defeat, all records of the Fell were expunged from mortal record to hide the existence of vampires.

Fell Hunter: The first vampires. Soldiers exposed to Fell blood became strong and fast enough to fight Fell in the service to humanity. Though the first Fell Hunters were turned by accident, many were turned on purpose after the phenomenon was studied. In those days, being a vampire was considered a sacrifice for the greater good. Most Fell Hunters died fighting monsters.

Fell Keys: Thirteen in total, referring to a set of rings with gemstones of pure magic. Each one represents one of the schools of fae magic and grants the wearer great power.

Fell Madness: The boogeyman of vampirism. First manifested in Fell Hunters when they consumed too much Fell blood. Fell Madness gives vampires black veins, a mouthful of sharp teeth, and endless hunger for blood. Very little is known about the affliction because those that manifested it were swiftly executed. In modern day, the affliction can be cured by an Alchemyst's potion.

The Gift: Some vampires manifest the Gift rather than the abilities of their bloodline. They are capable of healing others from even the worst of mortal wounds. The Gift leaves if a vampire uses it to harm or kill others.

Heaven-Hell Accords: A set of rules agreed on between angels and demons as it concerns their interaction with Earth. As the Everlasting War is based off of balance, if a demon is summoned to Earth, an angel is allowed through The Veil to hunt it down. Resurrections of newly created angels or demons is strictly forbidden. Hell attacks, Heaven defends. Demons historically have bent these rules to the breaking point.

Lifemate: A perfect match to a vampire. It is possible to identify a lifemate on sight and many vampires describe the sensation as being as subtle as a punch to the gut. A lifemate is usually a vampire's perfect opposite. It is possible for a vampire to have more than one lifemate, but the phenomenon is exceedingly rare as most vampires don't survive to an advanced age if they lose their first lifemate.

Nephilim: A person with angel parentage, who is capable of wielding light magic. Nephilim are considered extinct in modern day due to The Veil and the Heaven-Hell Accords.

Nyixa Island: A chunk of The Fell Lands that the Fell managed to drag to Earth. It is a relatively large island with the Dark Eye at its center. After the Fell were defeated, vampires made it their seat of power before it was sunk to the bottom of the ocean in a bid to eradicate Fell Madness. It has only resurfaced recently in modern times and is considered inhabitable.

Occultarus: A tool used by Sorcerers to concentrate their magic. Instead of using complicated gestures to summon magic, a Sorcerer can hold an occultarus and cast spells more quickly. An occultarus is a sphere of glass forged by dragon fire and contains concentrated magic within. The Eyes of Worlds were modeled after occultari and are giant versions of them.

Seelie Fae: Greater fae who aligned with angels before The Veil separated Faerie from Heaven and Hell. Their tongues are cursed to utter only the truth. While Faerie is at peace now, Seelie and Unseelie have historically been at war along the same lines as their patrons. Their sub-races are terran fae (earth), solar fae (fire), astral fae (water), and aether fae (wind).

Shifter: A fae or human with the soul of an animal within them. The denizens of Adrun all became shifters as the Fell curse cannot take root in a body with two souls within it. The creation of a shifter is a partnership and the resulting person can appear fully humanoid or gain physical characteristics of their animal side. Some shifters fully give in to the whims of their animal and never return to humanoid form.

Spark: A piece of a demon's soul that can be given to a "willing" person. A spark will slowly corrupt the person's soul until it resembles the same level of darkness as the original demon, twisting their personality in the process. A spark can out-live a demon if they are killed. Powerful demons can "resurrect" by taking over the body of a humanoid afflicted by their spark.

Spellbreaker: A fae skilled in reflecting or mitigating magic. A highly trained Spellbreaker can render a Sorcerer's magic useless.

Sorcerer: Originally a distinction for the rare fae who can control all thirteen schools of magic, this title is also awarded to the sub-class of vampire that has silver blood and the ability to control every school of fae magic. Sorcerers are highly trained and often manifest extra rare abilities called virtues. The five virtues are: true sight, future sight, empathy, druidism, and mediumship.

Unseelie Fae: Greater fae who aligned with demons before The Veil separated Faerie from Heaven and Hell. Their tongues are cursed to utter only lies. While Faerie is at peace now, Seelie and Unseelie have historically been at war along the same lines as their patrons. Their sub-races are curse fae (earth), destruction fae (fire), death fae (water), and blight fae (wind).

Vampire: Descendants of the original Fell Hunters, spread by their cursed blood. The existence of vampires has become a myth to modern mortals as the purpose of vampires has tarnished from war heroes into former mortals trying to avoid their mortal coil. Contrary to popular myth, vampires are not walking corpses; they eat, breathe, and reproduce, though the chance of conception narrows as a vampire ages. Young vampires act a lot like humans with a taste for blood, though as they age they grow more powerful and inhuman. Vampires manifest an aura, which communicate to each other how old and powerful they are.

The Veil: A magical barrier that separates Earth and Faerie from the realms of Heaven and Hell. Anchored in place by the Eyes of Worlds, it's been in place for over a thousand Earth years and prevented the worlds from coming to ruin by being battle-grounds for angels and demons.

Cast of Characters

Modern Day Vampires
Residents of New York City's covens.

Alexander Rehnquist

A vampire nearing his five hundredth year. Master of Coven Rehnquist and skilled shapeshifter. He is bitter rivals with Bryant Collins and lost his first lifemate due to the conflict between their covens. Fate crossed him one night and he ended up partnered with a second lifemate, Violet Reynolds.

Violet Reynolds

Formerly a mortal zookeeper, Violet was exposed to vampirism after Lucia secretly turned her into a kind of vampire that hadn't been seen in a thousand years. She became a silver-blooded Sorceress, learned how to master her magic, and captured Alex's love.

Julian Fairfax

One of the officers of Coven Rehnquist. The only vampire who mysteriously manifests an icy cold aura. He searched for his life-mate for hundreds of years until they were united via Lucia's machinations. He was viciously hunted by Lucia due to him killing her obsession. Possesses the Winter Key.

Olivia Cooper

A struggling mortal actress who was kidnapped to New York. She knows of the vampire world due to her best friend, Charlotte, but was quickly over her head after taking in Violet's blood and turning into an Alchemyst. She developed magical empathy and used it to save her Ancient allies from Jazrach's corruption. Due to her blood and quick thinking, she transformed a portal manifesting a connection between Earth and Hell into one that linked Earth to Adrun instead. Possesses the Shadow Key.

Charlotte Smith

Olivia's best friend and the only dhampir around. She is loyal and protective of her friend, joining Coven Rehnquist when Olivia did. She joins the supernatural police and becomes Armando's patrol partner when Julian retires.

Armando Nizzola

Julian's cousin and a member of the supernatural police. He is Charlotte's lifemate and earns her affection in the Christmas special *Dhampir's Wish*.

Bryant Collins

A bitter rival to Alex and Coven Rehnquist. He owns the telecommunications company Haven and thus members of his coven are referred to as Haveners. He is an Ancient and a religious zealot, believing the Light Key is his by his faith. He allied with Lucia thinking he could finally crush Coven Rehnquist with her might and magic, instead realizing his mistake too late after she got his entire coven killed and sacrificed his wife's heart to power a portal. He now seeks repentance for his misguided ideals.

Kim Cox

Bryant Collins's wife, known for her sadistic personality and enjoyment of torturing others. She is deceased as of *The Winter Key*.

Cossette Deveaux

The Ancient leader of the most powerful coven in New York City. She is an albino and a rare vampire who possesses future sight. She is stuck in the body of a little girl due to the twisted ideals of her vampire master. Due to her unique circumstances, her mind is damaged. She usually acts like a cheerful and sweet girl, but sometimes shows hints of her age as she delivers prophecies of the future.

Ancients

Surviving Fell Hunters whose bloodlines have shaped the vampire world in their absence.

Adrius

King of Adrun

Strongest Fell Hunter and owner of the Shield Key. He fell into a deep pit of depression to be separated from his lifemate, Nyah. Possessed every vampiric ability until he became a shifter by bonding to the spirit of the dragon Zerenth.

Lucia

The first vampire Sorceress and briefly Queen of Vampires in *Blood Curse* while struggling with the titular curse. Nyixa was sunk partially to contain her evil.

Gwendolyn Firetree

A nephilim who represents the grace of duty. Conspired to sink Nyixa in *Blood Curse* to contain Fell Madness and Lucia. She has committed her immortal existence to curbing the damage of old vampires on the brink of Fell Madness by making them mysteriously "disappear."

Sirius

Blood Prince Sirius, the Dawn

Adrius's second-in-command and brother. Was once a kind and giving man, but emerged from his thousand-year rest bitter, angry, and unable to fully control the whims of his inner beast. He is a shapeshifter and possesses the ability to walk in daylight without harm.

Korin
Blood Prince Korin, the Bane
The gentle giant of the Ancients, a steady and quiet personality. He is a blood tracker.

Neala
Blood Princess Neala, the Wraith
A mute orphan raised by Gabriel and Gwendolyn. She defied the odds and survived the Fell Crisis, though she sustained several terrible wounds that scarred her face and chest. Despite being an illusionist, she refuses to hide her scars or make herself more attractive and feminine. Loved and lost her first mate, Marcus Hartson, to Lucia's machinations.

Elandros
Blood Prince Elandros, the Legion
Squire to Gabriel Legion and also his murderer due to unfortunate circumstances. Possessed the ability to make minor illnesses and blights. After being blackmailed for the rest of his life by Lucia, he confessed his crime to Gwendolyn and was forgiven. Deceased as of *The Winter Key*.

Jaromir
Blood Prince Jaromir, the Mender
The doctor of the surviving Ancients. He was in possession of the Gift until he was briefly afflicted with Fell Madness in *The Winter Key*. He believes himself incomplete without his Gift.

Qin
Blood Prince Qin, the Ascended
He is considered a greedy coward by his peers, as he took a payment from Lucia and went into hiding, never to be seen again.

Taryn

Blood Prince Taryn, the Blade
Lucia's bodyguard due to taking a stage three love potion and being enslaved by his emotions. While he was immediately driven to Fell Madness upon being released from her control, he found his peace and center by becoming a druid as of *Queen's Return*.

Marcus Hartson

A close friend to the Ancients and Neala's former mate. After his mating bond was severed by Lucia, he was poisoned by her cursed blood and grew increasingly insane as the years passed. Died in an honorable duel with his son Julian after he drove the family to the brink of ruin from countless wars with other vampires. Deceased as of *Blood Curse*.

Adrun

A land of shifters and eternal darkness, full of life despite the odds.

Nyah

Queen of Adrun
Banished to the Fell Lands in *Blood Curse* due to Lucia's machinations for her throne. Instead of dying in the desolate land, Nyah used her Alchemyst blood to cure the Fell around her one at a time and establish life with the help of the Spring and Autumn Keys. Once her people discovered they could become shifters to permanently stave off the Fell curse, she was crowned Queen of Adrun and ruled with an empty throne beside her until she was reunited with her lifemate, Adrius. She is a shifter bonded to the greater wolf spirit Night's Howl.

Swift Spirit

A shy druid accustomed to taking the form of her beast, a red fox.

Izell Firebrand

Considered to be the oldest fae alive. She is King Oberon's granddaughter and the first Archfae of the astral fae people. She's been through a lot and has learned to keep her true thoughts hidden under a thick layer of cynicism. Bonded to the spirit of her familiar in life, the golden dragon Queldian. She's a distant ancestor to Keegan Firetree, much to his chagrin.

Cedric Applewhite
A half-fae, half-human born in Adrun. He inherited an enchanted lute from his grandfather and became a self-taught musician. He is known for his energy and enthusiasm.

Chandra
Blood Princess Chandra, the Dreamer
The only Ancient locked into the Fell Lands alongside Nyah. She shed her vampirism and bonded to an earth spirit, becoming the head druid of Adrun. She now believes in peace, love, and parties, and gladly helped Taryn escape the grip of his rage.

Caladorn Nightweaver
An astral fae Blade who lost his wife tragically when they were both afflicted by the Fell curse. He surrendered his newborn daughter, Sorsha, to Neala and promised to repay the favor one day. He serves Nyah as her general and has developed an icy façade to endure his immortality alone.

Calinhes Nightweaver
An incredibly powerful Sorcerer who was afflicted with the Fell curse while defending an academy full of fae children. He became the leader of the Fell, crowned the Fell Emperor, and became the reason the Fell came to Earth due to his keen mind and magical prowess surviving the transition. His familiar was Zerenth and the dragon mourned Calinhes's death for an eternity, refusing to believe his master turned into a monster until confronted by the facts. Deceased as of *Blood Curse*.

Other

Sorsha Shadestone
An astral fae Sorceress with the true sight ability. She was born in

the Fell Lands, but her father gave her to Neala to raise, who adopted her alongside her brother-by-circumstance, Keegan. She is petite, sweet, and still sometimes acts like a teenager when she lets her guard down.

Keegan Firetree

An astral fae Blade who comes off tight-lipped and reserved. He was adopted by Neala alongside Sorsha and took on his adoptive mother's warrior persona. He is considered to be very powerful due to bonding with a fire dragon as his familiar.

Ashaela Dread

A cagy and sarcastic Unseelie fae who accompanies Sorsha and Keegan. She is a Spellbreaker and trained assassin who relies heavily on her shadow magic.

Soren

A humble man who is Adrius's guardian angel.

Gabriel Legion

In life, a vampire named for the amount of Fell he killed. In death, an angelic soldier whom has returned to Earth to hunt Jazrach. He was the original commander of the Fell Hunters before his untimely death.

Jazrach

A greater demon of corruption whom was unwillingly sacrificed to create the Dark Eye of Worlds. He plotted to escape his prison and eventually stole a living body to wreak havoc and spread his corruption.

www.ingramcontent.com/pod-product-compliance
Lightning Source LLC
Chambersburg PA
CBHW061655190726
48289CB00006B/1887